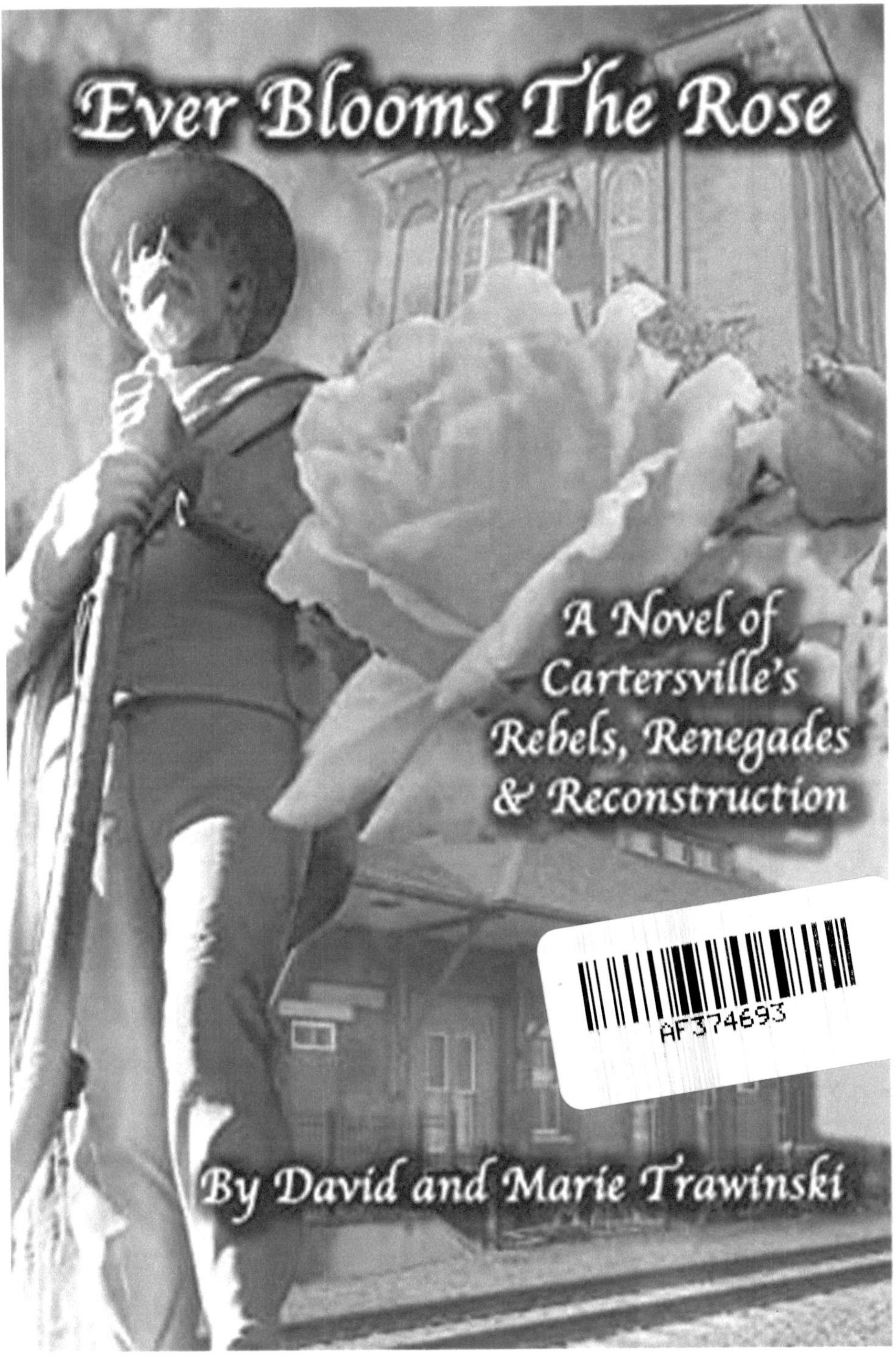

Ever Blooms The Rose

A Novel of Cartersville's Rebels, Renegades & Reconstruction

By David and Marie Trawinski

DANTE
ASSOCIATES

*This Book is Dedicated to The Memory of
The Man Who Inspired Us All
To Live A Life Rich in Faith
And Rooted Deeply In Family.*

Our Brother,

Michael Lee Trawinski

The authors wish to express our thanks to the following who contributed so significantly to the historical sourcing of this novel:

The Bartow History Museum and their Archives, Director Trey Gaines, Archives Assistant Sandy Moore, and especially Registrar Tina Shadden.

The Rose Lawn Museum in Cartersville, their Director, Jane Drew, and her assistant, Catrina Shepard.

The Euharlee Welcome Center & History Museum, and their Director Katie O. Gobbi.

The Etowah Valley Historical Society, and their Vice-President, Joe Head.

The Bartow County Library Reference Section in Cartersville for access to its collection: ***War of The Rebellion: Official Records of the Union and Confederate Armies.***

Thank you also to Dekie Hicks of Rome, Georgia, and the Rome Area Writers Group for their warm welcome of us into the area's writing community.

And Very Special Thanks to Miss Pat Taff of the Bartow History Museum, for welcoming and befriending the authors and our family into the community of Cartersville.

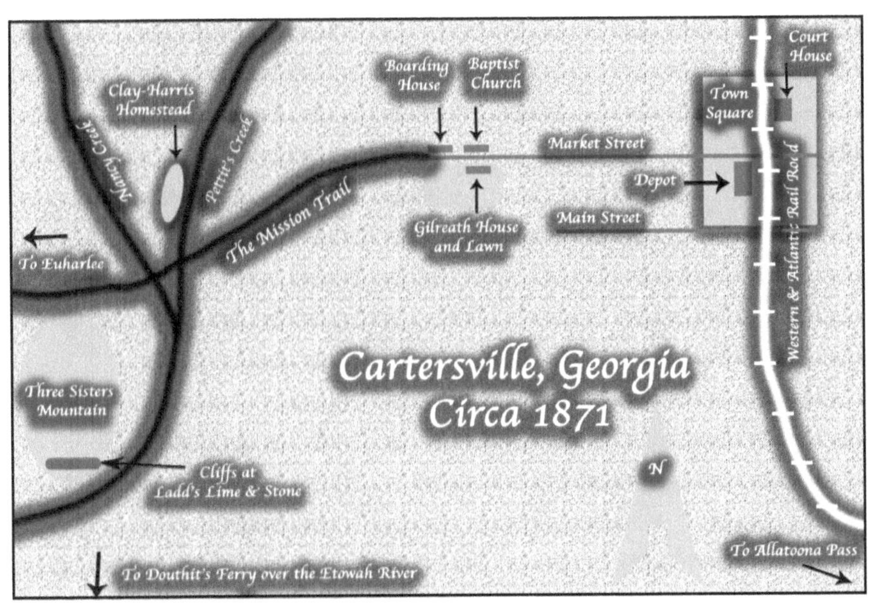

Image 1 - Map of Cartersville circa 1871

CHRONOLOGY OF REFERENCED CIVIL WAR EVENTS

President Lincoln Takes Office	March 4th, 1861
Attack on Fort Sumter	April 12th, 1861
Baltimore Mob Riot on Union Troops	April 19th, 1861
Battle of First Manassas (Bull Run)	July 21st, 1861
Battle of Sharpsburg (Antietam)	September 17th, 1862
Battle of Fredericksburg	December 11th to 13th, 1862
Battle of Chancellorsville	April 30th to May 6th, 1863
Battle of Gettysburg	July 1st to July 3rd, 1863
Battle of Chickamauga	September 18th to 20th, 1863
Union Army Invades Bartow (Cass) County	May 1864
Battle of Kennesaw Mountain	June 27th, 1864
Battle/Siege of Atlanta	July 22nd to September 1st, 1864
Union Troops Enter Atlanta	September 2nd, 1864
Truce to Evacuate Civilians from Atlanta	September 11th to 21st, 1864
Battle of Allatoona Pass	October 5th, 1864
Ten Murdered Union Troops found in Cassville	October 11th, 1864
Burning of Cassville (Manassas)	November 5th, 1864
Burning of Kingston and Cartersville	November 12th, 1864
Burning of Atlanta/March to the Sea Begins	November 15th, 1864
Sherman's March to the Sea Ends at Savannah	December 21st, 1864
Fall of Richmond	April 2nd, 1865
Lee Surrenders to Grant (Appomattox Court House)	April 9th, 1865
President Lincoln Assassinated	April 14th, 1865
Johnston Surrenders to Sherman (Carolina)	April 17th, 1865

<u>*Image 2 - First Bloom of the Rose*</u>

"As delicate a scent as has ever reached a living thing's nose,
Is the breath of Our Lord, In the first bloom of a Summer's rose"

(Source: Rose image adapted from fablesandflora.wordpress.com)

1

THE BURNING OF CARTERSVILLE
THE NIGHT OF NOVEMBER 12TH, 1864

He stood in darkness.

A thick, heavy darkness that had totally enveloped him. Not only that of the cold autumn night, as he stood alone upon the dirt and gravel path awaiting his fate, but also the darkness in which a wounded soul takes refuge after having been discarded by those around him.

He thought about his physical limitations, then just as quickly decided they didn't matter. The six men on horseback approaching his homestead were less than a quarter mile in front of him. He was all that stood between them and it. They would soon be upon him, and he knew what he must do, his limitations be damned.

Ahead, the four torches rippled and snapped in the still blackness of the night. The fact that the night was itself calm only heightened the awareness of the Union soldiers. Caution demanded that these torch bearers and their two officers move forward slowly.

However, the calm of the night had already been pierced with the pungent smoke that permeated through the otherwise crisp, clean air. It hung pregnant with the sour smell of burnt tar and smoke. The smell stuck to the lone figure standing in the darkness like the failures of his recent past. It was the smell of the town of Cartersville burning just over the ridge at the hands of Sherman's Union Army.

The Federals had taken everything from him. They had taken his youth, his energy, and his innocence. Tonight, they came to take the only things he had left in this life – his family and the farm on which they barely survived.

He could hear them clearly now. The light of their flames had not yet fallen upon him. They were unaware of his presence within the shroud of the black night.

"Sergeant, are you certain this is the right path to *his* farm?" asked the officer leading the procession.

"Yes, Captain. The townsman said to follow Market Street until it led to the Mission Trail. Then, just after crossing the first creek, proceed along the path following the tree-line to the right. His farm should be just ahead where the tree-line pinches closest to the creek. This was exactly his description, Captain."

"Can we be sure the townsman wasn't deceiving us, Sergeant?" nervously asked the captain. "He could be sending us into an ambush."

The sergeant thought his captain to be too cautious a man to lead others.

"Yes, I am sure, Captain. That bastard knows we spared his property for this information, and should it prove false, he also knows we would return to burn his home and business to the ground. For certain, this is the way to the rebel's farm. We will find it shortly, and it will burn for his sins against the Union Army at Antietam."

With this, the sergeant spat upon the ground. Just as he did, the first torch bearer called out, "Sir! There he be! Directly ahead of us."

The captain searched the darkness to see the flicker of the torches highlight a gaunt figure. The light of their flames washed upon him like waves upon a rocky shoreline. Some twenty yards separated the singular man from the group of six horse soldiers. The sergeant then barked an order that resulted in the four torch bearers fanning out, before stopping in their newly spaced positions. At that point, they were then able to draw weapons with their free hands.

Ahead of them stood the solitary figure, tall and thin, covered in his long-coat that stretched down to the top of his worn boots. On his head he wore a tattered field hat. The flames cast enough light upon the figure to reveal the color of the red soil that stained everything he wore.

They could see he was armed. In his right hand he held a British Enfield rifled musket. Each of the six men knew this to be a muzzle loader – capable of firing a single shot before it would require a reload down its barrel. Even if this man was as good as the legends about him, the weapon would surely kill only one of them.

They much more feared the weapons at his hips. His long-coat had been pulled back on either side to reveal a matching pair of Colt Navy revolvers.

The soldiers could not see his left hand, which appeared to be stuffed awkwardly into the pocket of the long-coat. They wondered if it was grasping another weapon as well.

"Drop the guns, Reb, or we'll open fire upon you, by thunder!" yelled out the sergeant.

The clay-stained man remained silent, standing eerily still before them. He held the rifle by its stock beneath the barrel, away from its trigger, pointed upward to the sky. He took in the spread of the six men, measuring with his eyes the order with which he would be forced to kill them. After a long pause, he finally spoke.

"I am not fixin' to surrender my weapons," he said softly, in response to the sergeant.

"Speak up like a man, you Rebel bastard, or we'll cut you down, here and now," barked the sergeant excitedly.

The solitary figure before them refused to answer. Instead, he just watched the six men with eyes that anticipated not only their actions, but also their reactions to what he was about to do.

"Are you Virgil Clay-Harris?" asked the captain in an authoritative voice.

A heavy second hung between the two men. The smell of the torches mixed with the already acrid odor of smoke and tar. With every breath the man on foot drew, his memory flashed, recalling his exploits in the war. His nerves tightened, but not disabling so.

"I am so named," said the Southerner.

"The man the locals call the hero of Antietam?" continued the captain.

The man knew if he did not kill these six Union soldiers, they would not only burn his farm, but also kill the family that he had sent to hide in the woods. These Bluebellies were most dangerous when they had strength in numbers.

"T'ain't not one of the townsfolks here would ever use that name. *Antietam* is a Yankee name, for a Yankee victory. The proper name of that battle was *Sharpsburg*. And there was no heroes at Sharpsburg, just the dead and them that mourn 'em."

The soldiers on horseback shuffled fore and aft upon their mounts, cautious of the danger of an ambush. The captain advanced his mare until he was looming over the Southerner.

The captain spoke even more confidently now. "It is said that you killed fifteen good Union men at Antietam, as the Confederate army was retreating. It is also said that your rifle was the main reason that General McClellan refused to pursue General Lee's Army of Northern Virginia across the Potomac River. Hear tell, son, the Rebs call you the Savior of Sharpsburg."

The thin, earth-stained man before them locked eyes with the captain. "They called me that once, but not no more, Cap'n. I swore my days of killing are plum over...", he looked in a penetrating way into the captain's tense eyes, before adding, "... unless y'all force me to kill again here tonight."

The Union captain could feel the imposing threat within the man standing so defiantly before him. He knew he was dealing with a wounded animal, backed into a corner by its pursuers. The leader of the soldiers felt unthreatened, however, as his squad had the man outnumbered six-to-one.

"Drop the Enfield and the Colts and step aside, son. By order of the Union Army, we are here to burn your farm and requisition any livestock that you may have," the Union captain said in a superior and lofty tone.

The man in the long-coat laughed aloud. "Livestock! Can't y'all see we is starving to death. We been for some time long. T'ain't been any cattle or hogs around here for years now. No chickens, neither. We been living on weeds and any critters from the ground or the woods we can shoot. No Sir! No! I am not stepping aside, and I am not throwing down my guns. I will not allow y'all to destroy the only slim bit of life which we got left."

"Then, it will be our pleasure to kill you here tonight," said the sergeant.

With the sergeant having said this, the Southerner, in a rapid, singular motion of his right hand, pitched his rifle slightly upwards. He released the grip on its stock and worked his hand to find the trigger while gravity brought its barrel down. Shouldering the butt, he aimed it dead upon the captain. This action was swift and totally unexpected, catching the six men by complete surprise.

By the time they realized what was happening, the man had their captain in his Enfield's sights. The same captain, who so audaciously had not even bothered to draw his own revolver, dared not reach for it at that point.

"I don't reckon to kill nobody," said the man on foot, "but if y'all force me to, your captain will be the first to die. You will not be burning my home tonight, so all y'all can turn tail and git on back to town."

The Southerner stared coldly at the captain, focused on the weapon he wore on his hip – a single Colt Navy revolver, very much like his own pair. Most likely it was resting on an empty chamber, meaning this six-shooter perhaps had only five rounds loaded.

The Southerner's gunsmith father had given him his revolvers, which drew him to think to himself, *My Diddy claimed this land after the Cherokee was driven off it in '38. He worked this crick panning for gold until his back was lame and his family was poorer than the dirt I now stand on. Only thing my Diddy left me was these pair of Colt Navies, and by the Lord's grace, I will use them to scare off these Yankees tonight. Or, if need be, I will use their own weapons to kill the lot of 'em.*

His thoughts were snapped by a response from another of the Union soldiers.

"You're the only one going to die tonight, for sure, you Rebel bastard," said the sergeant in an angry taunt. He could not believe this dirty scrap of a man dared defy their torching party. The fury in the sergeant's voice ran a chill of fear through his captain, who stared at the musket pointed at his chest. The man behind the Enfield was not concerned over the sergeant's threat.

"Hold your positions, men. No one fires upon this man without my order," pleaded the captain. His voice wobbled nervously as he gazed down the barrel of the weapon.

The tension of the situation had ratcheted. The sergeant watched the Southerner closely. He showed no emotion. His face was cold; his eyes were two black slates. He held the rifle trained on his superior with his right hand only, the stock butted against his shoulder. The sergeant still could not see the rebel's left hand, and he wondered what the man was keeping it free for.

"Men, I command you to fire upon this bastard! How dare he defy the Union Army," spat out the sergeant.

"No! No! No! Hold your fire, that's an order," screamed the panicked captain.

At that point, a new voice spoke out, surprising not only the six Union soldiers, but the Southerner as well.

"Best y'all listen to your cap'n," came the smooth, slick voice from the darkness behind them all.

The soldiers on horseback, save the captain, all glanced behind them to find a second Southerner. This man was dressed all in black and seemed to float upon his dark mare. He did not have the earthy stain of the first Southerner that stood before them all. This man's clothes, his hat, his boots reflected the pride with which he carried himself. His horse was groomed, his saddle had a finery to it that was evident even in the fringe of darkness from which he emerged.

The man in black was holding a Henry repeating rifle, similar to those that had just been made available to the Union Army. He held it pointed squarely at the sergeant's chest.

"First Yankee to cock a hammer dies tonight. Now, you boys needn't die at all, but so help me God, you even think about firing them weapons and it'll be the last thing yer ever to think about. All y'all lower them guns, right now."

The sergeant began to turn his weapon to the man behind them. Before he could aim it in his direction, the man dressed in black fired over his head, freezing everyone. With a speed surprising them all, the second Southerner fluidly re-cocked the rifle's lever and re-trained the weapon upon the sergeant.

Every man knew the math, as the Henry could hold up to fifteen rounds. It had been known to the Confederates as the damn Union gun that could be loaded on Sunday and fired all week. Yet, this night, it was a dangerous advantage in the hands of this rebel.

"You are not listening, Sargen'. Now, I reckon that should my friend Clay in front of y'all here take out yer Cap'n, and I fire upon you right after, the rest of these here men will scatter like cats. Not that we wouldn't be happy to cut 'em down, each and every yella' one of 'em."

It was then that they all saw it for the first time. It drew a primal fear from within each of the men, with at least one soldier gulping aloud in an attempt to suppress his revulsion. The man in black's face had now come fully into the light. It came alive and danced in the flickering torchlight with the movement of shadows.

Some of the shadows were from the black hair that dangled beneath the brim of his hat. Some were from the trimmed beard that framed his white face. Mostly, however, it was the shadow that danced upon the right side of his face that morbidly seized their attention.

For there, his face bore a swollen raised scar that ridged from the corner of his eye until it spread gruesomely down to his mouth. Here it smoothed in a sickeningly awkward flat that merged with his upper and lower lips. All along its ragged length, it cast an ebbing shadow across the smooth cheek skin that youthfully lay just behind it.

"Now, I reckon you boys ain't to have the big night y'all had hoped for," the man in black continued. "Y'all figured, iffen we burn down the rebel sharpshooter's farm, then we will ourselves become heroes. Took it upon yerselves, didn't y'all. The Union Army wouldn't send only six of y'all out this far. Problem is, y'all didn't reckon with who yer dealin'. Hell, Clay here could have picked y'all off coming up the dirt path by these pines. I sure would have, were it me, but that's just Clay for ya. The boy won't hurt a soul, lessen he has to."

The sergeant glared at the man and realized that even though his soldiers outnumbered them, the two Southerners had them in a dire position. Should the soldiers begin to act, he and his captain would surely be lost.

"You dare not kill members of the Union Army. You'll have the entirety of General Sherman's Corps hunting you down! You are a pea-wit to even threaten us!" said the sergeant, his gun still lowered to the ground.

The man in black ignored the sergeant's utterance.

"Last I heard, some ten Union soldiers were found dead in Cassville last month, and the mighty Union Army never found the renegades that caught and executed them, now, did they, Sargen'?"

The comment struck at the core of the six soldiers. The guerrillas in these foothills had taken Union soldiers' lives seemingly at will. While it was only a nuisance to the Army as a whole, these six Yankee Blue-Devils realized just how deadly a situation they had walked into.

Despite this, the sergeant thought he could scare both of the Southerners into lowering their rifles.

"Son, Cartersville burns tonight because of those cowardly killings of our boys. If you harm any of us, our Army will only inflict even greater pain upon the citizens of this area..."

"Stop callin' me son, you Yankee bastard. Y'ain't man enough to be ma' paw," seethed the second Southerner at the sergeant from atop his black mount.

"General Sherman's troops will hunt you down and see you hung..." responded the sergeant.

"I doubt it, Sargen'. Way I reckon, iffen we lay y'all in this here field tonight, come mornin' the Army will write y'all off as a bunch of deserters. Even if they don't, they'll never find your bodies, let alone us. Unlike Clay here, I already have the whole of the Confederate Army looking for me for desertion. They ain't found me yet. Word has it your army, with or without the six of y'all, will be off on the morra', moving south past what's left of Atlanta. So, you boys can go back to camp tonight and join that army when the mornin' dawns, or y'all can die here tonight. Make yer choice."

Atlanta had already been taken and laid waste by Sherman's troops. General Sherman had returned to Bartow county, some forty miles north of the city, only when Confederate General John Bell Hood had decided to attack the Union's supply lines into Atlanta. The railroad was attacked between it and Chattanooga. This tactic resulted in the major conflagration that came to be known as the Battle of Allatoona Pass.

"Now throw down your weapons," said the man in black, from behind the Henry repeating rifle that he had scavenged from that very battlefield.

The captain, having said nothing through all this, just continued to stare down the barrel of the first Southerner's Enfield. The sergeant had earlier ordered his men to lower their weapons, but none had, as of yet, surrendered their guns.

"We are soldiers. We will pay no heed to your ultimatum," said the sergeant bravely.

The man with the scarred face scoffed at the sergeant's response.

"Well, thar ya' go, Sergeant, with yer fancy words. Hell, this ain't no '*allteematum*'. It be nothin' more than a promise. Ma personal promise that y'all either turn and run, or we will run all y'all into the Georgia soil. Just like me and Clay did to you Yankees at Chickamauga. As I said, it's yer choice."

The captain was still frozen in fear. The sergeant calculated their odds, despite the two rebel scoundrels having caught them unawares.

"It's still only the two of you against six of us. I don't think we will be surrendering anything to either of you."

"Well, I reckon this will change your mind," said the man in black, at which point he whistled loudly. From the trees, five men bearing identical Henry repeating rifles walked out into sight. "Now, for the last time, throw down your revolvers and save us from having to pick 'em out from under your dead bodies."

The four torch bearers one-by-one threw down their army revolvers. The sergeant delayed surrendering his own until two of the men on foot came within extremely close range, their rifles aimed directly at his chest from only a few feet away. He then reluctantly threw down his revolver, as well as the Spencer rifle that had been sheathed in his saddle.

"Y'all leave your ammunition too. Everything you got on yerselves..."

The captain remained frozen in terror. One of the renegades walked up to his mount, and slowly relieved him of his weapons and ammunition.

The man in black spoke next. "Keep them torches lit so y'all can follow the path back yonder to the Mission Trail, but as ya' cross that crick, I am expecting y'all will drop them torches into the water as a sign yer won't be coming back. Otherwise, y'all come back, and we will kill every last one of ya'. Got it?"

"How are we supposed to explain losing our weapons?" asked the sergeant.

The man in black leaned forward in his saddle, and with the barrel of his revolver pushed up on the brim of his hat. "How does this strike y'all – tell the almighty Union Army that y'all had a hare-brained scheme to come out here and kill a near defenseless one-armed man, and he took your weapons away from y'all."

He saw the confusion on the faces of the soldiers.

"Hell, y'all didn't know Clay has only one arm? My good Lord, y'all come out here not knowing you was picking a fight with a cripple? Sure 'nuff, he lost his left arm below the elbow during the war. Same day I got this..."

As he said this, he traced the outline of his scar with the barrel of his revolver. "Like I said, though, but not before we killed us a mess of Yankees. Clay got discharged with his wound, but they expected me to keep killin' y'all with this little scar, so I up and deserted. I reckon' the Confederate Army was right though, 'cause I am surely still capable of killin' more Yankees. Don't tempt me tonight."

The soldiers were now all taken with fear, not knowing if the renegades would shoot them in the back as soon as they turned to find their way back to the main road and into town.

"That's enough jawing for one night," said the man in black, "now git!"

Having said this, he fired his rifle into the air a second time to get the Yankees moving. Each soldier glanced momentarily at the soiled man on foot with the Enfield as they turned their horses to ride back. Clay could feel them gazing upon the left sleeve of his coat, which he had stuffed with rags to conceal his lost lower limb.

Once they were out of earshot, the man in black ordered his men to retrieve the surrendered weapons and ammunition, and to bring him the revolvers.

"Give that Spencer rifle to Clay," said the leader of the renegades, "It's only a seven-shot repeater, but it's better than that muzzle loader he has. I am not even sure how that sergeant got it, they's s'pose to have been issued Henry rifles."

One of the renegades, known to Clay only as "Flinch", handed him the Spencer. Flinch was second in command to the man on horseback, Willet Blackwell.

Clay took the rifle and walked up to Blackwell. "Willet, I owe you a bale of thanks. I was likely about to die here tonight. Let's say this makes us even."

Willet Blackwell, from atop his horse, laughed aloud.

"Clay, I'm pert sure ya' would have killed two or three of them Yankees, before they would have got you. Outside chance ya' might e'en got 'em all. I am just sure glad I saw them torches coming out of town from atop the mountain. We barely made it here in time. Yer maw and little Truitt in the cabin?"

"They was. I sent them to the back woods to hide," said Clay. "No less, y'all saved them both, too."

"And what about Deekie? She out there, too?" asked Willet brashly.

The question caused Clay to tense up. The girl was a sore point between the two men.

"You know she is. Like I said, Willet, you and me, we's even now," said Clay, with the air of a man releasing another from servitude.

"Like Hell we are, Clay," responded Willet with fervor. "Ya' saved my life, for sure at Chickamauga. Then ya' left me to live the rest of it with this," he said, pointing again to the ghastly scar upon his face. "And on top of all that, ya' went and stole my girl from me. I don't think we're even at all."

Clay could sense the hostility in his voice but wondered how much of it was directed at him, and how much was reserved for the girl.

"Willet, ya' know Deekie come to me only after ya' drove her off. You shouldn't have been takin' what life has handed ya' out on her. She was beat half to death when she got here."

Willet Blackwell, who had been looking down at Flinch, without raising his head, arched his right eye angrily at Clay. A suppressed rage wept forever from that eye in the form of that tortuous scar.

"Like I said, Clay, we's a long way from even," said Willet. His men had brought the captured weapons, handing them up to him.

"Give me that Colt Navy first," he ordered. The marauder Flinch handed him the captured revolver and Willet removed the .36 caliber rounds from it.

"Good news, Clay. This Navy's been modified to take bullet cartridges just like yours. It don't have your daddy's smithmarks on it though. Somebody else's work, this conversion. I might guess you could use the ammunition, but I am keeping this Navy pistol as a souvenir."

Willet passed the metallic cartridges to Flinch, who, in turn, handed the rounds to Clay. He took them into his right hand as he awkwardly rested the Enfield and Spencer rifles against what remained of his left arm.

Willet then moved onto the rest of the revolvers. These were Union standard issue .44 caliber Army Colt revolvers, which were what his own men had, at least since they had murdered the ten Union soldiers in October.

"Why didn't ya' just let 'em kill me, Willet?" asked Clay. "It wouldn't have been on you, not for letting them Yankees do what they do."

Both men could hear the same words in their minds – **No harm to you, no harm to me, forever, no matter what!**

Willet stopped his task of removing the bullets from the weapons. He looked at Clay with a widening grin. Clay sensed the mock respect that now registered upon Willet's scarred face.

"I most nearly did, Clay. Just to see how you were gonna take on them boys with a single musket ball. I know for a fact that them pretty Navies are empty, that you been out of ammunition for them for a while now. Them pistols are something fierce lookin', I give ya' that, but how were you gonna take on them soldiers after ya' killed their Cap'n? Were ya' gonna dive at his body and grab his revolver? I gotta admit there was a piece of me that really wanted to see how many of them Yankees you would've killed. Besides, Clay, we have our deal, don't we? **No harm to you, no harm to me** – remember?"

Clay remembered the deal they had made as they marched away in defeat from Gettysburg. He could never forget that devil's pact he had made with Willet.

Willet went back to removing the rounds. "Why didn't I let them kill you?" he began again after no response from Clay, "cause they all Yankees. Damn Yankees who got no proper right killin' no one down here - not that it ever stops 'em."

Clay at this point felt exposed. Willet and he had been through so much of the war together that they well enough knew the weaknesses and strengths of each other. They knew each other to be steadfast in battle. Yet, they also knew it was dealing with the aftermath of the fighting that tore each man down to his essence. Their reaction to the horrors of the war was what separated the two young men.

Clay always thought it a sin, what the war had done to his friend, Willet. The man he knew so well could not bear the disgrace of his disfigurement, and it stoked a mighty anger within him.

"I will make it up to you, Willet. I promise you," said Clay earnestly.

"Ya' wanna make it up to me, then join us. At least y'all would be fed somethin' proper, and not starvin' to death slow like ya' already is. We could use a sharpshooter like you. I know you can still shoot, even without that left forearm. I can set you up with a proper rifle. Like these new Henries, or you can stick with that Spencer I just give ya'."

Clay merely held up his left arm, the rags falling from the sleeve of his long-coat. The lower half of the sleeve dangled down limply, clearly acknowledging the lack of a limb beneath it.

"It's not your hands I want, Clay," said Willet in response. "It's yer eye I need. With yer eye, it don't matter what yer shootin', you could hold off all of Sherman's, Thomas' and maybe even Grant's armies put together."

Clay lowered his head at the proposition. It was one that had been put to him by Willet not long after they had returned from war. Willet had been given the task of escorting Clay back from Chickamauga, where they had both been severely injured. When they had returned to Cartersville, and Willet saw the hero's welcome that Clay received, it fanned the flames of a rage that had already been building within him. It was then he decided not to return to the Confederate Army. Willet Blackwell had decided to desert.

"Come join our guerrilla army, killin' Union soldiers as they come through North Georgia," Willet said again, as he had many times since then. "I would have killed these men tonight had they not already had you in their sights, Clay. And I know ya' wouldn't take kindly to me and my men shooting them in the back on yer spread."

Clay could see Willet and his men doing just that in his mind. Cold blooded murder it would have been, and for Willet, not a sin so long as they wore the Blue.

"I told you before, I ain't going to be one of yer renegades, Willet. I am done with killin' and stealing," said Clay strongly.

He thought of the ten missing Union soldiers found murdered in October in Cassville. He knew this had been the work of Willet's gang of marauders.

"Why not? The Yankees are still killin' and stealin'. Besides, ya' certainly would have killed these men here tonight, Clay. As many as you could of. I seen it in yer eyes. I know that look in ya'. I've seen it before."

Clay knew he had. The war had marked them both. But, Clay was trying to wash away its stain. Willet was still swimming in its darkness.

"Only had they made me, Willet. Only had they made me."

"Well, Clay, that there is yer problem, and it's going to get you killed one day," Willet said flatly.

"Maybe so, Willet. I guess I had my share of killin'. Enough for one lifetime," responded Clay.

"So be it. And it will be a short lifetime, if ya' live by that creed." answered Willet. "You still might just have to do some killin' tonight. The Yankees yonder is comin' up on the crick. Let's see what they is gonna do."

As the two looked back upon the far-off soldiers crossing the creek, the four torches dropped one-by-one into its swift running waters. The night returned to full darkness, but the smell of the burning town of Cartersville continued to sicken the air.

"I don't reckon they will be back," said Willet, "but just to be sure, you, yer little brother and yer maw should come up to Three Sisters mountain for the night." Willet then had just finished removing the rounds from the captured revolvers.

"No, I stood ma ground, and we will stay here. Anyone comes back, then I will pick them off at long distance with the Spencer." Clay knew he could never join Willet up on the mountain, to do so would lead to the end of what scraps of respect he still had for himself.

"Iffen that be what ya' want," said Willet. "I give you a lot of credit, boy, standing up to them six Yankees with a single shot musket, two empty Colts, and missing half yer left arm. You sure got some balls on you, boy."

Clay had ignored his comment. Instead, he backed up to the discussion a few moments before. "Willet, you didn't mention Deekie. You only said me, Maw and Truitt should come up the mountain. You would leave Deekie to fend for herself?"

The comment caught Willet off-guard. His face expressed nothing, just a stillness that hid his feeling of rage that the man before him would once again come back to the issue that had ripped them asunder – the girl.

"Deekie seems to be able to take care of herself, or else she will find some softhearted fool who will take care of her. Anyhow, she knows her way up Three Sisters. She can come back to me any time she wants to."

Three Sisters Mountain was west of Cartersville, between the town and the mills of Euharlee. Atop it had been the encampment of Willet's marauders, ever since he had banded these thugs and deserters together. It was in this camp atop the mountain where Willet had beat Deekie within inches of her life. It was then that she came to Clay.

Willet then rode off as his men disappeared back into the pines to retrieve their hidden horses. Clay turned to walk back to his family's cabin, which really was nothing more than a single room shack. A shack upon a farm that was nothing more than a few acres of Georgia clay, yielding barely enough to keep them all alive.

As he walked back to this modest homestead, Clay's twelve-year-old brother, Truitt, ran up to him in a frenzy.

"Who dun gat shot?" asked the winded child, having run at great speed from the woods behind the shack.

"Nobody's hurt, Truitt. Willet and his gang just done drove off them boys..."

"Are we safe now, Clay?" asked his brother excitedly.

"Yes, Truitt, I reckon we's safe," said Clay.

"Thanks to Willet and his renegades?" asked Truitt.

"Yup, liken I said, thanks to Willet," Clay said somewhat dejectedly.

"*Huzzah!*" exclaimed Truitt, "I want to grow up and join them someday."

"You will do nothin' such. Diddy always said you were special smart. We're going to get you some more schoolin', boy, so you can make us all proud one day."

"I won't never be able to make people proud of me as they already are of you, Clay," said Truitt, envious of his big brother.

Clay looked down at the child walking alongside him. "Don't mix up people likin' me, just cause I killed a mess of Yankees in the war, with the pride of gainin' somethin' special for yerself. You got it in ya', Truitt, to do somethin' really special."

His young brother would not relent. "They all say you're a hero, Clay. The folk in town, I mean."

"They don't know what a real hero is. Look it what the war did to me," said Clay, rubbing the stump of his left arm, "it done gone and left me a cripple. You know what a real hero is, Truitt? A man who takes care of his kin is a real hero. How in blazes is a cripple ever goin' to take care of his kin? Now, go git Maw and Deekie out from their hiding place in the woods."

Truitt looked at his older brother, his young faced pained as if to speak the next few words.

"Maw says Deekie's a tramp, Clay. Says she's no better than that strumpet that Diddy ran off with to Texas. I reckon Diddy leavin' us like that while you were gone to war means he'll never be a real hero, does it Clay?"

Clay seethed knowing that his maw had poisoned his young brother with her venom. So, her husband had run off with another woman, younger still by nearly half than her. Of course, she had every right to be bitter with her missing husband. But to poison her own son against his father, there was something outright vicious in that.

"You listen to me, Truitt. You listen to me hard, now! You forget yerself about Diddy. Maw is just still mad something fierce with him. And Deekie's had a hard go of life, so far. She's just trying to survive this war, like the rest of us. Now, go and git them, and don't listen to Maw. She's just become another bitter war-sister. And forget about Willet and his gang. That's no life for you, boy. You are going to do better than all of us, ya' hear, better than all of us, by far."

2

IN THE ASHES OF CARTERSVILLE
THE NIGHT OF NOVEMBER 15TH, 1864

Even for this time of war and suffering, it had been quite an eventful ten days in Bartow County. On Tuesday past, the eighth of November, Abraham Lincoln had been overwhelmingly re-elected as President of the North. He soundly defeated George B. McClellan, the very general who had failed to pursue Robert E. Lee's Army of Northern Virginia as it withdrew from the Battle of Antietam. The folk of Bartow County were sure McClellan's timidity was due to the sharpshooting of their town's own Virgil Clay-Harris, but they were wrong. And "Clay" was either too disinterested or too tired of the killing during this war to have corrected any of them.

Only months earlier, many thought Lincoln was ripe to lose that election. The war had stalled early in its fourth year, and many Northerners were calling for a negotiated peace with the Confederates. To do so would have recognized the South as a separate country. This would have brought the international recognition as a sovereign state, that had until then, evaded the Confederacy. The candidate McClellan was suggesting a negotiated end to the war. Lincoln would never do so. Given the country was so tired of the massive loss of life on both sides, few Northerners were willing to vote for more years of battle. Therefore, few of them were likely to vote for Lincoln.

Then, before the Fall election, General Grant had General Sherman thunder into Northern Georgia in May. They took siege of Atlanta by late July, and only then could the Northerners begin to see that both Atlanta and the South would soon fall. Given this change of fortune, Lincoln was re-elected handily, his constituents buoyed by the knowledge that not only would the war be soon over, but that the Union would indeed stay intact. General McClellan's political career failed as soundly as his military career had.

After the election, the decision was made to burn Atlanta to rubble. Sherman already had the city evacuated. On November 15th, 1864, Atlanta was engulfed in the flames of Union torches, rendering it useless to the rebel war apparatus.

Ten days before this, the city of Cassville had been burned to the ground, also on the orders of General William T. Sherman, who had remarked that he intended to make Georgia howl. The Union Army had been encamped in Bartow County since mid-May, after skirmishes at the Octagon House in Adairsville, and later Cassville, as well as near the Etowah River. Even today the Cartersville train depot bears the bullet holes of skirmishing between the two armies.

After Union troops had pressed their campaign in late June at Kennesaw Mountain, they continued to drive through Marietta on to the outskirts of the city of Atlanta. The continual tactic of fighting and falling back eventually cost the Confederate General Joseph E. Johnston his command. General John Bell Hood was selected by Confederate President Jefferson Davis to replace Johnston. Hood was known as a more aggressive General, although the situation he inherited in Atlanta was intolerable.

The Union Army held the city of Atlanta under siege for over a month, with shelling through late July and all of August. Eventually, General Hood had no recourse but to evacuate his army from the city on the first of September. His troops destroyed the ammunition and explosives as they left, such that they would not fall into the hands of Sherman's troops. The Union Army entered the decimated city the next day.

On the eleventh day of the September, a ten-day truce was

observed by Generals Sherman and Hood to allow the remaining civilians to leave the rubble that was then Atlanta.

After withdrawing his troops from the city, General Hood commenced a series of actions intended to disrupt the Union supply lines into Atlanta. His true intent was to draw General Sherman northward from the city, which initially was effective. On the fifth of October, the Battle of Allatoona Pass was fought, at the narrowest section along the Union controlled railroad. While the Confederates outnumbered the Union forces, this was offset by the Federals having a well-situated defensive position. Also, the Yankees had been equipped with the latest weaponry, the fifteen shot Henry repeating rifles.

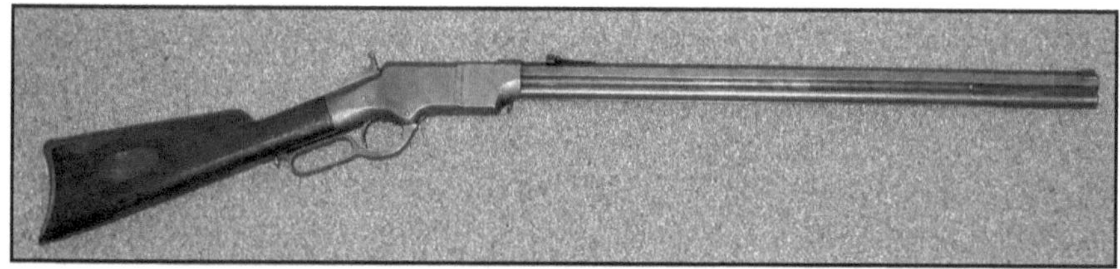

Image 3 - "Those Damn Henry Rifles"
Source: commons.Wikipedia.org

The fighting at Allatoona Pass was particularly bloody. With Federal forts atop both sides of the deep cut of the railway pass through the rocky terrain, along with the Union firepower of "those damn Henry rifles", the Confederates were unable to take this strategic objective. Eventually, the Rebel forces retreated to New Hope Church in nearby Paulding County.

With some fifteen-hundred causalities on both sides of the fighting, other opportunities were afforded those desperate enough to undertake them. From the corpses of the Union dead, Willet Blackwell's men scavenged a small number of the deadly Henry repeating rifles during the night. The newly pilfered firepower only emboldened these renegades.

Throughout the month of October in 1864, renegade actions against the occupying Union Army ensued. On the eleventh of October, the dead bodies of ten Union soldiers captured and murdered by the local guerrillas were found strewn across the grounds of the Cassville Female College. Confederate guerrilla actions in the county became significant enough to risk the wrath of General Sherman. He directed that if the abduction and murder of Union soldiers did not cease, the towns of Kingston, Cassville and Cartersville would be burned.

In retaliation, on Saturday, the fifth of November, the County seat of Cassville, was utterly destroyed, reducing the town to cinders and ash with only free-standing chimneys remaining. Those chimneys would come, in time, to be called Sherman's Sentinels all across Georgia. The only few wood structures that were spared by the Federals at Cassville were those for use as hospitals and churches.

Many assumed this obliteration was due to the fact that in 1861, following the first Battle of Bull Run in Manassas, Virginia, Cassville had formally changed its name to Manassas, Georgia. This was as a tribute to the glorious Confederate victory.

This was the battle at which the emerging Rebel commander Thomas J. Jackson's regiment, under heavy enemy fire, was said to have been "standing still like a stone wall." The name "Stonewall" stuck to Jackson for the short duration of his life, and throughout history thereafter.

At the same time that Cassville changed its name, Cass County elected to change its name to Bartow County. Originally, it was named before the war for General Lewis Cass, a Yankee who served as Secretary of War under President Andrew Jackson. The county was renamed after General Francis S. Bartow, a former U.S. Congressman, Georgia Militia Officer, and founding member of the Confederate government. He was killed at the first battle of Manassas.

Popular belief was that Cassville's name change to Manassas had brought out the fury of the Blue Devils. The actual reason for the utter destruction was more likely the fact that Cassville, or Manassas, was the administrative seat of the county. As such, it had to be destroyed. Sherman was adamant on leaving a wake of annihilation as he moved through Georgia. Burning was his terror of choice. Cassville was razed, obliterated so utterly that the city was never to be rebuilt to its former prominence.

On the following Wednesday, the ninth of November, General Sherman received approval via telegraph from General Ulysses S. Grant for his "March to the Sea" while residing in the nearby town of Kingston, Georgia. It was from there that he dispatched his operational orders to his commanders.

On Saturday, the twelfth of November, Sherman and his staff departed from Kingston, burning its train depot and structures of military utility. Sherman had reached Cartersville by noon, and reportedly lunched upon the massive porch at the old Park Hotel on the town's square. After which, he crossed the street to the train depot and communicated via telegraph his final instructions to General George Thomas in Nashville. After completing his communications, the telegraph lines were cut, and General Sherman was not in touch with the rest of the Union Army again until he entered Savannah in late December 1864.

Image 4 – Old Park Hotel in Cartersville
(courtesy of Etowah Valley Historic Society)

That afternoon the troops began moving out of Cartersville. The train depot, and many other prominent structures along the town square were set ablaze. Few structures were spared the torch. One was the Milam home that had served as the quarters of the Union officers. Another was the Tumlin house that had served as the Union Headquarters.

It was later that very night that an ambitious captain led a raiding party intent on burning the outlying farm of Virgil Clay-Harris, veteran of the battles of Sharpsburg, Gettysburg, and Chickamauga.

A few nights later, the Union troops having moved south, left a charred town of Cartersville in its wake. On the night of the fifteenth of November, as the Union troops departed the evacuated city of Atlanta to move "South to the Sea", the remaining shelled rubble of that city was set ablaze. The fire so engulfed the siege wreckage of Atlanta that it is worthy of being remembered as the funeral pyre of the Confederacy.

That very evening in the ashen rubble of Cartersville, in the darkness of the square, the embers only having recently cooled, there moved a thick, portly shadow from burned-out building to burned-out building.

The chubby, soot-streaked figure used his long stick to stir the ashen rubble of the burnt buildings. He would scour for anything usable left behind in the ashes, although mostly his stick would turn up only an occasional hot ember. He wore a bandana over his face to protect him from the smoke that still smoldered.

He was not having a very productive night, having found only soot, but he was sure there might be some kind of metal bounty – coins, skillets, guns, whatever – that he might recover from the ash. For the fat man knew that in the dire situation in which the county found itself, any metal object he might have found would be of some value. So, he continued to poke through the ashen ruins.

As he raked his stick through what used to be the general store, he noticed a shape off in his side-sight in a corner that remained partially unburnt. It was then near two in the morning, and the figure was too large to be a dog. It blended in to the soot covered remains that were no higher than his knees.

The hair on his arm stood in panic, as he feared perhaps it was a small black bear that had wandered down from the mountains. His heart was racing until he realized the figure was still. Not likely a bear at all. It appeared to be a corpse covered in soot propped up against the blackened stones that once had served as the corner fireplace in the storefront.

What was this body doing here? Had it been in the fire? If so, this much of it would not have been left. It might have something valuable on it – maybe a watch or a ring. He began to move slowly toward it under the moonless night sky, when suddenly he froze as the black figure stirred.

"I figured you'd be out here tonight looking for scraps of other folk's lives to steal, Chatmon," said the blackened figure as it raised its head and the hat upon it.

"Holy Moses, Willet, ya' dunned scared me half to death," said the chubby old man, regaining his breath. "All dressed in black like that, I figured ya' for a burned corpse."

"Ya' know why I dress in black, Chatmon? Same reason as you smeared soot all over yerself when ya' first come out tonight. To blend into the darkness." Willet had slowly raised himself to stand, and fat Chester Chatmon could see the scar across his face. A tremor of fear ran through him.

"Ya' know, Chatmon, with that thing across yer face ya' look like the horse thief ya' are..." continued Willet.

"Willet, this here's for the smoke," said Chatmon pulling the bandana down off his face.

"Well it sure ain't to disguise ya', cause yer the only person in this town that has any meat on his bones. How you stay so sloppy fat when near everyone else is fixin' to starve' to death, hereabouts?"

Suddenly, the relief that Chatmon had on discovering his "corpse" was really his partner in thievery, Willet, transformed itself into a rush of concern.

"I don't know what yer gittin' at, Willet..." said Chatmon, as he thought to himself *How long have I been tradin' in rustled cattle and horses from you and your boys Willet? Ever since you come back from Chickamauga.* "I guess I been just plum lucky," he said aloud.

"Lucky, alright, Chatmon. Just look around what's left of town here. Yers is the only business that weren't burned to the ground. Ol' Chatmon's livery stable still stands, now that's what I call lucky."

Willet drew his gun slowly and leveled the barrel at the old man.

Chatmon drew back in fear.

"I think ya' been makin' yer own luck, Chatmon," said the scarred-faced man in black. "Ya' been heard to say them very words."

Chatmon began to tremble, holding onto his tall walking stick with both hands, as if somehow that stiffened the spine that now shook inside him.

"Ya' also been heard talking to them Yankee soldiers. Ya' gave up Virgil Clay-Harris' farm to them, just so they wouldn't burn yer stables, didn't ya'?"

"No, no, I would never do that. Near everyone knows that Clay's a hero, saved the whole Army of Northern Virginia at Sharpsburg by killin' them Yanks as Lee retreated. Scared them from gittin' our boys. No, I couldn't never turn on Clay. The Yanks just wanted my stables for musterin' their own horses, that's the only reason they didn't burn it down."

"And yer house, too, Chatmon? Why ya' sweatin' like a pig? You lyin' to me?"

"Well, ...well, my house is attached to my stables, so they burn one, they'd already gone and burned the other. No, Willet, you got this all wrong."

Willet could smell the sweat that was now running down Chatmon's face.

"Except my boys been talkin' to the townsfolks. Ol' lady Landis said she saw you pleadin' with that cap'n and sergean' just as they was about to torch yer place. You gave them Clay, and then convinced them they'd be heroes to the Union if they burnt-out that Sharpshooter. They had never even heard of him, had they?"

Willet raised his gun to Chatmon's face and cocked back the hammer. "Had they?"

Chatmon's face rippled as the muscles below the skin trembled in fear. His mouth turned down at the corners, as tears flooded from his eyes. And he began to stammer out a response that was nothin' more than a pitiful sobbing squeal.

"They was going to burn it all, my stables, my house, everything I got. I wasn't going to have nothin' left. I'd be as poor as every-body else in this here town. So, I figured Clay would see 'em comin', maybe kill the lot of 'em. Hell, even if they burned his place, ain't like that Clay-Harris family had nuthin' to begin wit'. So, he loses a shack, better that than me losin' everything."

Chester Chatmon, fear splashed across his sweat drenched face, looked for forgiveness in the scarred face of Willet Blackwell.

"Yer pitiful, Chatmon, cryin' like a baby. You know I'm surprised they didn't come back and burn yer place to the ground after we run them Yankees off."

"Please don't shoot me, Willet. How long have we been doin' business? I been buyin' the stuff your boys been raidin' from folks for God knows how long. Don't shoot me, I'll give ya' a better deal on anything yer boys bring in, just don't shoot me."

Willet turned his gun to the ground, uncocking the hammer. "Quit yer wimperin', ya' fat bastard. I'm not going to shoot you. But it bothers me that you would have sold out Clay just to cover yer own ass. Makes me wonder who else ya' might give up next. Maybe somebody you was in cahoots wit'."

With this Willet walked past the trembling fat man who had just pleaded for his life. Chatmon collapsed to his knees, sniffling like a cried-out child. "I would never give ya' up, Willet. Honest, on my wife's grave. I would never give ya' up to no one, Willet."

Chatmon caught his breath as realized he had just dodged a brush with death at the hands of Blackwell. He thought to himself he would have to do something when the sun rose to ease Willet's fears. For Chatmon had learned that Willet was not a man he was willing to feud with.

That's when the old man felt the hand come from behind him grabbing his hair and yanking his head back with great force. Out of the corner of his terrified eye, he saw the knife come from over the other shoulder.

He could clearly see etched in its blade the letters WEB next to an engraved Stars and Bars of the Confederacy. Chatmon began to convulse uncontrollable in fear.

Then, in an instant, the blade slit a bloody arc across his throat, just above his hanging bandana, that burned like a heated wire pulled under his skin. He felt the hand release his head, as he dropped to the floor among the burned remains of the general store. He thrashed on the ground, his hands at his throat. He could taste the ash along with the fear in his mouth. He could hear the gurgling noises as his body involuntarily panicked. He gasped for the air he could not draw, his terror intensified as he watched his own blood, black in the night, mix with the soot into a demonic slurry.

Willet Blackwell stood over him until he died. He cleaned the knife on the leg of Chatmon's trousers, then slowly slid it into the sheath inside his boot. When he was sure fat Chester was dead, he turned to walk away, saying, "No, Chatmon, I don't reckon yer be givin' nobody else up to nobody."

3

THE WAR AND ITS ECHOES
FALL 1864 – FALL 1869

Four long, hard years had passed since the end of the fighting. In the South, the post-war misery passed over no one. The United States Congress had ruled it illegal for the Confederate war debts to be repaid, although they honored all debts incurred by the Union Army. As such, those who toiled on behalf of the Confederacy had lost nearly everything, either having been paid in currency that was worthless, or holding debt that could never be legally repaid.

The plague of loss afflicting Southerners extended all the way to the White House. Upon the assassination of Abraham Lincoln at the hands of John Wilkes Booth, the newly elected Vice-President, Andrew Johnson of Tennessee, ascended to the Presidency. Lincoln had broken with his first term running mate, Hannibal Hamlin, to select a pro-Union Southern Democrat in the 1864 election. His intent was to form a National Unity Government as opposed to a strictly Republican administration. Ironically, the nation found itself having resolved the fighting of the Civil War, only to find a Southern Democrat residing in the White House.

One of Andrew Johnson's first directives was an amnesty of all soldiers who had fought for the Confederacy. Those specifically exempted from the amnesty, such as anyone holding rank above Colonel in the Confederate military, or serving in position within the Confederate Government, were allowed to apply for a presidential pardon. In a little over one year, President Johnson had issued over 12,600 pardons.

This overly generous clemency and the attempt at Presidential Reconstruction only angered and emboldened the Radical Republicans in Congress. Johnson's Presidential Reconstruction left most decisions in the hands of the Southern states, who quickly enacted their own "black codes" limiting the liberties of the freed slaves.

President Johnson soon was at open war with the Republican dominated Congress. They battled viciously over the severity of the proposed Congressional Reconstruction of the South. One of his first entanglements with the legislative body was over the law passed by Congress establishing the Federal Freedmen's Bureau. The intent of this measure was to provide assistance to the newly freed slaves from the actions of their own state and local governments. The Freedmen's Bureau would have the power to invalidate contracts and actions limiting the rights of the newly freed Negroes. The President saw it as another Federal overreach upon states' rights.

Johnson quickly vetoed the measure, only to have the Congress rapidly override his veto, thus passing it into law. This sequence of events soon became commonplace for many bills from the Congress having to do with the Reconstruction of the South.

A rift had grown between Johnson and his Secretary of War, Edwin Stanton, who had been appointed by Lincoln. In fact, Stanton had been one of the key architects of the Union War effort, and he generally sided with the Republicans in Congress on Reconstruction issues.

Congress had passed a law, again over Johnson's veto, called the Tenure of Office Act, which severely limited the President's power to dismiss members of his own cabinet. The law was surely unconstitutional as a restriction on Presidential power. It was repealed twenty years later without ever having been challenged to the Supreme Court.

When Johnson attempted to dismiss Stanton in 1867, the fuse of impeachment was lit. This represented the first time that a sitting president was impeached, and it stood as the only presidential impeachment for well over one hundred years.

It may well have been history's sequence of events that saved Johnson from being removed from office. When Johnson ascended to the Presidency, the office of Vice President remained vacant, per the rules of succession at the time. Given this, the next in-line to the White House was the President Pro Tempore of the Senate, Ohio Senator Benjamin Wade. Senator Wade was progressive beyond his times, going so far as favoring the right for women to vote, even in the 1860's.

Thus, with Wade waiting in the wings of the Presidency, Johnson was found not guilty in his trial in the Senate by a single vote. Perhaps that is why in 1871 the New Orleans Times called the life of Benjamin Wade "a profane history".

President Johnson served out Lincoln's second term but failed to secure the Democratic nomination for the 1868 election. After Ulysses S. Grant was voted into office, Johnson returned to Tennessee. His vindication would come six years later, when he was elected to the United States Senate. He remains the only President to serve in the Senate after leaving the White House. However, only months after being sworn in as a Senator, Johnson would die as the result of a crippling stroke.

Despite the tribulations of President Johnson, and the suffering of the ruling classes of the South, it was the working families who were hit the hardest in post-war Georgia. Poor by any means before the war, they lived in destitution since its end. Livestock and farm animals were slow to be available to them. Beasts of burden to work their fields were even scarcer. Meat, in general, was unavailable to the poor.

The few who had meat often had no means with which to preserve it, as salt was still a scarce commodity years after the fighting had ceased. The efficiency of the Union naval blockade against the Confederacy had such a devastating effect, despite it being lifted after the war, commodities such as sugar, spices, and salt were nearly unobtainable for years to the common man.

The newly freed slaves, or Freedmen, suffered equally alongside the poor whites of the South. Many would lose hope. Many would lose everything.

Perhaps the cruelest stroke of all was that in many cases the shackles of slavery were replaced with the bindings of inequitable legal contracts for their services. In several cases, the plantation owners took advantage of the ignorance of those Negroes to whom they had previously denied the most fundamental elements of education.

Image 5 – First Bartow County Courthouse in Cartersville (Constructed 1869-1873)

Yet, there were indeed shifting tides within the North Georgia county. Cassville, having been utterly destroyed by the Union Army, was never rebuilt to its former prominence. The town was no longer worthy of being the seat of the county government. For even had it been rebuilt, the town lacked the key technical advantage so critical in the time period – the railroads did not run through Cassville. There was a depot in Cass Station, but this was somewhat removed from the town.

The railroads, which were rebuilt by the Federal Government after the war, did indeed stop in downtown Cartersville. The Western and Atlantic Railroad Depot was reopened on the town square, and the delegates of Bartow County decided to move the county seat to Cartersville in 1867.

The new courthouse was being built just down the tracks from the same depot that Sherman had burned in November of 1864. The courthouse was paid for with private funds from the citizens, and its construction was a source of civic pride to the town.

Clay continued to scratch out a living from the land on the banks of Pettit's Creek left to him by his departed father. He struggled to raise enough crops to feed himself, his mother, and his younger brother Truitt. All the while Clay tortured his own mind, wondering what would ever have drawn his gun-smith father to abandon his family, and take up with another woman in far-off Texas.

Clay was adamant that Truitt continue his schooling, for which he had a natural aptitude. Clay had lived his life without education and could see the respect that well-learned people garnered in town. Truitt would be schooled, no matter the cost to the family. Clay considered this essential for the generations of Clay-Harris to follow, lest they should live in the hardship that defined his life.

Clay had known Deekie since they both were children. He and Willet and she had played in the caves of Three Sisters Mountain together. The three of them had grown up just outside the pleasant little town before the war. In fact, Deekie had been there at the Cartersville depot that day he and Willet had boarded the train to leave to fight the Federals.

She was Willet's girl then. She had given herself to Blackwell for the first-time only days before they left. She waited anxiously during the early war years for their return. She prayed every day for their safety. After each battle, she waited days, if not weeks, in agony for letters from either of them, to know if they had survived.

She was there the day Willet brought Clay back from the war, both of them having been butchered in the Battle of Chickamauga.

The war had wounded Deekie as much as her two friends. She had been born into a good working-class family, like Willet's, somewhat better off than Clay's. But that family seemed to be torn apart by her arrival, with her mother dying just days after her childbirth.

Her father named her DeKalb, after his departed wife's family. The girl grew, but never into that formal name. She came to be known to all as "Deekie".

She was raised as one might expect a widowed man might raise a child, more as a boy than the young girl she was. She loved her father dearly, especially when he so affectionately called her "*Deeks*".

When she was sixteen, her father had gone to war as well, leaving her in the care of a neighbor's family. Her father did not return, as he was killed the next year at Chancellorsville by a Yankee in an area known only as The Wilderness.

It was the same battle that ultimately took Stonewall Jackson's life. Accidentally shot by his own men, Jackson died of pneumonia after being treated for his battle wounds.

With the loss of her father, the war had left her all alone as a seventeen-year-old girl with no other family in town. Deekie moved back into her childhood home. She tried to keep it going from her father's modest savings, but these soon ran out and the house was lost.

Deekie thought she could rebuild her life with the return of her two wounded childhood friends from the fighting at Chickamauga. She noticed the physical changes – Willet's horribly scarred face and Clay's amputated left arm - immediately. It took her much longer to notice the changes in their personalities.

Clay, who she had always called by his given name "Virgil" since childhood , was terribly ill when Willet brought him back home. He ran a severe fever, and all feared he would succumb to it. His maw attended him for two days, but had decided that he would not live, and thought it merciful to allow nature to take its course.

Deekie refused to accept this. She came into the shack and

nursed Clay back to health. After several days by his side, his fever finally broke as Deekie administered over him.

This became the root of animosity between Deekie and Clay's maw – that the young girl had tended to her son after the old woman herself had given up on him. Just as the same woman had been given up on by her own philandering husband with that harlot in Texas.

After nursing her friend Virgil back to health, and having earned the contempt of Clay's maw, Deekie left the cabin.

With nowhere else to go, Deekie took up with Willet. He had just set up camp atop Three Sisters Mountain, by an old Indian stone settlement there. Many said it was an ancient site, outdating the burial mounds in nearby Etowah. Willet had moved into the abandoned site and set up large canvas tents that he had stolen since being back in town.

Initially, Willet was hiding alone from the Confederate Army he had deserted, but while she was with him he brought together the five men who would become his gang of renegades. They followed Willet because of his personal magnetism, the same characteristic that had drawn her to him years ago.

This is when she noticed the differences between her two friends. The contrast was stark, with each of them struggling in their own ways.

While Clay recovered from his wounds, he sank deeper and deeper into silence. He would not speak of the war, and when she pushed the subject upon him, he would become rigid and unfriendly to her.

On the contrary, Willet loved to speak of the war. He would rattle off all the details of the various battles – Sharpsburg, Gettysburg, and even the days leading up to Chickamauga. Yet, he would never speak of that final battle itself, or of how he and Clay had come to be wounded.

Willet took glee in recounting the many Yankees he had killed in the war. He spoke of it incessantly. He had a lust for it that went unfulfilled. He began drinking more and more with his new gang. They drank anything they could steal.

And they would steal anything they damn well pleased.

One cold December night, Willet had been drinking in camp when he became impatient and aggressive towards Deekie. He began to abuse her physically that night, slapping and dragging her. She had never seen this behavior in him before but told herself it was something from the war that he would outgrow. Willet laid his hands on her no more that winter and begged her to forgive him for having ever done so.

Then, in the Spring of 1864, long after Willet and Clay had escaped from the jaws of the war, that deadliest of conflagrations came to their county with a fury, as if it was a starving beast hunting the two of them.

In May of 1864, the Yankees came into Bartow county under the command of General William T. Sherman. Having the Federals in his homeland drove Willet absolutely livid. All he could talk of was killing the invading Yankees.

Several months rolled on, before Willet's frustrations, compounded by his weakness for drink, led him to bring abuse upon Deekie a second time. Again, he profusely apologized to her the next day, but despite his pleadings for her to stay, despite his promises to never allow this brutality to recur, it did. The frequency of the slapping and shoving slowly increased. With each occurrence, he became slightly more physical with her. Then, one night in September, he told Deekie, as he assaulted her, that she had brought this abuse upon herself. It was then that she knew she would have to leave him for her own safety, but she still had nowhere else to go.

In October of that year, the rage in him exploded. Willet and his gang of marauders had left her alone in camp, as they often had. Deekie knew they would go on raiding parties to rustle livestock or steal whatever they might have come to need. But this time was different, they were gone much longer, and the relative calm of their absence steeped an ominous foreboding in her.

They had disappeared for many days – nearly two weeks - and returned with no bounty whatsoever, except Union handguns and those damn Henry rifles.

The camp was quiet for the first few days upon their return. The men seemed to share in an unspeakable tainting of a great crime. Slowly their guilt was replaced by a mock bravado that was to shelter them from their conscience.

It was a few days later when she first heard them speak of it around the camp. They had captured and executed ten Union soldiers and dumped the bodies in Cassville on the grounds of the Women's College. Willet had satisfied his bloodlust. For a while, anyway.

Deekie made the mistake of asking him how they could kill these men in cold blood.

"It was easy, girl, they was Yankees," said Willet. He had been drinking whiskey, and she should have known better than to say what she said next.

"They were men, Willet. With kin waiting for them to come home from this war, just like I waited for you. You didn't kill these men in battle. You captured them as stragglers and then executed them like they was criminals."

"Open yer damn eyes, Deekie. Look around this land. They are criminals. Can't you see the suffering?" An anger had seeped into Willet's voice.

"I can't believe you and your men did this. Is this for what Clay saved your life at Chickamauga?"

The last comment enraged him. It was then that Willet had closed the palm with which he had only been slapping Deekie into a fist.

"You ungrateful little bitch. He left me with this carved-up face for people to stare at for the rest of my life. I would have been better off iffen he would have let that Bluebelly kill me."

"So, it is true, Clay did save ya' from the Yankees at Chickamauga. And this is what you do with the life he gave ya'?"

Willet exploded into furious rage. His drunken frustration became a violent storm upon her. Despite her screams and cries, no one else in camp came to her aid. He expended his every guilt upon her, until his own exhaustion overcame him.

That night, after he passed out, Deekie collected every ounce of her remaining strength, and somehow overcame the excruciating pain of the horribly inflicted wounds. She ran from him. She knew if she failed to do so, no matter the sorrow he expressed on the morn, his next beating would surely kill her.

Image 6 – Three Sisters Mountain

Deekie left the camp. The other men had been drinking as well, and the entire camp was in a drunken stupor. She slowly worked her way down from the mountain, constantly looking over her shoulder. Every noise of the night raised the greatest fear in her. She came upon the Mission Trail, and having nowhere else to go, she headed towards town.

As she came upon Pettit's Creek, she became weak with pain and was overcome by her own emotion. She thought of her old friend Virgil, and she dragged her bruised body to his cabin door. And that was how Deekie had come to be with Clay.

4

SURVIVING THE DROUGHT
1865 TO 1869

Deekie had come to Clay bruised and battered. She was as frightened as the whipped stray she had become. She needed someplace where more than anything else she could feel safe.

Clay attended to Deekie, making her feel welcome in the one room shack. His maw protested, and in a way that Deekie could not help but hear. "That woman don't need be here, Clay. We barely got enough for the three of us to live off of. Send her back to Willet."

"No, mama, I can't do that," Clay responded flatly. "I will not send her back to the man who did this to her. We'll make do."

"Then we'll all starve, boy," responded his maw.

"Then we'll all starve together," he said, staring at the bruised skin of his childhood friend. *How could Willet lay hands on her this way?* he wondered.

Clay had come across any number of strays over the years. It was his experience that they would only cower so much before they turned on those that abused them.

Clay told Deekie as she healed, "Girl, ya' stay by mah side as long as ya' need. Give mah maw no mind, she done been twisted by Diddy's leavin."

"Virgil, I swear I won't be no trouble a t'all. I can he'p you in the fields. I can he'p Truitt with his schoolin'. Maybe I can even he'p ya' with some learning for yerself."

Clay had always been aware of his lack of education. During the war, while he met many soldiers, most even more simple than himself, Clay had been exposed to some of the most educated men he had ever met – the Rebel officers. They spoke elegantly, acted gallantly and fought fiercely for their lands.

Clay wanted this path to an elevated lifestyle to one day be the legacy he left for the generations of the Clay-Harris family to come. He hoped Truitt's schooling would lead to great things, which one day might wash away the shame of their run-away paw. Or even Clay's being wounded and left lame from the war. He was dead set on Truitt receiving all the education he possibly could.

This would leave only Clay and Deekie to work the soil. This would be done without the aid of any plow-horse or ox. While the Yankees promised the newly freed slaves "forty acres and a mule", no such working creatures were made available to the poor farmers such as Clay.

Each day, the two of them exhausted themselves. With Clay having only one good arm, Deekie's help was desperately needed. She became his hands. Clay spent the first week teaching her how to tie the basic knots they would need about the farm. He was frustrated trying to teach without the ability to demonstrate himself. He took to crude drawings to show her. Slowly, she took to his verbal and drawn directions and learned the art of his craft.

Soon she had tied the ropes into crude harnesses that allowed Clay to pull a makeshift plow. His sweat would cleave the hardened soil like the beast of burden that the war had left him. His days left his back marked with the burns of poverty.

Deekie continued to follow Clay into the fields each day like a shadow. The Southern sun weathered them both, the exertion of their toils only magnifying its effects. Deekie was not welcome in the cabin throughout the day, where Clay's maw constantly harassed her.

Each day was like the day before, with Deekie leaving the shack early to work with Clay. Their days together were mostly quiet, with Clay's silence seemingly deepening each year after the war.

Deekie learned to speak only when necessary, as this seemed preferable to Clay, and this reserved quiet came to suit her.

Each night, when she returned alongside Clay, Deekie was still subjected to the older woman's insults until Clay would be forced to quiet his hostile maw. After whatever dinner they might be lucky enough to have, the exhausted Deekie would sleep on the floor on a tick mattress alongside Clay in the corner of the single large room.

This only stirred further hatred in the bitter heart of the old woman. She could not bear to see her own son, alongside this vagabond girl, when she herself was shamed to sleep alone. Despite all this, in Deekie an intimacy with Clay was spawning.

Their relationship had become as hard as the land they worked together. She had come to him bruised and bloodied, and he took her in. Neither out of love nor duty, Clay just took her in as the stray she had become. He had given her a home and a purpose, and she was ever grateful for both. More than anything, she felt safe, free from physical abuse, even if she was continually verbally harassed by the old bitter woman that Clay's maw had become.

It was during Deekie's first summer living with Clay in '65 when the inevitable happened. The war had just ended. Clay and Deekie had been working the fields under the scorching sun. This was Deekie's greatest joy, being alongside Clay and working the land.

One late summer day, having toiled under the relentless sun, they were both covered in sweat, and their bodies dripped like ripened fruit. They had decided to cool themselves upon the tree-lined banks of the creek.

Clay kneeled in the creek to wet his bandana with which to wash his face and cool his neck. Deekie stripped out of the ragged dress she had worn in the field. She stood naked before him for the first time, unashamed, before joining him in the cool waters of the creek.

Being alone with her in this way stirred feelings in Clay he did not understand. Her naked body, her bruises long healed, was surely as beautiful as any creation of the Lord that had ever been placed before him. Her tired frame was seemingly refreshed by their newborn intimacy. Deep within him stirred a longing for her, making him for the first time in his life regret never having had experienced this feeling before. Yet, at the same time, Clay felt he was betraying her, felt he was taking advantage of her in this way. He also could not help but think of Willet, and this act of betrayal to his friend.

Deekie came to Clay in the creek. She took the wet bandana from his hand and dipped it again in the cool, running water. She then washed his face and hair tenderly with it. The cascading water drenched his shirt, soothing him.

Clay looked into her young weathered face, and despite her skin having been hardened by the sun, her eyes had a softness of longing for him. She reached around him with the bandana to splash his neck, her breasts pressing hard against the soiled shirt upon his chest.

He looked deeper into her tender eyes. He saw her vulnerability, but in a manner tremendously different from when she had first come to him, bruised and battered. She was no longer the whipped and beaten animal cast carelessly aside.

She was now willing to show him, that under the hardened exterior she had been forced to adopt, lay the sensitivity of a young woman who had grown to first respect, and then to admire, the man before her. The man who had given her a life again. A safe life.

Her vulnerability was now not of the flesh, but of the heart.

She reached with the soothing wet bandana under his field shirt and found the deep burns that marred his neck and back. These were from the plow's rope harness, which she herself had fashioned. Her knots had scarred him, as much as the fall of any man's whip. As her gentle touch tended to his scars, she drew his mouth down to hers. The desire within her trembled as she pressed herself upon him, melting her mouth into his, her hands under his drenched field shirt pulling his scarred back hard into her. In that precious second, her body told him of its all-consuming yearning to fuse into one with his.

Clay's response was awkward at first. He could not deny his feelings for her, but now these were being pulled from him by the runaway desire within her. He dared not pull away from her, fearing the rejection might drive her away permanently. Slowly, he admitted to himself during that probing kiss that he wished not to pull away at all. It was just that he kept hearing Willet's voice in his mind telling him he should do so.

Deekie gently pulled her lips from his. She slowly unbuttoned his drenched shirt. She could feel him wrench his crippled left arm away from her. She tenderly undraped his form revealing his muscular chest and upper right arm. His left arm was somewhat withered and truncated clumsily below the elbow.

She tossed his creek-drenched and sweat-stained shirt onto the muddy banks of the stream.

Clay had been shielding his stubbed forearm with his body, but Deekie was intent on exploring it. She knew how sensitive he had been about it since returning from the war. She longed to tell him through her actions that she loved all of him, even that which had been so brutally butchered in battle.

She cupped her hand behind his elbow, then pulled it gently from behind him. He resisted, yet she only persisted more vigorously. Clay's embarrassment slowly disappeared as Deekie leaned to gently kiss the mangled skin of his arm's healed wound.

Without looking up at him, she said aloud, "Virgil, I know this part of you was taken away, but it don't matter. You have showed me great kindness, and now, if you will let me, I will pay you back. I am thankful for everything you done for me. Let me share the only thing I have left – my heart."

Deekie then washed his left arm with the cool waters of the creek.

It was perhaps the first time since the war that Clay had come to terms with his infirmity. That day in the creek, it did not make him any less of a man, and he found solace in that she desired him. The voice of Willet protested louder in his mind, but slowly it was pushed away by his innermost desires. Clay yielded to her, and she was tender to him.

Not long after that encounter, a devastating drought overtook the county. The fields withered, and the creek ran dry as if the damnation of the Yankees was not severe enough. Then came the damnation of nature itself. It was as if the continual tears of the loss of the war had drained the very Southern skies themselves.

Deekie and Clay were able to manage a modest crop from their land, but only through the sacrifice of their tremendous combined efforts. This deepening hardship only brought them closer together. They slowly grew into a single entity, one that Deekie felt would last forever.

They were not quite lovers, although they continued to share pleasure with each other. They were both the wounded and the protector, and each of them knew that at alternating times they were to play each role. They shared the closest of bonds, for each had been wounded, and each had been healed. But what each did not realize was that the healing of the other was painfully incomplete.

The drought persisted, so severely that many left the area to resettle in the new western territories of the nation. Deekie and Clay knew this plot of land was their last refuge, and they defended the fields of their homestead against the ravages of the burning sun.

Each day at dawn, they would begin the long march to find water. Often having to walk as far as the Etowah River at Rowland's Bend, where they would fill leather bags with as much water as Clay could carry on the tree limb he had improvised as a yoke across his shoulders. It was not uncommon for a second drawing to be made later in the day at the height of summer. By the burden of these efforts alone were they able to grow enough food to barely feed the four mouths of the shack.

The drought stretched into a second year. Their hardships continued. North Georgia families suffered, as they had during the devastating procession of Sherman across the area. In addition to the destruction, burning and looting of his army, the railways were intentionally destroyed by the Federals, denying their use to the Confederates.

Sherman had the rails of the remaining lines between North

Georgia and Atlanta twisted into mangled, unusable scraps of iron. These were left along the path of the former tracks, often wrapped in a contorted manner around the trunk of a large tree. These mangled rails came to be known as "Sherman's Neckties".

The Union did undertake the reconstruction of the railroads after the war, but during this period they were unusable. Famine set in from the ongoing drought, and food from other areas could not be shipped in by train to relieve the widespread hunger.

Even medicines could not be obtained to relieve the suffering of the resulting extensive illness cast upon the land.

Deekie and Clay hunkered down, redoubling their efforts to keep the family fed. They continued to walk miles for the slightest bits of water they could draw, and through their tremendous efforts, they continued to produce just enough food to keep them all from starving.

Their words were few. There was no luxury of laughter, no pride in their persisting. There was only survival. Subsistence was the bond that connected them at the deepest level. It was more primal than even the rawest desires they still satisfied in each other.

Still, over these years, Deekie and Clay remained inseparable. The fields yielded more crops as the weather improved and their skills increased. The skies finally opened, and the dry creek began to flow yet again. Soon, there was a modest surplus with which they could barter for other necessities. Their labors bore fruit, but their existence was still unbearably hard.

As time went by, Deekie spoke more to him, often inquiring about the war. Clay had remained quiet, refusing to address what had happened in battle. Deekie persisted in her attempt to draw him out of his isolation.

He continued to tense uncomfortably whenever she approached the subject, but she had an unquenchable desire to know exactly what had happened to her two childhood friends. To the only two men she had ever shared herself with.

Deep within them, Clay and Deekie knew they did not fully love each other, but they continued to steal comfort from their common hardship in each other's arms as the opportunities presented themselves. One afternoon, they rested from their labor under the cool canopy of the dense pine forest. They had just finished satisfying their desires. Her head laid upon his chest as they rested.

"Virgil," she began, with her being the only person to call him by his Christian name, "how is it you never talk about what you and Willet went through durin' the war?"

Her fingers curiously searched the creviced skin of the scarred stump of his arm. Upon presenting her question, she could feel him pull it away from her. She could feel his body tense beneath her.

"You can tell me, Virgil. Tell me all about what you and Willet went through while y'all was away."

She thought to herself that it had been years since the war was over, and that the salve of time would allow him to recall it, to get it out of his blood.

She did not realize that the terror of taking the lives of other men would forever be embedded deep within his veins.

"Deekie," he responded with a tense exhaustion that seemed to drive out the relaxed state he had enjoyed moments before, "we done been through this so many times. I'm fixin' to tell ya' for the last time, that is somethin' I never want to talk about. Not with you, not with no one."

She paused, having expected his response. Yet, she had over the past few years crafted different strategies to draw the discussion from him.

"Ya' remember the day I come to the depot to see you and Willet off to war?" Her voice was nostalgic.

"I remember ya' come to see Willet off, you was his girl then," answered Clay.

"You boys were so eager." In the long second she paused, she could feel his chest stiffen further beneath her. "Y'all looked so fresh in your uniforms…"

"That's because we had not a stitch of an idea what we was headin' off into." said Clay. "We had no idea what war was about. Not a lick."

"What did you think it would be?" She could feel a twitch ripple through him.

"We didn't know nuthin'. We thought it was gonna be some great adventure, some way to cover ourselves in glory."

Deekie repositioned her naked self upon his chest. She had now gotten further than she had expected, although she could sense the tension building within him.

"Virgil," she said, drawing his name out in a smooth coil, "You did cover yourself in glory. Ya' killed all them Yankees at Sharpsburg."

His voice became flat and rigid. "I told ya' I am not talking about that, woman."

Deekie decided to push just a little bit further. She traced her fingers in the small hollow at the base of his throat, as if to coax out the words that continued to elude her.

He swallowed gently. As she had pressed herself upon him, he became more and more aware of the weight of her body upon his chest. He was beginning to feel more and more driven into the soil. He became entrapped by her words.

"They say you killed some fifteen Yankees with your long-range rifle. Convinced General McClellan not to follow General Lee's army back into Virginia. They say you saved the Army of Northern Virginia that day…"

The response beneath Deekie was as rapid as if the earth had violently shaken. Clay exploded upward, sweat dripping from his brow. Not the fine beads of sweat from their natural act moments before, but a drenching sweat of uncontrolled terror.

He grabbed her arm with his one hand. His grip was fearfully tight to her. His arm shook itself with tremors. Soon, he was shaking her cruelly.

"They got it all wrong, Deekie. I told ya' I didn't wanna talk about this. Don't you go and listen to what these ignorant townsfolk say. They don't know, they wasn't there. Fifteen Yankees laid low. I wish it were only that many. It were at least twice that. Where did all this long-range sharpshooting talk come from? I can tell ya' that there ain't no glory in shooting boys at thirty yards. Ya' hear me. I could hear them Yankees dyin', wheezin', spitting up blood as they drew their last breaths and called out fer their mamas. I could see their eyes when they knew they was all but dead. Don't you ever ask me about his again, ya' hear me. Well, do ya' hear me?"

Clay had not realized the force with which he had shaken her. His voice had found level after increasing level of agitation as he spoke. Deekie had pulled away from him, her eyes flooded with tears from the explosion she had triggered. In her eyes burned a terror he had not seen in her since that first night she came to him from Willet Blackwell.

"Don't hurt me, Virgil," she cried at him.

He was frozen by the comment. He could never think to hurt her. Yet, he had just done exactly that. He tried to wrap his only good arm around her, but she pulled away further from him.

"Don't you never hurt me, Virgil" she said, "Or ya' won't never see me again'!"

Clay looked at his empty hand. It shook in tremor as he had recalled the killings of Sharpsburg. His heart raced. He had transferred his horrors upon her.

"I'm sorry, Deekie. I didn't mean to blow up at ya' like Willet done," said Clay. He realized that as she had drawn out the terrors of war in him, his response had drawn out the terrors of the war's abuse that echoed in her.

Deekie collected herself. She stared at him, never having seen him anger to this point. It reminded her of the rage of Willet.

"Willet never had a problem talking about killin' Yankees, Virgil," she sneered at him. "He would get drunk and brag about it. He liked killing them, 'specially them soldiers he and his gang killed after the Yankees come around here."

Clay looked at her in confusion. He remembered the bruises and marks on her back.

"It sure didn't look that way the night ya' come to me," he said.

Deekie was now pulling her clothes on. She was still frightened of the man she had just shared herself with.

"He never got tired talkin' of the war. And he never punched me before, Virgil, 'til the first time I asked him if you really saved his life at Chickamauga. He had slapped me something fierce many times, but it was that night that he nearly beat me to death."

"What?" said Clay. She had never talked about that night, the night she had left Willet and come to him, just as he had never talked about the war.

"He flew into a rage, Virgil. Slapped me until his palm turned into a fist. After that he kept punchin' me with all his might, until I laid bloodied on the dirt at his feet. Then he started whippin' me with them leather cords he carries." Now her voice had worked itself into a frenzy.

"All I done was ask him about Chickamauga," she cried.

Clay just looked at her. Within him, the remnants of war surged. He remembered Chickamauga, that first major battle on Georgia soil. He could smell the smoke, see the sprawl of the dead, and hear the panicked flight of the Yankees realizing they had lost in a terrible way.

Then he remembered being with Willet, side by side, when they were unexpectedly charged.

"What happened to you two there?!" she screamed at him. "What happened to y'all? That's all I want to know…"

The edge of anger in her voice was lined with the fear of a woman who had perhaps just lost her last safe haven.

She was vulnerable, for she had again given herself to him, and he had hurt her in a way she feared more than death.

"I will never lay a hand on you again, Deekie. I promise. I am so sorry to make you remember all he did to you."

She looked at him again, not believing what he was saying. She had heard the same words from Willet, only to have the violence against her return.

"This ain't got nothing to do with Willet, Virgil. This here is you and me. You are the kindest man I ever had met, but you can change so fast into somethin' violent and fierce. Like a wounded animal. It scares me."

He knew it to be true. He could often feel the tension build in him when people pushed him on about the war before he would lash out without warning.

"It scares me, Virgil," she said a second time. "I want to feel safe. I need somebody to make me feel safe."

He took her in his arm.

"I am so sorry, Deekie. I will never lay harm on you agin'." He wondered if he would ever be able to heal the fear he had inflicted upon her.

"You ever touch me again like that, Virgil Clay-Harris, and I will kill ya' where ya' sleep."

Her eyes burned with a mixture of fury and fear that told him she spoke the truth.

5

JUDGEMENTS AND JURISDICTIONS
SUMMER OF 1870

Following the end of the war, Union troops were stationed in the South not only to provide protection to those slaves freed from the plantations and other servitude, but also to assure that the re-establishment of civil governments in the former Confederacy would not revert to retribution against these new citizens. The Confederate governments had been dissolved. In 1866, following the Republican dominance in the mid-term elections, in an affront to President Johnson, Congress directed that Union commanders be given control of the five military districts of the South. These represented the ten States that had not ratified the fourteenth amendment, assuring equal rights to the freed slaves, until each state could write new constitutions that would be approved by the Union.

A year after the war concluded in 1865, the administration of law in Georgia was restructured. What had previously been deemed the Inferior Courts of Georgia (as opposed to the Superior Courts) were now restructured as County Courts within the state. With this, it became clear that a new courthouse was needed for Bartow County. In December 1866, it was announced that the citizens of Cartersville would construct a courthouse at the townspeople's expense on the condition it be located in the town of Cartersville.

The courthouse location decision was put to a vote, and the

issue was decided by a margin of 1085 votes for Cartersville over 919 votes for Cass Station. Cass Station had been the railroad depot closest to the former County Seat of Cassville.

The new Cartersville courthouse was to be built alongside the Western & Atlantic Railroad tracks in the town square. The courthouse was begun in 1867, and by 1870 the Courtroom upon the second floor of the structure was rendering verdicts, although construction was not completed until 1873.

It was in that summer of 1870, that Truitt Clay-Harris, then eighteen years of age, began his apprenticeship for the Clerk of the Court. His schooling had been accelerated, given his abilities, and even though he did not come from a prominent family of the county, his abilities were recognized in the appointment.

His duties were primarily associated with case documentation, but also he was responsible for the handling, logging and safekeeping of physical evidence. He was apprenticed to a newly elected Clerk of the Court, Conyers W. Trippe.

The county judge presiding was J. R. Ferris. Judge Ferris was an anomaly within the early years of Reconstruction. He was a meticulous judge, who prided himself on the procedural underpinnings of his court.

It was said that Judge Ferris once dismissed a case against a vagabond accused of aggravated assault against a white woman of the county because the evidence introduced in court had been misplaced before the end of the trial. The man walked out the courthouse completely free at the ruling of Judge Ferris, although he was found drowned in the Etowah River a short time thereafter. However dutiful he was to the procedural aspects within his courthouse, Judge Jesse Ferris was an unabashed Southerner who found nothing felonious in the vigilante justice administered beyond his court's realm.

Juxtaposed to Judge Ferris was Clerk of the Court Conyers W. Trippe. He was an ambitious man. Ambitious to a fault. Rather than execute the responsibilities of his office, he was constantly in search of his next appointment. Thus, he delegated nearly all the responsibilities of the Clerk of the Court to his apprentice, save for the signing of documents requiring a formal signature.

It was a hot summer day in August 1870, in the courtroom when Judge Ferris, Clerk Conyers Trippe and his new apprentice, Truitt Clay-Harris, were challenged to understand the elocution of the town's first resident Carpetbagger – an Irish gentleman from Boston who had been appointed the county's first representative of the Federal Freedmen's Bureau.

The man spoke unlike any Yankee appointed up until that time by the bureaucracy of the Federal Reconstruction. His voice was high, despite that the girth of the fellow otherwise suggested a depth of timbre. The brogue of his speech rolled high and low and high again, as if floating on a wave.

This was apropos, as the gentleman, one Colin Brannigan, was himself an immigrant from across the Atlantic, from the emerald isle of Ireland.

Colin Brannigan had been in the United States for over 20 years, having emigrated during the height of the great Potato Famine in 1848. He had quickly established himself as a merchant among the ever-growing Irish population of Boston. He became prosperous, and with the protection of the Irish mobsters in that port, he soon became a prominent businessman.

Brannigan soon realized he could profit from the war when it came to be. He did this by taking a bounty for each Irish youth he talked into volunteering. Then, after the conscription was enacted by Lincoln in 1863, he profited from the selling of replacement soldiers to wealthy families. Their sons could be spared the ravages of war if a replacement soldier was arranged. Brannigan was quick to establish an informal service where the destitute poor of Boston could be enticed to enlist in the Union Army for a fee offered by himself.

The sum offered by Brannigan to the immigrant poor was more than they could expect to earn in Boston in several years hard labor. Often the money went directly to their families to keep them fed and sheltered through the harsh New England winters. What these volunteer replacements did not know was that the monies which they collected were usually less than one-third of the huge sums demanded by Brannigan from the wealthiest families to keep their sons from the dangers of the war. And so, with every Irish life that he gambled on the battlefields far to the south of his home in Boston, Colin Brannigan greatly enriched himself.

In 1866, the year after the war had been decided, given his new-found wealth, he sent for his widowed sister in Dublin to come join him in America. The response that came back was stunning to him - his sister was dying of the Consumption. She was near death, and as such unable to make the crossing. Even had she the energy, no ship would allow her contagious body aboard it. Instead, she pleaded with her brother to take her daughter, his niece, Ever Nic Lochlain. They agreed Ever would join her Uncle, but not until after her mother passed.

Colin's sister lingered and suffered. She finally came to her end in the Fall of 1869. True to his word, Colin Brannigan sent for his niece. She would join her uncle in Boston the following Spring.

She came to America with the anglicized name of Ever McLaughlin and joined her uncle in his stately townhome residence only a short distance removed from the Boston Common.

Soon after she had joined him, her Uncle Colin had heard through his contacts in Boston's political circles that politicians in New York State had connections within the administration of President Ulysses S. Grant. They were selling titles to lucrative government positions in the South. Brannigan invested a sizable portion of his wealth in procuring a Freedmen's Bureau Administrator position for North Georgia. In addition to his government salary, the position came with the right to open a Freedmen's Savings Institution. With this, he intended to enrich himself upon the savings of the newly freed slaves of the South.

"So, Mister Brannigan, you come before the court to register your application for the Freedman's Savings Institution as proscribed in Federal law?" queried Judge Ferris.

"Aye, your honor," his r's rolling like the waters of a raging mountain stream, "I come before ya', a simple, humble representative of the Government, brought here by the duties of me service."

"Well, Mister Brannigan, in these parts the Federal Government is found to be neither simple, humble nor of service very often," responded the judge, with great laughter filling the courthouse.

It was Colin Brannigan's first engagement with the officials of the South. He was unprepared for the not-so-passive distrust of Northerners to be found in this community. However, the Irishman refused to allow this to defer him from his undertaking.

"Aye, your honor," he continued nervously after the peal of laughter had faded throughout the quiet din of the courthouse. It was an uncomfortably warm day. Brannigan could feel the sweat collecting under his suit jacket.

He could hear the birds squalling outside as the courtroom windows were open for ventilation. "I myself come originally from a land where the Government is indeed mistrusted."

"Sir," the judge interrupted, "I was told you are an American citizen from Boston appointed by the administration of President Grant. Is this not so?"

"Aye, this is *terrrue*, your honor," said Brannigan. "However, it is also *terrrue* that before I became a naturalized citizen of this country, I was born and raised in the land of Eire. That is Ireland, your honor, a land of great natural beauty."

"So, Mr. Brannigan," the judge pursued his inquiry, "what would prompt you to leave such a wonderful setting?"

Colin Brannigan looked nervously around the courtroom, the seats filled with the town businessmen who had come to see this Carpetbagger in the flesh.

"I had to leave the lush green land of my youth, your honor, because while my eyes could feast on its beauty, alas, my stomach could not. There was a great famine there when I left for America, as I suspect you have heard, in the 1840's. I came to settle in Boston, where I was soon enough exposed to the ways of this great nation."

A stirring of malice swelled amongst the gallery. The judge pounded his gavel, demanding order.

"The ways of Boston are not the ways of Bartow County, Mr. Brannigan," said the judge, spawning another ripple of laughter through the room. "Yet, there is a common experience that you have had with the folk of this county – that is an undeserved, but crippling, hunger. Unfortunately, due to the excessive and unnecessary violence thrust upon this community during the Great Conflict, many county residents have suffered and many more died of the famine brought on by the drought here as well."

The judged paused to a volley of "Here, here" and even one "Amen, it's true" coming from the spectators. The judge waited for silence to return before continuing the proceeding.

Brannigan began to speak when he was abruptly halted by the raised hand of Judge Ferris, who had pulled out his pocket watch, and was inspecting it closely behind the bench. Then he paused for a second, as if performing some mental calculation with great dedication of thought, before he began to speak rapidly.

"The drought that was brought upon us in the succeeding years only exasperated the suffering of our citizens. Many from these parts had moved westward searching for their own opportunities of ample food and water and provisions for their families. So, your experience, Sir, is in accordance with that which much of this community has endured. I see no reason to prolong these proceedings. Your application is in order, and I hereby declare it approved. Good luck, Mr. Brannigan. It is 2:15 and I rather strongly suggest we depart the courtroom."

Brannigan, proud of his ability to reach common ground with the judge and the business community began to indulge himself in gratitude to the court.

"Your Honor, if it pleases the court, I would like to confer my great appreciation of the rapid approval you have given to my undertaking..."

But, as the Irishman continued to talk, the judge stood erect and began to move to the doorway behind him. The gallery also began clearing, not intending to heed the Carpetbagger's discourse even in the least.

Turning at the rear courthouse door, Judge Ferris said to the Irishman, talking over him, "It indeed does not please the court, because..."

At that point the Judge himself was drowned out by a piercing whistle from the depot across the street. Soon the courthouse shook with a low rumble as the train pulled out from the depot. Billows of thick, dark coal smoke cascaded through the open windows. Young Truitt Clay-Harris tried in vain to close them before the train engine passed by. The smoke was heavy with a gritty coal ash that dusted the entire courtroom, including Colin Brannigan and Truitt. These were the only two men still in the now vacuous space, as everyone else had slipped out at the train whistle.

"It would appear, my young friend, that perhaps this community erred in placing the courthouse so close to the railroad," said Colin Brannigan.

Truitt Clay-Harris looked up at the soot covered Irishman and knew he need pay this Carpetbagger no undue respect. He replied snidely, "Perhaps if those who come before the court paid more attention to the train schedules and limited the length of their presentations before the bench, we would all find ourselves in a bit less of a mess."

6

PROMISE OF THE ROSE
SUMMER 1870

Earlier that Summer in 1870, Truitt's older brother Virgil, known throughout the community simply as "Clay", had made a fateful decision. He could no longer continue to work the fields with Deekie. The work was wearing them both into an early grave. They had watched each other grow hard, and their skin leathery under the scorching Southern sun.

Deekie had become, if possible, even more quiet and withdrawn since Clay had handled her so roughly the summer before. She had not offered herself again to him since that day. She just pulled away from him in both feelings and physical distance. She slept in the same one room shack, but no longer alongside Clay. She had taken over the corner farthest from Clay's maw. Clay slept between them. Truitt had the perch of the small loft that overhung them all.

Clay had come to suspect that Deekie might leave them all at her first opportunity. Though she never failed to follow him into the fields, nor do anything that Clay requested while there, she continued to draw into herself, to cut herself off from him.

That is when Clay made his fateful decision. He could no longer work the fields.

Four former slaves he had known from one of the plantations on the Etowah River had come to him to offer a proposition. Clay knew them all well. They were good men, although Clay would admit he had reservations in dealing with them now as equals.

"Mistah Clay, you ain't but working a small patch of dat land dat yer daddy leff ya'. Nows that the crick is runnin' again, we can work dem entire fields for ya', and weez o'ready got us a pack mule to do it proper. We can split the crops at harvest fiffy-fiffy, and everybody come out better than now. Weez gets to sells our haff, yer gets at lease twice assun much as what ya' can grow yerse'f today, and yer stop wearing that poor pretty woman down to a stump. Whaddya' says, Mistah Clay?"

Clay could not reject the benefits of the freedmen's proposal. It made too much sense all way around. Clay's pride would be wounded, as the local folk came to hear of it, but Clay knew he could nurse his pride on a full belly and clear conscience knowing that everyone else – his maw, Truitt, and Deekie - was cared for.

"Come on, now, Mistah Clay," said the leader of the group, "Weez cants afford no land o' our own ta work, and you cants affords not to have us work yo' land." The man extended his arm.

With a handshake Clay turned his family farm over to the four share-croppers. It was Clay's decision as head of the homestead, but that did not keep his maw from being furious.

"You 'spects me to have slaves working this property day-in, day-out. First yer Diddy runs off with a common harlot, and now my son sells me out to a bunch of slaves."

"Wars over, Mama," fired back Clay, "and they's not slaves no more. They's freedmen now. They's just looking to survive like we all is. And three hands alone t'ain't enough to keep working even a small parcel of our fields. I refuse to go on being half starved, fully tuckered and still dirt poor."

His maw raised her shrill, aged voice in protest. "There ain't no shame in being poor, Clay. Poor folks' the most righteous folk I ever known. You need to learn this, Son."

"T'ain't never said I was 'shamed, Mama," declared Clay.

"Oh, my boy, you gots plenny of shame on yerself, layin with that woman, that tramp. Y'all think nobody notices, but the whole town talks about you two. Send her back to Willet, where she belongs."

"She ain't goin' back to Willet, Mama. I told ya' before, Deekie is here so long as she wants to be." The fire rose up within him. "I don't give a damn what these townspeople think, anyhow. I am not livin' to impress them, Mama."

"Just who exactly you livin' to impress, boy?" she snapped with a salted tongue.

"Me, Mama. I am livin' to impress me and only me. I got to do somethin' in this life other than kill other men. I got to do somethin' good, Mama, while I still can."

"Then do what Truitt done did. Go git yerself a job. Leave me here with a bunch of slaves working our fields and go git yerself a job. Shame yerself some more, my boy, begging for a job that no man in his right mind is going to give to a crippled, one-armed man."

She had worked herself up into a frenzy. She began coughing the hoarse, cracking cough that had been affecting her for some time. She wiped her mouth with a rag, glanced at it briefly before folding it in her palms and slipping it into her apron.

"Look what you dun brought on me, Clay," she said, but not literally showing him the blood in her rag that she had been hiding from him for some time. "I am ashamed to have given birth to a misfit like you, boy."

She had intended to embarrass him into changing his mind. Instead she had only convinced him more firmly of his path forward. "Jest go git yerself a job, boy, but don't drag yer hide around here when they reject you for the cripple that you are."

"That is exactly what I plan to do, Mama. I am a one-armed man, t'ain't no denying that, but I t'ain't no cripple. No cripple would have gotten us through the drought the way that I did. No, I dun proved to myself I am a man, not a cripple. And yes, I intend to find me some payin' work, just as Truitt dun, so we can all be a li'l better off."

"Then you best take yer tramp wit' ya'. Cause she ain't no near welcome in this cabin all day long. Not so long as I am livin' here."

"Mama," Clay said, "Since Diddy been off you t'ain't nuthin but a sour scold. My advice to you is give yer thoughts no tongue, or one day someone's likely to cut it out of yer mouth."

"You just try, Son," she said, and began coughing anew.

"Oh, It won't be me, Mama. Last person it will be is me," Clay said.

The next day Virgil Clay-Harris set off before the dawn looking for work. He found the town was quick to want to talk about his exploits at Sharpsburg, but Clay would not engage that discussion. When the talk turned to his looking for work, the polite would simply say "but, Clay, you got only one arm, son, how can ya' pull yer weight?"

Day after day he continued to search for work. The Ferryman across the river told him he was a great man, "but ya' know I would be endangerin' my passengers by hirin' a man limited like yerself."

Clay presented himself at the mining operation that had been opened by Alonzo C. Ladd on the back of Three Sisters Mountain, the very mountain that Willet Blackwell's renegades were camped upon. The Ladd's Lime and Stone Company had begun excavating the labrynth of caves that ran throughout the south-end of what the locals were now just beginning to call Quarry Mountain. These were the very caves he, Deekie and Willet played in as children.

Clay thought this was, perhaps, his best chance in finding honest work. He presented himself to the quarry's boss.

"Sir, I know these caves. Grew up in 'em. Played here as a boy. Surely that familiarity counts for something."

"I would hire you in a second, Clay," said the foreman of the operation, "but it would cause me a riot among the other workers, don't ya' see. They are bustin' their skins each and every day. For me to bring in a man like yourself, Clay, who can't carry his own weight, the rest of the guys would slow-down if not stop working altogether."

Clay lowered his head dejectedly. The quarry boss continued, "Hell, Clay, I might as well bring in a woman, at least she could tie off the carts and cinch the mules. Nothing personal, Clay, but I just can't use ya'. Wish for sure I could."

Clay pressed on, determined to make something useful of himself. Each day he walked further and further in the summer's heat looking for his opportunity. He soon heard that Western and Atlantic Railroad was hiring men to maintain the tracks. He walked the better part of the day to Stegall Station, across the Etowah.

The Railroad man laughed aloud when Clay cut off the war talk and asked for a job. Clay offered himself for any sort of manual labor that might be needed.

"Son, you ever see the line of men I get here when there's work to be had? If you did, you might notice that whether they are white men, or freed men, but son, they all have two arms. This is a real man's day of work, Clay."

Clay politely thanked the man for his time, before he walked away from the station. A heavy embarrassment weighted his heart. He was finding exactly what his maw had predicted. The town had no use for him beyond war stories.

It was late in the day when he reached Cartersville. Disparaged, he pulled himself back through town on his way home. Clay walked dejectedly along Market Street, past the remains of the Baptist Church which had, years earlier, been destroyed by the Union Army. He came to a stop in front of Miss Howell's boarding house next door. He watched the swarm of activity still ongoing across the street, with workmen in the process of updating Nelson Gilreath's cottage. It was then that he heard a fracas rising up from across the lawn.

"Clay! Clay!" yelled out old man Woodard, the overseer of the property for Mister Gilreath. Horace Woodard had been overseeing the improvements being made by Gilreath.

Nelson Gilreath had been born in Greenville, South Carolina in 1814. After marrying, he relocated to Cartersville in 1837, and became a respected local merchant for many years before the war. Over time, he had become a very prominent business leader within the town. After Cartersville was officially incorporated as a town in the early 1850's, he had searched for a prominent home on the new town's west side, for much of his trading was with the town of Euharlee and its nearby mission.

In 1863, Gilreath had bought and cleared the lot on Market Street, with ready access to the Mission Trail. There, he had built a small three-room cottage, although it seemed more like a mansion to Clay.

The home's location turned out to be only a short mile or so from Clay's farm. Gilreath was now renovating the cottage to make it more suitable to a man of his position. Horace and his men were bringing the cottage up to date with something called the Second Empire architectural style.

"I been keepin' watch for you, son," said old man Woodard. "For someone who, I been told, passes by here near every day, you sure are a hard man to pin down."

"I hope all is well with you, Horace," said Clay, pleased to see the man he had long respected. Clay had crossed the street and came over to the Gilreaths' lawn, at least alongside the decorative wrought-iron fence that had recently been installed surrounding it.

Image 7 – Nelson Gilreath's Cottage
(Courtesy of The Rose Lawn Museum)

"Clay, let me get right down to business. I come to hear you lookin' for a job. Is that true?" asked ol' Horace.

"Yes, 'tis" said Clay dejectedly, "but everyone just sees me as a war cripple. They love to talk of the war, just not of hiring the one-armed man it left behind ."

"Hell, son, I ain't never known no cripple could do all you can do," said Woodard. "Ain't it true you kept that farm o' yours going through the drought when other fully abled men was packing up and movin' west?"

"I reckon so," said Clay modestly.

"Look here, Clay. We done cleared this lot. All the heavy liftin' is done now. I need a groundsman. Someone who can tame this here lawn. Care for it, make it grow. You could do that, son. You could tend to this lot, couldn't you?"

"I reckon I could, but..."

"Clay, now I am gonna be square with ya', there's a catch," said the overseer.

"Well, Horace, I might be 'spectin' such..."

"Clay, Mrs. Gilreath wants to put in rose beds. Seen some up at what's left of Godfrey Barnsley's Woodlands earlier this year. Just bowled her over, son. Now it is all she talks about. I want you to oversee their planting. You could grow them to something that will please Mr. Gilreath's wife. And truth be known, son, she is not the easiest of women to please."

"I dunno nothin' about growin' no roses, Horace," admitted Clay. He could not imagine tending to flowers. Working a lawn was respectable work, but the idea of looking after flower bushes brought a pall of shame upon him.

"I know yer don't, son. But even with most of the Barnsley family having relocated to New Orleans, Mrs. Gilreath dun' got the folks who planted them at the Woodlands to share wit' her how it's dun'. She just needs someone to do the doin', if you get my gist."

"Horace, I know you seen that I am a little short on hands here," said Clay.

"Son, I can hire all the hands we need to get this goin'," said the overseer, "but t'ain't hands I need. What I need is a tender heart."

Clay was dumbstruck at the comment. "What you talkin 'bout, Horace?"

"Clay, these things need carin' after. Patience and a tender touch, I am told. I reckon anyone who can raise enough food to feed his family durin' the severest drought we 'bout ever seen can surely convince a few rosebushes to grow. Besides, me and my men are going to be real busy here. Mister Gilreath has us renovating his cottage and is talking of adding rooms to it soon. On top of that, he has us helping to rebuild the Baptist Church across the street. Damn shame how that twister ripped it up in '68, after the Yankees having' dun' tore it up during the war. What do ya' say, Clay? I can pay ya' a fare wage."

Clay hesitated. He nearly turned down the offer, thinking it was only made from the kindness of his family's old friend, Horace. Besides, Clay was sure Nelson Gilreath would not take kindly to having his lawn attended to by a one-armed man.

"You talk it over with the Mister Gilreath and I will let you know once I got his nod..." began Clay.

"Already done, son. I ran it past him last week. He was right excited about it. He likes the idea of the hero of Sharpsburg being seen on his lawn, day-in, day-out."

Clay felt that his friend had been laying in wait for his response.

"Horace, I greatly appreciate this offer, but t'ain't nuthin' more than charity, and I got too much ..." Clay began to say before being thunderously interrupted.

"Charity? Charity, my rump, Clay! If you can't make them bushes bloom and prosper, I fully intend to fire your hide and find someone who can. Now, I am fixin' to get angry, son. You either are looking for work, or you're not. I am offering good honest work, no strings attached. So, are you gonna come work for ol' Horace, or ain't ya'?"

With this, the old man thrust out his arm, extending his hand to shake on the deal. Clay looked at him momentarily, before reaching out to take his hand and shake it firmly.

7

THE COLT NAVIES
SUMMER, 1870

Knowing he would soon be working throughout the day, Clay decided it was time to teach Deekie to defend herself. She had proven herself resourceful and strong-willed. Despite this, a woman alone in the fields of the farm throughout the day could be a target for the baser intentions of idle men. Clay did not concern himself with the Freedmen who would be working his fields as sharecroppers. He knew these men, and their presence on the farm gave him solace.

It was the passers-by along the Mission Trail that concerned him. There were still many men who had no work to fill their days. The sight of a young woman alone in a field could be an invitation for diversion that could quickly turn into trouble of a major sort.

"These here is the only things that my Diddy left me when I was off at war, other than the mouths of Truitt and Maw to feed," Clay said to Deekie.

They were standing in the field behind the house where it rose onto a forested upslope. Clay had picked this location because the hillside would engulf the rounds fired, and the large stump of the tree that Truitt had cut for him recently offered a stand for target practice. He handed one of the two matching large pistols to Deekie.

"I am going to teach you to shoot, girl. You need to know how to defend yerself when I'm not near..."

She took the gun from him with great trepidation. "Virgil, I can't do this. Surely not with these guns."

"Naw, they's just guns. Just cause my Diddy left 'em for me, don't let that fret you none."

She held the Navy Colt revolver in her two hands, awkwardly.

"It's not that, Clay, but this thing is heavy. I am not sure I got the *strumpf* to handle this. And I am afeard it will kick like a mule."

The 1851 Colt Navy revolvers were indeed massive weapons. Unlike the Colt revolvers used by the military during the war, these had octagonal shaped barrels instead of round. Their cylinders - that is, the part that revolved - were round and smooth, save for their decorative engraving. They had none of the scalloped notching that would become common in later Colt handguns.

Despite their heft, these revolvers were actually known for their reduced size. They were significantly smaller than the earlier Colt's Dragoons that were so massive they could not effectively be worn by the shooter. Instead, Dragoons were generally sheathed in a saddle holster. They became known as horse-guns.

The Colt Navy had its surfaces finished in a blued-metal coating that appeared near black. The guns were originally percussion revolvers, which meant each cylinder chamber had to be loaded with a charge and ball, much like a musket, using the plunger built-in underneath the barrel.

However, the guns given to Clay by his gunsmith father had been converted to fire metallic cartridges, or bullets. The Colt company itself had manufactured thousands of these percussion fire weapons. After the war, the company focused on the conversion of these guns to accept metallic cartridges. This was done by trimming back the cylinders and in the resulting gap installing a breech plate. Thus, the guns could then be rear-loaded, a much faster process. The final modification was the addition of an ejector rod to push out the metal casings of the fired cartridges.

But Clay's Colt Navies were converted much earlier, when the patent for the conversion process was still held by another company. This meant his guns were converted illegally, and Clay had long figured this was, most likely, what took his daddy off to Texas. There, the need for fast reloading of weapons by cowhands and bushwhackers alike would prove a prosperous opportunity for a skilled gunsmith.

"Now, I know you is worried 'bout the kick, girl," Clay said to Deekie, "but the thang 'bout guns is that the bigger the weapon, the lessen the kick. So, these guns, they fire real smooth-like."

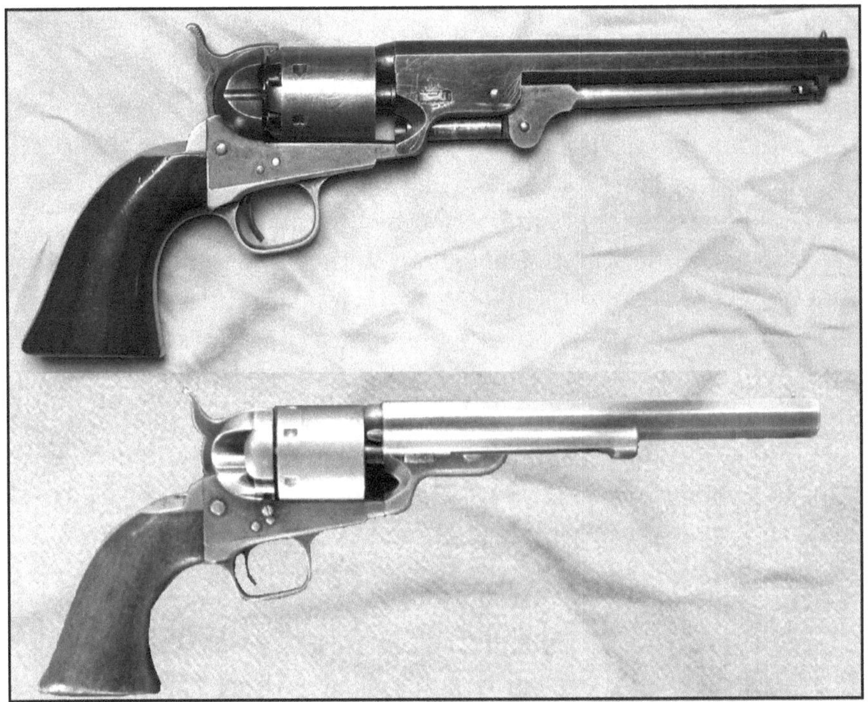

Image 8 – Colt Navy Revolvers (1851 on top, conversion below)
Source: fr.wikipedia.org

Clay raised the Navy and aimed it at a large empty can he had placed upon the stump. The massive gun fired, belching forth a mix of smoke and flame from its unusually long barrel. The round caught the metal can at its base, and in response kicked upwards into the air in an energetic spiral. He then fired at it several times as it lay on the ground, three times more pitching the can into the air, missing it only once.

Clay then taught Deekie how to eject the cartridge casings. It was a very awkward maneuver for the one-handed man. The breech plate had a loading gate that had to be opened, the cylinder turned to allow each chamber to align with the ejector rod. Then that rod had to be pushed from the front alongside the barrel to eject the casings.

Deekie took to it quickly, and having both her own God-given appendages, was much more proficient at the process then Clay himself was. Loading the cartridges was a much simpler activity, just rotating the cylinder until a cartridge could be slid into one of the six chambers. Clay taught her as he was taught, leaving one chamber empty to avoid an accidental firing.

Clay reset the large empty, and by that point, perforated metal can back onto the stump. Deekie raised the gun, holding it so stiffly that her arm began to move in a slight circular motion as she readied to fire. She cocked back the hammer and began to tighten further, anticipating the shot and its kick. She fired, jerking the trigger, and missing her target completely.

"You is fearing that gun far too much, girl," he said to her, "and you is dropping that muzzle just as you jerk that trigger. Ya' gots to relax."

Clay took the weapon from her. He aimed it at the target.

"Now just fire a couple more rounds at that can but pull that trigger so smooth that you'll be surprised when the round fires." He squeezed the trigger lightly, and the can jumped from the stump into the air."

Clay gave the gun back to her, and quickly reset the can on the stump.

"Go 'head and try that. And relax yer arm a little, it helps lessen the kick that you feel."

Deekie did as he said. She held her arm less stiffly and squeezed the trigger as gently as she could. Her second shot sent a puff of dirt flailing up about three inches in front of the stump.

"Relax, girl. As long as you is behind that barrel and not in front of it, that gun ain't gonna bite ya'."

"I'm trying, Virgil, but this is so new to me…"

She pulled back the hammer with her thumb and squeezed off another round, and instantaneously a large chunk of the stump aside the can flew off excitedly.

"Let me show ya' how to line up them sights," said Clay.

He came in close behind her, putting his cheek as close to hers as he could. He held his hand over hers, but only her finger was on the trigger.

"Just line up the top of the hammer with that front site like so," his breathe was hot on her ear, "Fire when ready."

She squeezed the trigger, and the kick of the gun seemed to travel through them both. The can departed the stump wildly, the round tearing it nearly in two along the front side.

Clay could feel her excitement as she spun to face him. He had to stop her, and not removing his hand from hers, pointed the gun to the dirt just in front of them.

"Ya' dun good, girl. But ya' has to remember to never point this thing at anything you don't plan to fire at. Me, most of all."

"Virgil, this is fun. I want to fire some more."

He replaced the mangled can and she became very proficient in hitting it. By the end of their session, Clay was confident she could handle the weapon.

"Virgil, I got another question," began Deekie, "your Daddy was never in the Navy, how did he get this gun?"

Clay laughed at her question.

"These guns is called Navies 'cause of these ship designs that are scrawled into the side of this revolving cylinder. See here?"

He pointed to the design features.

"T'ain't got nothing to do with the real Navy, t'all. Other than its 'spose to be a naval battle where the Texican Navy bested Mexico. Colt had this pretty picture cut into the cylinder of every Colt Navy gun. My Diddy said it was his attempt to honor the Texans, as they was one of Colt's biggest customers. Now, I am givin' you one of these here guns along with this belt and holster, and I want you to wear it every day. I'll keep the other."

"You sure, Virgil? These bein' the guns your Daddy left for ya', and all."

"Sure, I am sure. They will protect what's the most important part of my life, girl. You!"

She smiled when he said this. For the first time since the incident in the pines, she began to feel ever so slightly closer to him again.

8

GLIMPSE OF AN ANGEL
OCTOBER 1870

That summer Clay began his job as caretaker of the grounds of Nelson Gilreath's home. It did not pay much, but what he earned was a Godsend to him. Coupled with the monies he would make by selling his portion of the sharecroppers' harvest from his lands, and the much larger salary his younger brother brought in from being an apprentice at the courthouse, the family's future began to look up. For the first time since the war ended, they did not have to rely solely on what the soil produced, or animals they hunted from the woods.

The transition was one that affected all parties. Clay had the physical transition of mastering a series of chores that were previously unfamiliar to him. Using a scythe to cut the lawn was difficult, but by using his good hand counterbalanced with his left stump, he soon became proficient, if not adept. Similarly, every new task he was presented became a puzzle to be solved – *How do I do this task, given my limitations, such that I'm as capable as any two-armed man?*

For Clay's maw, the transition was more severe. Both her sons were now gone all day. She had made it known to all parties that Deekie was not welcome in the cabin without Clay, and truth be known, not even with Clay.

The fact of the matter was that Clay's maw was fighting a battle of her own. She had been coughing up blood for some time and was concerned that she had contracted the Consumption. She feared, if indeed it was this killer disease, she might pass it on to her sons, given the close quarters in which they lived. She would have tried to give it intentionally to that girl chasing after her boy, if she didn't think that the stray runt wouldn't just pass it on again to Clay.

Clay's maw severely resented the girl. Had she not come to live with them, there would have been more food for her and her two boys. Less food made them all weaker. Weak bodies get sick. Clay's maw so blamed her illness on Deekie.

His maw also had to deal with the fact that she was sharing her days with the former slaves who worked her fields. They stayed away from her in the shack, and she from them in the fields, but this did not release her from the shame that somehow she had been lowered to their level. It never occurred to her that they had only been unshackled from the bondage of the plantations to be elevated to the lowest rung of human condition – the starving poor.

For Truitt, the transition was one of dealing with how the community had come to view his brother. The former hero – the so-called Savior of Sharpsburg – was being openly discussed in town as a charity case undertaken by the businessman Nelson Gilreath. This caused young Truitt an embarrassment in the brother that he had once idolized.

The greatest transition of all was thrust upon Deekie. Every day, she would walk the mile or so with her Virgil to the Gilreath house, despite his telling her it was not necessary. At the end of his day, she waited for him to walk back home, rain or shine.

It was the hours in-between that weighed on her like the sands of time. Not welcome in the cabin, not wishing to associate with the freedmen working the family's fields, her days became a vast nothingness that she soon came to dread. She would walk into the town, until it came to be known to her that she was the talk of the townsfolk – this woman in the field dress holstering the massive Colt Navy revolver. Her days betrayed her, the boredom sucked the very life from her. She longed for the days that she and her Virgil worked but only a portion of the family's lands. It was arduous labor, but their sweat produced the very foods off which they lived. It had been honest, respectful work.

Her days had become nothing more than a morning walk with Clay and an evening's return, the hours between dragged weary with uselessness. Even worse, she had finally forgiven Clay in her heart for his violence to her in the pines, but with his new job, he seemed to be drawn away from her.

Clay took to his tasks with a vigor she had not anticipated. Horace the head-groundskeeper soon realized he could rely on Clay in all matters. The rose bushes so desired by Nelson Gilreath's wife were planted and cared for by Clay. He hoped that soon they would be approaching their first bloom. His every thought was to those roses, seemingly with no attention left for her.

Horace began using Clay for other tasks as well. Having observed how readily he managed the buckboard wagon behind a pair of horses, Horace would soon send Clay around town to pick up supplies and occasionally visitors that came to stay with the Gilreaths. Clay enjoyed the freedom of being behind the horses along his regular rides to the mills along the Etowah River. He would also travel to the farms of the area to pick up meats and fowl that were only by then beginning to become more common again.

It was the early fall of 1870 when he first laid eyes on his "angel". Clay was spending the morning removing a tenacious vine from a garden trellis. It had grown thick and became wickedly entwined around the structure. It was a delicate task, as Mrs. Gilreath had let it be known she expected the trellis not to be damaged. The shoots and shafts of the vine each ensnarled the slats of the wooden lattice until the original structure was near unrecognizable.

For whatever reason, perhaps from his experiences in the war, Clay likened the vines to the corruption that ensnarls the hearts of men. No one lie, no one blackened thought was of itself of much concern. But when these were left to thicken, and began to multiply, to wind round and reinforce each other, it soon produced a stranglehold that no knife's edge could simply slice through.

Through the partially cleared trellis, Clay soon spotted the Irish Carpetbagger Brannigan across Market Street. Clay saw him often, as he boarded in one of the grand houses along the road. The man had come to Cartersville, and in only a few months, like the evil shoots of vine Clay had spent so much tedious effort clearing, the Irishman had ensnarled himself in the most delicate workings of the town.

As head of the Federal Freedman's Bureau he was granted the authority to invalidate contracts made between the local plantation owners and the area's freedmen, if he deemed them to be taking advantage of the former slaves. And indeed throughout the South, many attempted to replace the bondage of slavery with the subservience of inequitable legal contracts.

It soon became known that the Carpetbagger, in all his finery and prestige, could be bought. If he threatened to invalidate the contract between a local plantation owner and the freedmen he employed, a bribe was known to dissuade his interests. In this way, Colin Brannigan became vastly wealthier than he had been when he arrived.

In addition to his role in local contractual matters, Brannigan had created the Freedmen's Savings Institution. Here, black laborers could deposit their funds with the confidence of the United States Government. What was not known, was that he then reinvested these funds, skimming nearly half of the earnings for himself before dispersing the rest to his clients.

As he watched the Irishman across the street, Clay continued to cut through the hardened thickets of vines, peeling back its wooden greedy fingers from their grasp upon the delicate trellis. It was only then that he noticed the purest of souls walking alongside the Carpetbagger.

She was unlike any girl he had ever laid eyes on in his life. Her dress was of an indescribable elegance, free flowing on the light, cool gust carrying the reddened leaves of fall. Her walk was delicate, her gait was measured and reserved. Her skin was pale but luminous, like a precious porcelain. The hair that framed her face was a sensitive shade of ginger red, perfectly complementing her complexion. Her hair was thickened by tight ringlets that could only have been the result of the delicate touch of God's gracious hand.

Clay could not take his eyes from her. It was as if she represented everything pure and good, walking astride the blackened corruption of the Carpetbagger. Clay watched her young form walk up the steps to the porch of the home in which they would both be lodged. She carried herself with such a reserved grace and dignity that he could not forget her. He thought about her throughout the day until Deekie showed herself, waiting on her walk home along the Mission Trail with her Virgil.

Along that walk, she asked him how his day was. He told her about the tedious task of removing the vines from the trellis. He did not mention the girl. He instead asked about her day.

"I am sorry, Virgil, I could not take the boredom any longer. Day after day, week after week of nothing…"

"What did you do, Deekie?" asked Clay, recognizing the remorse in her voice.

"I went up to Three Sisters Mountain. I walked clear up to the top."

"Did you see Willet?" asked Clay with a voice of sharpened concern.

"Yes, of course, I did," she replied. "He asked me why I was there."

"And what did ya' tell him?" asked Clay.

"I told him I was bored, bored something bad, Virgil."

"Be careful, girl, remember what he did to you…"

"He was quite nice to me, today, Virgil. Told me I always had a home there. Told me it would be anything but boring."

"Deekie, he beat you half to death! That's why ya' come to me in the first place."

"Virgil, he's changed. He was kind to me. He seemed real interested in me. I just can't stand being ignored no longer, being throwed aside no more."

"No one's throwing you aside, girl. Promise me you won't go up there again. That's nowhere for you to be."

"Virgil, he asked after you, too. Asked how you was doing as the merchant's charity case."

The comment sliced through Clay with the impact of a sharpened saber. "I don't want to hear no more."

"Willet noticed the Colt Navy I was holstering. Asked after it."

"What'd he ask, Deekie?"

"He asked, 'Did Clay give you that gun to protect yerself from the likes of me?' I told him you was just worried about me in general."

"What'd he say?" asked Clay tersely.

"He just laughed. Showed me his Colt Navy. Told me he got it protecting you that night the town was burned. He said he was glad you had other people looking out for you now. I reckon he meant old Horace and the merchant Gilreath."

Clay had not cared about the talk of the townspeople that his brother had relayed to him. He was happy to have his job, it gave him pride. But the comments of Willet, as relayed by Deekie, cut him to the quick. And she seemed to take a sick pleasure in telling them to him. Was she striking back at him for making her days so unbearable?

"Virgil, when I come back from the mountain, I walked to town and on the square I heard two women saying that the Carpetbagger has done brought his niece to town from Boston."

Clay's blood pumped excitedly though him. "Sure 'nuff, his niece you say?"

"She's Irish, just like him. The women said she had the prettiest head of red hair you ever seen. A real lady, 'cept she's only sixteen years old. A proper girl, I suppose. And guess what her name is?" Deekie was almost giggling at this point.

"I couldn't fix a guess," said Clay, trying to hide his interest.

"Ever. Like in 'Forever and Ever'. Her name is Ever McLaughlin." Now she was giggling.

"Well, that's a pretty name," quipped Clay.

"Virgil, it surely is a silly name," Deekie said, slapping his arm. "Who on earth names their baby girl 'Ever'?"

"Don't laugh because ya' never heard it. Maybe it's a regular name over there."

"No. Mary or Colleen is a regular name for an Irish girl, not 'Ever'. Come on, Virgil, you ain't never been to Ireland."

No, but I killed my share of Irish boys during the war, he thought. *Maybe Ever is a perfect name for an Irish child, after all.*

9

AN UNEXPECTED RECEPTION
OCTOBER 1870

Colin Brannigan had a long morning's ride mostly behind him. He had ridden alone by horseback down from Cartersville, crossing the Etowah river on the new toll bridge at the location where Douthit's ferry once ran. He then rode further to reach the plantation at the point where Pumpkin Vine Creek flowed into the river. There stood one of the finest plantation homes to survive the war – River's Bend.

As the Irishman approached the magnificently maintained home, he noticed the path from the main road was paved with crushed red cinders, representing an expense that few other homes in the area could afford to match. As he approached the grand house, he counted no less than a dozen freed men working the grounds. He estimated that there could be that many again of freed men and women employed in the interior of the home as well.

A young black man met Brannigan in front of the home's central portico. He was dressed as an indoor servant might be expected, with fine clothing of waistcoat and britches, his shoes intensively shined.

"Welcome to River's Bend, Suh!" he said emphatically. As has been stated, his clothes had the finery of a house servant, but among his duties was the reception of guests to the home. The young man, taking Brannigan's steed by the bridle, had placed an elaborately decorated mahogany box aside the horse to assist the Irishman's dismount.

"Well, thank you, my good man," said Brannigan cheerfully as he swung his leg over the steed in his dismount. "I presume you will be showing me inside for my calling on Colonel Austell."

"Suh, the Colonel will be receiving you here on the porch," said the young man, raising his arm to the table and two chairs just a few steps above them.

"Well, I guess I should not be surprised," responded Brannigan as he slowly stepped upwards to the porch, "but after all I had heard of Southern hospitality, I at least expected the good Colonel to receive me in his home for our discussion."

"Hospitality only requires that I receive you here at River's Bend, Mr. Brannigan. It does not dictate *where* in my home I might choose to do so. We are under the roof of the porch, so you are within the confines of my home, Sir. Thank you, Thomas, you are free to return to your other duties."

The commanding voice of Silas P. Austell projected strongly ahead of him as he walked slowly out from the mansion's interior. It carried across the outdoor setting with authority. His dress was immaculate, as his suit of crisp linen was accompanied with the nearly mandatory wide brimmed hat protecting his fine, sharp features from the Southern sun.

Colin Brannigan could see that the Colonel was intent on providing him a somewhat unwelcome ear. The Irishman decided to prick back at the gentleman before him.

"It hardly looks like your servants are free at all, Colonel," began Brannigan. They sat, and the Colonel stared intently at his guest. A service bell was set on the table, but the Colonel did not reach for it. Instead, in a few seconds a black woman servant came from within the house with a silver tray containing a delicate china coffeepot, accompanied by Sterling silver serving pieces containing fresh cream and sugar. They waited patiently as she poured the hot coffee into the matching cups and saucers, already laid before them. She smiled courteously at the houseguest before returning to the interior with the silver tray.

Brannigan reached for the coffee, although after his travel under the morning's sun, he would have desired a cold glass of lemonade much more.

The Irishman suspected the Colonel had intentional denied him this refreshment, so Colin Brannigan sipped the scalding hot coffee, thanking his host for knowing exactly what he desired.

"Well, Sir, I can see your resplendent wealth – this lovely river home, your many servants, your having those things so hard to come by after the war – coffee, with sugar no less."

"I was warned that you, Sir, were a man quick to the point," began the Colonel as he stared at his guest across the cast iron table. Its black flat metal surface stood in defiant contrast to the white glossy painted wood of the porch structure.

The Colonel continued, "Also, Sir, I was told you enjoyed jabbing the sharp end of the stick of your Yankee authority into the eyes of your Southern hosts. So, my guest, I come to our discussion with my eyes wide open."

"And the doors of your home pulled tight," added Brannigan, almost without thought. Clearly the landowners of the area had been discussing the methods of the Irishman's office. Perhaps he needed to soften his approach and appeal to this man's vanity. He scolded himself for having snapped his last comment in response.

"My good Colonel," he began again, "what I mean to say is that surely you are a man of influence. How else could you have dissuaded the Union Army from burning this beautiful home during their war-time occupation here. She's as fine a mansion as sits along the river, Sir. I would love a tour of your most magnificent home."

The Colonel smirked at this rapprochement. "That she is, Mr. Brannigan, as you say, as fine as any home along the river. What makes her so charming is that she has never been entered by any Union Soldier or Northern Carpetbagger, such as yourself."

The message was unmistakable to Brannigan – the Colonel fully intended to resist his guest with every fiber of his Southern being.

"So, I see, Colonel," said the Irishman, "then allow me to get down to business. I understand you employ some two dozen freed men and women here at River's Bend."

"More like thirty, Sir," corrected the Colonel, "including those working at the mill along the river behind the house."

"And these freedmen, including the womenfolk, are all under contract to you, Sir?" followed Brannigan.

"Yes, Mr. Brannigan, that they are. Very much so under legal contracts to this home. I pay one of the highest wages in the county, and you will find that each and every one of them is very happy to be in my employ."

The Colonel beamed proudly at Brannigan, but he already knew the Irishman's next move.

"Well, Colonel, I am sure I need not remind you that ..."

Colonel Austell cut his guest off abruptly, "... That your office has the power to, based on the bills established by the United States Congress, and signed into law by President Ulysses S. Grant, has the power to nullify any and all contracts deemed to be inequitable to the Freedmen bound by them. And you fully intend to remind me that you, Sir, under those laws, are the deciding principle authority as to what is deemed inequitable, and which contracts are to be nullified."

Colin Brannigan had just been quoted verbatim, or nearly enough so, the very words he had shared with the other landowners of the area. The only aspect difference was the lilting brogue of his Irish tongue had been replaced by the defiant and seething Southern delivery of Colonel Austell.

"And yes, my bureaucratic fellow, I know the rest of your routine as well," said the Colonel in his superior manner. "You will next tell me that you, of course, have only the best intentions of the Freedmen in mind ..."

"Which I do, of course," interjected Brannigan.

"... and that while your review of their contracts here at River's Bend could likely turn up inequities, this inconvenience could all be avoided by my making a 'donation' to your Freedmen's Foundation

Fund, as several of my fellow landowners have already seen fit to do."

The Colonel paused, seething in contempt for the Northerner who sat before him. Colin Brannigan, while feeling somewhat like a man whose misdeeds had been exposed, was nonetheless ready to begin the negotiation of the 'donation'.

Colonel Austell stayed seated, saying nothing. The tension in the air between the two men was palpable, and with every second of damning silence, Colin Brannigan began to realize that there was no negotiation forthcoming.

Colonel Austell then stood up from the table and leaned over the Irishman.

"Well, Mr. Brannigan, I see you as nothing more than the greedy Northern Carpetbagger that you are. As I have said to my fellow land-owners, for me to accept your offer, as many of them have, would simply make me consider myself nothing more than a 'Scalawag'. Now, as I am sure you are now coming to understand, I am a man who takes every effort to know his foes. Learned that in earnest during the war, I did. My efforts have revealed to me that you, while having painted yourself a great American merchant success from your beloved home of Ireland, were in fact a dastardly vulture preying upon your own im-migrant countrymen. I know that you, Sir, had sold your Irish boys into the war, treating them as a new commodity into which you could profit. You profited from their spilled blood during the war, and now you wish to profit from the new situation of these freed slaves. Not for their betterment, but only for your own enrichment.'

Colin Brannigan stood from the table slowly, so that the damna-tion of the Colonel was no longer raining down upon him.

"Colonel Austell," he began slowly from a level perspective, "you have built a great undertaking here, Sir. I have the power of my of-fice that can break your contracts with these freed men and women. Your undertakings here would soon wither and die without the cheap labor contracts into which you have hoodwinked these former slaves. I advise you to take measure of the opportunity I have laid before you."

The Colonel stared back at the man before him.

"Mr. Brannigan, I have indeed taken measure of you, Sir. I will be making no 'donations' to your fund, Sir. Now, you have my answer, and I will be taking leave of you, Sir."

Brannigan could not believe how rudely he had been received. Austell was the first landowner to refuse the Freedmen's Bureau Administrator's offer.

"You are making a terrible error in judgement," responded Brannigan, his R's rolling like the river's waters over the rocks behind them. "You, Colonel, are taking on the full might and majesty of the United States of America."

"Well, at least it won't be the first time, Mr. Brannigan. As for the majesty, the government has cloaked itself in this term a little too broadly, although we Southern men see nothing majestic about our Yankee overseers. Relative to their might, even the Union Soldiers are not on every corner, nor in every field, nor around every bend."

"Are you threatening me, Colonel?" asked Brannigan outrightly.

"No, Sir, to the contrary. I wish you a most safe and prosperous journey home. It is just that these woods are full of renegades who deeply resent the presence of you Northerner's in our home. I just would hate for you to become confronted by one of these rascals, as Carpetbaggers do make for opportune targets. Now, Sir, I am busy at hand with a home and a mill to run, so do take leave of me, directly!"

Colin Brannigan could not believe that this staunch Southerner was not only rejecting his offer of non-interference, but clearly threatening him with bodily harm.

"That I will do, Colonel," said Brannigan coldly, "but be forewarned, I will begin challenging your contracts in court with the intention of invalidating them, Sir, unless you reconsider immediately."

"I fully expect nothing less from you, Mr. Brannigan," said the Colonel as he walked away from the cast iron table and headed to the massive oak doors of the home. "We have graciously watered your mount, so please be so kind as to remove yourself from the grounds of River's Bend."

Colonel Austell entered the house, the massive doors closing behind him with finality. An old disheveled Negro field hand brought Brannigan's horse to the grounds before the porch.

"Thank you, my good man," said Brannigan as he took the horse's reins, "I fully intend to improve your condition here."

The Negro gazed upon him awkwardly.

It was then that Colin Brannigan realized that the intricately designed mahogany mount stand was nowhere to be found.

10

TOUCH OF AN ANGEL
NOVEMBER 1870

The morning was late, and a murder of crows cast a gliding premonition of shade across Nelson Gilreath's lawn. The sun had risen with an unexpected intensity. Between the birds' shadows, reddish-orange leaves fell in lazy spirals in these late days of Fall, 1870.

The sweat dripped from Clay's brow. Though the air was cool, his exertions were extreme. He unloaded flagstones with which he would place a garden walk among his rosebushes, with the expectation that they would one day bloom. He would lift and grasp each stack of stones with his good right arm, using the stump of his left arm to lean into and stabilize them.

Clay handled the stones with great care, as the cart on which they were stacked was supported by nothing more than two wheels and a hitch. After pulling the stones into place on the cart, Clay had leveled the hitch end by placing a strong length of oak under it. He had brought along this post on top the pile of flagstones. He took great care not to displace the oak prop, for fear of sending the cart leaning and dumping its load. Not that the stones would be hurt by the fall upon the grass, only that Clay imagined that there were many watchers waiting for him to fail. Waiting for the one-armed cripple to demonstrate he was not their equal.

Clay worked past his physical limitations, as always, but this work was strenuous. He was about halfway through the unloading when he first heard it. Sweet as music, light as a feather, a woman's laughter drifted to him from across Market Street. Less a hearty woman's laugh than the innocent mirth of a girl.

Clay looked up from his work to spot Ever sitting on the porch having a morning coffee with the proprietress of the boarding house, the widow Rebecca Howell. It was quite the contrast of youth and the aged and was told by their voices that carried across the lawn.

Ever's voice floated light as a fragrance, while widow Howell's sank from its own resonant heaviness. He also noticed today, as over the past few weeks, that the young Irish girl had been watching him.

Perhaps she had never seen a man with only one arm before? Surely, after the war there were many disfigured men throughout the county, if not the country. It was rare for this elegant young woman – he decided that she was too refined to be thought of as a mere girl – to venture far from the Howell boarding house. Perhaps, she had not come across the war veterans of the town, other than himself.

The porch of the widow Howell's boarding house looked directly onto the Gilreath lawn. Ever liked to sit outside, and to do so invariably meant to watch Clay undertake his tasks. He could feel her eyes on him, but why?

He thought it possible that she had the same feelings of him, perhaps, that he had of her. It was the intrigue of another so unlike anyone he had ever met. He was constantly sneaking glimpses of her, and on a few occasions their eyes met in a tangled mesh of clumsiness. She had arrived in-time to watch him plant the last of his neatly organized rows of rosebushes. They then grew well, but stubbornly refused to bloom.

Returning to his work, Clay lowered his head and the sweat dripping from him spotted the few stones which he had already laid in the grass. As he unloaded the remainder, he heard her laugh again. Without looking up he knew it to be married to her beautifully brimming smile, which he had already come to admire.

Like a puzzle, he assembled these fragments into a still some-what incomplete image of the proper young woman. All was there now – the beauty, the smile, the laugh, the elegance – only the most intimate of details were still missing. What was the scent of her nearness? What was the pacing of her conversation? What were her interests? How kind was her heart?

These eluded him, and he felt silly thinking of them. He had never had these types of thoughts about any woman before. He had never desired to be so close to anyone else in his life. Even her voice was only a ghost to him. It had carried lightly across the lawn before disappearing into only his memory. It was sweetly high-pitched, and though it was deep Fall, the voice sang in his ear like the first songs of the robins of Spring.

Clay could not understand why he could not stop thinking of her. It was not romantic at all. Clay had no desire in that way. What he did not understand was that she represented the innocence that had been taken so violently from himself.

Still thinking of her, he lifted another stack of flagstones with the strength of his right arm, stabilizing it again with the stump of his left. As he rotated his torso to clear the cart, he lost his grip and the top stone slid free. In its fall, it knocked free the oak post hold-ing up the front of the cart.

Clay instinctively dropped the stack of stones he had been han-dling and was just able to grasp the front of the cart before the re-maining load slid free. He lifted the hitch end to level the cart, but the oak prop lay just under his left arm. Had he had his full utility, he could have readily picked it up. But given his lack of a left fore-arm and hand, the oak post might as well have been a mile away. His stumped left arm was too weak to hold the cart level, so his only choice appeared to be to release the cart from his right hand and allow the remaining stones to spill to the ground. He refused to admit failure.

Clay then was able to contort himself to work his shoulder un-der the front lip of the cart, freeing his right hand, but it still could not quite reach the oak post. The weight of the stones and the cart was digging into the bones of his shoulder, creating an unbearable pain. He could release it and allow the stones to fall which certainly would have not damaged them. But he refused again to do so.

Clay would not give in. For he knew that for every strenuous task he undertook, there were always onlookers who waited for him to fail. To remind themselves that this man was in no way able-bodied. For he knew they considered themselves better than him.

The sweat poured off him as he searched for a solution to his predicament. The pain burrowed deeper into him, confusing his thought when he most needed it clear. It was then he knew he would have to give in, to admit failure.

"Sir, I am believing you might be needing this," the voice said, soft and sweet and for the first time close. He then felt the tender warmth of two alabaster hands, smooth and delicate, as they pressed the oak post into his free right hand.

"Thank you," Clay grunted coarsely, taking the post from her. He then groaned more loudly as he drove his aching shoulder into the source of its pain. The cart raised enough to allow Clay to prop it level again with the re-secured oak post.

Clay took a few steps and rested against the trunk of a small tree. He breathed heavily, drawing deep breaths as the searing pain in his shoulder seemed initially to intensify before it slowly began to fade.

He anticipated what she might next say to him, before he raised his eyes to her. *It is a good thing I saw you struggling,* he thought she might say, or even, *A man should take stock of his limitations.*

In the long seconds he waited to hear her judgement of him, he first noticed it – the scent. Her scent wafted ever so reluctantly through the space between them. At first it had been imperceptible, but as his deep breaths slowly shallowed, it gently built. It was delicate and helpless, and seemingly caressed the air that framed the space between them.

Then he placed it. It was the scent of the morning's dew splashed upon the petals of the rose. He had only smelled it once before in his life, as these bushes had not yet bloomed. During the war, they had bivouacked overnight on a farm in Winchester, Virginia in the early fall. He had awakened to it, as he had intentionally slept on the soft soil of the garden. It was the sweet morning's kiss of rosewater.

He looked up at her now. Before he spoke, he noticed the gentleness of the morning's glow haloing the delicate features of her face. Her smile was more radiant than the light cast upon it, as she waited patiently for him to fully catch his breath.

"Thank ya', Miss," he began, "I am much obliged to you for…"

"…Ever" she said simply, with an infectious smile that erased any memory of pain from his being. Her eyes were wide and large, and her pupils the most beautiful pale shade of green that he had ever seen.

"… for yer assistance, I was about to say." He was smiling also now, for somehow he could not help but. She had only said a few words, but her entire being had been poured deep into him. He felt refreshed.

"Miss Ever," she said delicately, "Tis my name, it is. I am told it is an unusual name in this land, but not in my own."

The lilt of her voice was a subtle cadence he immediately loved.

"It is a perfectly lovely name," he said, adding "in any land."

Her Irish pronunciation was a beautiful and pleasurable rendering of the name "Ava" blending smoothly into the word "air". Clay repeated it aloud *"Miss Avair"*.

"My full name is Ever McLaughlin and it is a pleasure to finally meet you, Mister Virgil Clay-Harris," she said, extending her right hand. Clay took it into his own, hoping she would not notice the excited pulse raging within him.

He was stunned that she already knew his name, but later thought he should not have been so. He had been the talk of the town for so long, most everybody knew him. Why should she be any different?

"Just call me Clay. Most folks here just call me Clay, always have. Seems to fit me like a second skin, I guess."

"So I will, Clay. And you can call me Ever."

She was tender, he thought. No, she was tenderness itself. He thought her perfect, like no one he had ever met. She was purity.

"No, Ma'am, for as long as I know you, you will always be Miss Ever to me."

"Well, Clay, I will allow you to return to your work. I would be lying, however, if I did not say that I look forward to talking with you again soon."

She smiled at him warmly, before turning to retrace her steps to the porch across Market Street. It was at that very moment that he first became aware that she appeared to have no interest in judging him.

11

EVER AND CLAY
JANUARY 1871

The winter of 1870-71 had set in with a vengeance. Clay continued to work the merchant Gilreath's grounds, although Horace Woodard, the overseer, kept a mind to assign him chores that brought him in, as much as possible, from the bitterest fingers of the Winter season.

Clay had continued his friendship with Ever as the muted colors of fall drained to the icy pale emptiness of winter. They were seen often walking the grounds together as Clay performed his chores. To say he was taken with the young woman would be a tremendous understatement. However, Clay never had an ember of earthly desire for her. In fact, he revered her purity, and found a solace in it, having seen and survived the darkness of men's hearts upon the grounds of battle. For Clay, imagining anything that would detract from the bliss of her naivety arose a fierce anger within him. He only desired to protect her innocence, and in no way could he envision himself taking advantage of her in this way.

It was certainly not that Ever was in any way undesirable. She had the alluring form of a young girl ripening into the fullness of a woman. Her beauty was layered upon this finely evolving figure as surely as the scent of the roses he tendered would one day be dusted atop their delicate blooms.

Ever's thoughts were likewise consumed with Clay as well. From her first day in this small Southern town, she had heard the tales told about him. How the hero of Sharpsburg had struggled after the war. The once proudest of the town's youth had been ravaged by the carnage of battle. The man who had saved his farm from drought was now forced to allow sharecroppers to work his fields. The one-armed man was forced to accept the charity of the merchant Gilreath, tending to a lawn scattered about with a few rows of delicate rose bushes that refused to bloom. Hardly the work for a real man, the town's people had told her, but then again the war had left him only half a man.

Ever McLaughlin did not believe this. Not at any level. Surely, Clay was compromised by his physical losses from the war. But what the young Ever saw, from a distance even before she first spoke to him, was a proud man. Though not a man who was so proud he refused to lower himself in order to provide for those that relied upon him. He had taken what many considered to be a job of little dignity. He considered the care and the needs of others, before caring about what others might say of him. He was a good man.

It was true that he was not a well-educated man and did not have the vocabulary of even his younger brother, the clerk's intern of the county court. It was true that Clay's appearance was rough, lacking all refinement whatsoever. And it was certainly true that he perhaps overly compensated for his disability, recognizing the looks of the town that were increasingly cast disparagingly upon him. Clay had become hardheaded in performing any task as well as any "fully-abled" man.

While Ever admitted to herself that perhaps pity may have initially caused her to become taken with him, she soon realized that there was not an ounce of pity that the man desired. He had taken every hardship that life had so unfairly cast upon him and made the most of his situation. He provided for himself, his mother, his younger brother, and most certainly for his woman. Ever had noticed that she stood protectively at his side each morning and evening. The same woman she had noticed walking past the Gilreath's grounds several times a day to catch sight of her man.

Ever came to know Clay through their burgeoning friendship as a man who had no airs about him. She sensed the goodness that permeated his being. It was innate within him. There was no anger, no sense of having been wronged by fate. No sense of hostility in any form.

She could not reconcile the kindness of the man with the tales of his killing Yankees during the war. The townspeople, who so loved to tell of his brutality on the battlefield, were quick to condemn him as being nothing more than a mere cripple. Ever found it hypocritical that the very folk that condemned him for his war wounds revered him for his slaughtering actions against the Yankees at Sharpsburg, Gettysburg and Chickamauga.

Ever knew these to be three of the bloodiest conflicts of the American Civil War. She had come to learn the first two, considered Northern victories, had cost both sides immeasurable loss of their greatest treasure – the promise of young life.

She thought it ironic that while Chickamauga was considered a great Rebel victory, it was the battle where Clay had lost his arm. And she was told, Clay's childhood friend, Willet Blackwell, had also in this same conflict been wounded, marking the young man forever with the ghastly scar.

Unlike Clay, Willet Blackwell was unable to accept his wounds of battle. The townspeople told of how he had deserted the Confederate Army after bringing Clay home to Cartersville. They told of the darkness in his heart. Of how he had surrounded himself with a band of renegades, murdering Yankee soldiers they found separated from their units throughout the county during the remainder of the war. They told of how his men became a gang of marauders after the war, stealing from the farmers and herders to not only support, but enrich, themselves.

Ever thought Willet was much like her own Uncle Colin. They both had no self-respect, and no limits upon the actions they would take to enrich themselves. After having lived in hardship in her native Ireland, after having watched her own good mother deteriorate at the hands of a ravaging disease, Ever regretted having to pack up her grief and travel to America. Once there, she regretted having to live in such undeserved comfort, under the guardianship of her wretched uncle.

Ever did not understand America, especially in its postwar present. She had known only that the country's North and South had fought a great war over slavery, and the conquering Northerners had rightfully eliminated the savage act.

She had come to despise the ferocious pride of the Northerners in the months she lived in Boston with her uncle. How they boasted of ridding the land of a great social tragedy. She came to loathe how they had failed to despise just how much precious blood - on both sides - was spilled to do so. She recalled learning of the rebellions of her own country against the English and saw great similarities in the two tragedies.

She thought of her uncle, and his greed. She detested how he aligned himself with the Northern politicians, so that he could profit from their cruel treatment of the conquered South.

She had been in Boston long enough to learn of the immigrant Irish families that were ravaged by the war. The lives of their young lads were cast as fodder onto the battlefields of Antietam, Fredericksburg, Gettysburg and so many other sites of horrifying sacrifice.

Ever soon became even more disturbed upon arriving in America's South. It was the South's animosity and hatred that she could not at first understand. The South's animosity towards those who imposed upon them the onerous requirements for rejoining the Union, from which they had so desperately wanted to separate themselves. The hatred for those Northerners who had so violently forced their numerical and logistical advantage upon the already suffering South. Ever soon came to see how they despised the Union which had invaded and devastated their homeland. The Union they were now forced to rejoin.

No amount of Northern oppression would force them to accept that it had all been for the greater good of the combined country. They had watched as the same Congress that had defeated them was stamping the South with the stain of its radical Reconstruction.

It was exactly this corrosive derision of their own countrymen that Ever could not comprehend. Yet, in Clay, she saw none of this. He never spoke of the war, of the Yankees, nor of the Carpetbaggers like her own uncle.

All she saw in him was a good man who had been forced to perform inherently unnatural hostile acts. A man who had somehow, unlike all those around him, had let go of all his hatred. He was now nothing more than a good man who was doing his very best to survive.

And Ever, who had seen first-hand the corruption of her Uncle Colin, and the derision of the Southern community around her towards him, came to cherish the goodness of Clay. The man who singularly seemed able to shed the stain of war.

And so, these two souls thickened into a dense and deep friendship. Each came to offer the other the comfort of common values.

12

BRIDGING THE PAST
MARCH 1871

The dawn was more than brisk. Indeed, it was a biting cold morning in late March 1871. Ever had climbed upon the buckboard wagon to be driven by Clay on a mission of compassionate support to the residents of Euharlee. The morning's angled sunlight cast upon her face in a translucence that made Clay even more reverential of the purity of the child. Her porcelain skin, so softly freckled with her youth, was framed by the radiance of the morning sun blazing in her curls of ginger red hair. The cold morning air that separated the few feet of space between them seemed to preserve the image forever in Clay's mind. This moment would burn like an ember within him as a conflict of emotions – the great joy of his spending the day with her alone cast against the dire grief of the occasion.

A few days past, during a raucous storm, a great tragedy had beset the neighboring town of Euharlee. At Tumlin's Mill, Captain Elihu G. Nelson and his two young sons crossed by wagon over the bridge that spanned Euharlee Creek. The storm that raged had turned the creek into a violently surging artery, its waters hammering at the bridge's supports as they surged downstream toward the Etowah River. As the wagon neared the far edge of the bridge, the structure yielded violently, casting the wagon and the three figures into the furious flowing knots of the torrents below.

Captain Nelson perished, but by the grace of the Lord, his two boys were rescued from the creek's violent waters. However, this was not the full scope of the tragedy, as a Negro man named Jim Watts drowned while attempting to recover the wagon from the creek's still deadly waters.

The town of Cartersville had collected dry-goods, foodstuffs and other materials in support of the affected families of Euharlee. Given his trading history with the town, Nelson Gilreath had led the effort and even volunteered his own wagon to transport the materials.

Clay was selected to make the deliveries. This was only appropriate as both Captain Elihu Nelson and Virgil Clay-Harris were military veterans of the War of The Rebellion.

It was when Colin Brannigan heard of the support mission that he demanded to participate. His rationale was that the Freedman Jim Watts was lost in the tragedy, and as administrator of the Federal Freedmen's Bureau, Brannigan demanded that he should accompany Clay on this most somber occasion. In reality, Colin Brannigan saw this as a venue to increase his good-standing among the freed slaves of the area.

This demand brought about great consternation among the citizens of Cartersville. Brannigan had already been recognized as a self-serving Yankee Carpetbagger. This intercession, if it were allowed, would totally detract from the compassion of one Southern community assisting another in a time of great need. The town residents violently resisted, but when Brannigan pushed back, a compromise was reached. His niece, Ever, was selected to accompany Clay in her uncle's stead. She had already, in her short time in the community, become respected for her deferential manners and grace. She would present the share of goods to be given to the family of Jim Watts.

Mrs. Gilreath had intended to join the two as a chaperone. On the morning of the delivery, she was in such great grief over the tragedy that she could not be raised from her bed. Some said she had the vapors. Others said she simply detested the bitter cold of the March morn.

Still, others yet suggested that she acted magnanimously. For if Mrs. Gilreath joined them, Ever would have been forced to sit amongst the goods in the rear of the wagon. Clay had to handle the reins. It would have been so improper to have tried to squeeze all three of them on the wagon's two-person bench.

In any case, Mrs. Gilreath did not join the couple, and after a brief discussion by Mr. Gilreath and several prominent citizens who had come to see the shipment off, it was decided that the need for a chaperone could be set aside given the circumstances. Clay was trusted by all to behave as a gentleman. Even Colin Brannigan agreed to allow the two to travel alone together.

Clay had a great joy in his heart for the succession of events that would allow him to be alone with Ever for most of the day. He took both reins into his good hand, and with a flick of his wrist, the wagon moved off slowly on to Market Street, toward the Mission Trail.

As they passed, the morning sun cast down brightly upon the tight clusters of rose bushes that had so far survived the harsh winter and had fresh shoots upon their stalks. Clay prayed that in the coming months they would release their beauty and bloom, not only for the Gilreaths, but also for Ever herself to enjoy from upon the boarding house porch. He looked forward to that day with great anticipation.

"You have done a fine job with those rose bushes, Clay," she said to him in her lilting brogue, "and they surely soon will yield the loveliest of blooms."

"Well, Miss Ever, iffen they decide to bloom, I reckon you will be the first to know," Clay responded.

"*We* need not worry about them, Clay," she said, "when the time is right, they will surely bloom. If *we* have patience, *we* will be rewarded."

She merely smiled at him as they moved slowly down the Mission Trail towards Euharlee. She had never offered him the least advice as how to tend to the bushes, but her use of the words "we" instead of "you" sent a thrill through him. He had felt for some time this had been their collective undertaking.

"Clay, I am very much looking forward to seeing the countryside outside of Cartersville," she said. "Uncle Colin has been so busy that he has been unable to take me on anything but the shortest of Sunday drives."

Clay smiled at her, knowing how confining a small town can be. *Having the same folks around you every day could at times feel suffocating*, he thought.

"You'll certainly see much of the county today, Miss Ever," he said. "I only wishen it'd be under better circumstances. The loss of Captain Nelson was a grim turn, no doubt about it."

She smiled sweetly. It seemed an odd response to him.

"Clay, what the Lord provides and what the Lord reaps is a mystery to us all, only because we are too imperfect to know His ways."

His first thought was that he found her perfect in every way. She was not in any manner unseemly, and certainly not self-centered. Clay had never heard her speak of her own wants or desires. He just enjoyed her companionship, her joy of life, and her unspoiled outlook on the world around her.

"Well, Miss Ever, it still is so very sad," he responded.

"It can be as heavy a sadness as one will ever bear," she said to him, "but it is never our place to question the ways of the Lord. I learned this in Ireland, Clay. My own mother watched so many taken by the famine, and she survived it all only to be taken herself by the Consumption. She is with the Lord now, and free from the burden of pain and fear. That is how one must come to understand death, Clay."

Clay looked at her as they proceeded down the dirt trail before them. She blushed in response. Clay thought of his own maw, who despite her best attempts, failed to hide the fact that she was now coughing up ever increasing amounts of blood.

"I am so very sorry for yer loss of yer mama, Miss Ever," said Clay.

"Thank you, Clay, but please mind my lack of manners," said Ever, as she interrupted his thoughts, "I am talking about death to a man who has seen more than his share of the taking of life. Forgive my forgetting of your being in the war. Sometimes I can be so naïve, can't I?"

Clay thought upon her comment. Without saying so, he deemed that the beauty of her soul stemmed from her compassion.

"Miss Ever, I seen more than my share of death, for sure. And I never seen a heart so true to the Lord as yers. I just can't come to grasp how the Lord can under any way allow one man to wage war on another."

It was a dilemma that he had quietly struggled with since the war, but he had never shared it aloud to anyone else before.

"Well, Clay, I think you just put a point on it. It is man who wages war, not the Lord. It comes as a consequence of the vices deep in men's hearts. The Lord does not allow it, Clay, other than he has given us all free will. War is nothing more than the clanging of men's wills against each other."

He knew she was right as soon as the words left her young lips. This was not a young lady of naivety, as she herself had said, but instead of a deep understanding of the world, he thought.

"Now I have a question for you, Clay. This is not a very comfortable wagon. Why on earth is it referred to as a 'buckboard'?"

Clay laughed. The wagon was nothing more than a flat cart with wheels drawn by the two horses to which they were hitched.

"Well, I guess the name come from the way it's built. Once upon a time these was just flat wagons, with the bench we're sittin' on hooked on up front here. Ya' sees where yer feet are restin'?"

Ever looked down at the angled board on which her feet were reposed. "Yes," she said.

"I guess somewhere along the way, some fella found out the hard way that this board was needed for in case the horse in front of him bucked up. That board is to keep the driver and passenger from gittin' kicked by the horse's bucks."

"So, I see, Clay," she responded, "that is the buck-board!" A smile washed over her innocent, young face.

"Ever since, peoples just called these 'buckboard wagons', or even simpler just 'buckboards'."

"Well that makes perfect sense," responded Ever.

"Most things do," said Clay carefully, "Iffen ya' willen to ask. That was a dandy of a question, though, Miss Ever."

It was about this time that they came to pass over Pettit's Creek, and Clay pointed out his homestead to Ever. She could only see the slightest glimpse of the cabin off in the distance to her right.

"It is such a delightful location, Clay. Your family must be so proud," she said to him. "Did your father settle this land?"

Clay thought before answering, somewhat ashamed of his response. Yet he could not be evasive to her. She was so easy to speak to, it gave him solace, as if he were confessing all of his and his family's shortcomings.

"We got his spread after the government drove off the Cherokee in '38. Mah Diddy had been a blacksmith, and he later learned himself gunsmithin'. But, I guess, he could be lazy something fierce. Instead of earning his livin' from black-smithin' or gun-smithin', he saved up all his money and bribed one of the men involved with conducting the Cherokee land lottery. He wanted this site because after the Dahlonega gold rush, he was sure he would find nuggets in this here crick. He'd heard the Cherokee had drawn gold here, themselves. He wanted the big claim, the easy money."

"Well, Clay, that is a trait found in men around the world, now, isn't it?" she said, thinking of her Uncle Colin.

"I reckon so. He and mah maw settled this stolen land. Mah Diddy built that there cabin with his own hands. He was right handy that way. He could fix anything. In fact, he was the one who told me about the buck-board name and all. Just seems like he could only work hard in spurts, cause once he got that shack built, all he would do was pan for gold. Never cleared them fields, not until we all almost starved to death. All he wanted to do was hit a rich strike in gold, which he never did. Not until the day he left us."

"Oh, Clay, I am so sorry. I did not realize you had lost your father to the Lord..." began Ever.

He laughed aloud at her comment. "I doubt whether the Lord would take a man like my Diddy. Might likely just send up the Devil to save my paw the travel."

"Oh, Clay, your father could not possibly be so vile," she said

"Well Miss Ever, turns out we just lost him to the next big money-making scheme. Ya' see, he and mah maw had a hard life on these grounds. But when I growed-up, he put me out to work in the fields while he panned that creek. He did learn me to shoot, and dang-good thing, because it kept us all alive at times."

"Oh, Clay, your family certainly had a rough toss before the war," she said.

"Well, it got worse. Just after I left for the war, Diddy went off to Texas to get some work as a gunsmith. He heard there was real money in it, supplying guns to cowhands and bushwhackers, if not to the Rebels themselves. He wanted to sell the spread of land here and have mama go with him. She wouldn't have none of it."

"So, I see, your mother is a sensible woman," said Ever.

Clay looked at her as if he did not understand what she had just said. "Well, I don't know about that. She was just getting tarred of his schemes. So, he went off to Texas alone. He took to makin' money down there illegally converting ball and cap pistols to take bullet cartridges."

"Why would that be illegal?" asked Ever.

"Cause another company held the patent for this. Hear tell, that didn't stop mah Diddy, tho'. He kept supplying them quick loadin' six shooters to anyone who would buy them. And on that frontier full of rustlers, raiders and ranch hands, there was a lot of folks willin' to pay good hard cash for a quick loading gun."

"And he never came back to share his wealth with you all?"

Clay turned his face away from her, but as he did, Ever saw a shadow of shame come upon it.

"While I was gone at war, Diddy come back to town with an-other woman. A young woman, who he told mama was a business partner. He put her up in town, and he stayed with mah Maw. He only stayed the one night, left me a pair of revolvers, and gave mah Maw some small portion of the money he had earned. Told her to git these guns to me. That they could save my life in the war. Then, mah Diddy run off with that other woman to Texas for good. Mah maw never saw him agin', and to this day is as bitter as turned cider. I feared she would kill him if she ever got the chance."

Ever listened to him, feeling the pain salted among his words.

"Did your mother ever get those guns to you during the war?" asked Ever.

"That was the most 'mazing part of all this. She used that money from Diddy to come to Richmond in '62 and she finally found me. Give me them bullet loadin' sixes and the ammunition my Diddy left behind."

"Did you ever find need to use them?"

"They was some proud guns, Miss Ever. Everybody wanted them. They was a pain to keep, I tell ya'. But they did come in handy later, worth all the fuss. Especially for Willet and me."

"Oh, my, Clay! Your family certainly has been through so much," she said with a tenderness that was without judgement. "Look, just ahead of us along the trail there. Isn't that the woman who is a friend of yours?"

Walking along the trail was Deekie. She was dressed in a heavy wool field dress that clung to the contours of her womanly form. Over her shoulders was a threadbare, but warm, shawl. The Colt Navy revolver was holstered amid her waist. Her body was taut with hardship. She looked up over her shoulder as the wagon overcame her. Deekie spied, with an accusing eye, her Virgil and the lovely girl, Ever, together. Clay felt the pain that ran through her bleak emptiness.

Deekie was now out of the cabin for the day, despite the cold bite of the morning. She knew she was not welcome there, so every day, bitter or temperate, rain or shine, she walked. Deekie waved tentatively to her Virgil, smiling curtly through the searing anguish of seeing him and the Irish girl together. Clay responded with a snap of his lone wrist, which the two-horse team took as an encouragement to break into a gallop. The buckboard immediately bounced along the trail, its contents threatening to rattle themselves onto the ground. Deekie was left behind in a swell of dust.

"Whoa," said Clay, wrestling with he two horses, fighting with his single hand to rein in the animals. He screamed at the team of two, "Settle yerselves, y'all!"

They had come to a stop some three hundred yards down the trail.

Ever had turned back looking upon Deekie, standing alone in the plume of dust that the animals had kicked up.

"Clay," she said frantically, "You must go back and apologize to her."

"Not, now, as we must git on to Euharlee. I will do it tonight when I see her, Miss Ever. She's knowin' I didn't mean that, she knows all about my limits, especially with these animals" he said, raising his shortened left limb.

Truth be told, Clay did not wish to go back to Deekie because he feared how she might react after having seen the two of them together. He decided to keep the two women apart, and again drove the buckboard forward.

"She is a very lovely woman, Clay," said Ever, turning around to look forward once more. "I always though the two of you made such a grand couple."

The comment took him by surprise. Deekie had none of Ever's refinements. Clay thought her hard and spent, and he cared for her as one cares for any other stray. Yet, Ever professed to see beauty in her, and in the two of them together.

"Ya' reckon she's pretty, do ya', Miss Ever?" asked Clay. "She's had a very hard life..."

"Her eyes are a stunning shade of blue, her hair a delightful auburn-blonde, and she has a peaceable strength about her, Clay. She is indeed a very beautiful woman."

"Miss Ever, iffen' I didn't know better," replied Clay, "I would think you were baiting me to disagree with ya'."

"You don't think she is lovely, Clay?" asked Ever. "Now don't be mistaking the parcel for the packaging..."

Clay thought for a moment about her comment. He had grown close to Deekie, only to be pushed away by her after the incident in the pines. He thought that since he had taken the job at the merchant's lawn, that she had only drifted away further from him.

"Let's just say that the war has left its mark on her, too," Clay said to Ever.

What he had failed to realize was that just before taking that job, she had warmed to him again. She had never felt closer to him then when he had taught her to shoot. He failed to see how touched she was when he gave her one of his cherished Colt Navies with which to protect herself. He missed noticing how her ears rang with joy when he spoke the words that she was the most important part of his life.

That was all before Clay began working the merchant Gilreath's lawn, before the elegant Miss Ever came into Clay's, and by extension, Deekie's lives. When that buckboard rushed on past her on the Mission Trail, with her man alongside that pretty, young red-headed girl, Deekie was left standing alone in a cloud of dirt that the couple kicked up together.

It was at this very moment, clouded in the dust of rejection, that Deekie felt humiliated by her Virgil. He favored the finely dressed and well-mannered Ever McLaughlin. Deekie then decided that she needed somewhere more welcoming to live, somewhere that she belonged. It was then that she decided to return to Three Sisters Mountain. To return to Willet Blackwell, as flawed a man as he was.

Virgil has cast me aside just as his daddy cast his maw aside, she thought, *for a younger, prettier woman. I refuse to live with him in shame.*

Deekie turned around and returned to the shack by the creek. This was the cabin where she had once nursed her Virgil back to health, when his own mother had given him up for dead.

She had made a decision, a very fateful one, at that. She was tired of living where she was not wanted. She had once come to feel unwanted during the war, when she was forced to live with her neighbors. Now, she certainly was no longer wanted at Virgil's cabin.

She entered the shack, and unleashed the wrath of Virgil's maw.

"So, now ya' runnin' off to yet but another man..." scowled the bitter woman, as Deekie grabbed her things about the cabin, "...go and git your scrawny backside out of my son's life."

"Virgil would have no life at all if I had let you cast his life away after Chickamauga," screamed Deekie in response.

"How dare ya', ya' little hussy. You had no right, then nor now, of wedgin' yerself in here. Just git, and don't turn yer sights on my boy ever agin'."

Deekie looked upon her with contempt. "I only hope that when yer time of need arises, yer Virgil treats ya' as badly as you did him!"

Having said this, Deekie left the shack, slamming its door with all the fury within her. She took with her the scant possessions, everything her life had amounted to, up to that point, and left for Three Sisters Mountain.

She would rather risk living a life of potential physical abuse with Willet than the verbal abuse of Virgil's maw. Most of all, she could not and would no longer continue to stand by and be ignored as her Virgil heaped his attention upon that Irish woman-child.

Deekie would not be waiting for him at the Gilreaths' lawn at the end of that day. Nor would she be waiting in the shack when her Virgil returned that night. And neither would his Colt Navy Revolver, for Deekie had taken the gun with her.

It was her only souvenir of her years with Virgil. A reminder of what could have been with him. And, just perhaps, it would be the only protection she would have against the dangers of the camp upon Three Sisters Mountain.

13

EUHARLEE
MARCH 1871

Clay and Ever drove on to Euharlee. They crossed the Etowah at Rowland's Ferry. Clay could not help but think of Deekie, as this was near the site that they once would walk to draw water at the height of the drought. He knew she would be angry at him, but thought he would fix this with her later that evening.

Having crossed the river, they made their way further west. They soon after came upon the collapsed bridge over Euharlee Creek at Tumlin's Mill. The creek was between them and the town of Euharlee. A makeshift raft ferry, of sorts, had been improvised for the crossing the creek, but it could not accommodate the weight of the fully laden wagon.

The creek was calm by then, and with the help of the local men of Euharlee, the goods brought by Clay and Ever were ferried across the creek. Each return of the ferry carried goods from the Tumlin Mill, as Clay had been directed by Nelson Gilreath to buy as much of the products from their mill as he could possibly transport back to Cartersville. This was another sign of his own personal support for the townspeople of Euharlee.

Finally, as the milled goods were loaded onto the buckboard, Clay and Ever were ferried across the creek's waters, which were presently very calm. As they crossed, Ever began to envision the good Captain Nelson struggling for his life while trying to save his children only days before in the furious flow of these very waters.

The sense of the community's loss stung with bitterness in the air. The elders of Euharlee seemed to be themselves awash in a state of shock. Captain Nelson, and his two young boys, had been the victim of inadequate safeguards for the creek's bridge, and every man and woman of the area knew this could readily have been any of themselves lost in the raging creek. Thanks to the providence of the Lord, the two Nelson Boys had survived.

Clay and Ever arrived on the opposite bank of the creek to encounter two groups of mourners. Closest to them were those mourning the loss of Captain Nelson. Behind them were the freedmen mourning Jim Watts.

Clay addressed the recently widowed wife of Captain Nelson. He read a declaration from the merchant Gilreath. This was a very difficult act for him, reading aloud before this many people. He became stumped only once, on the word "tragedy". Ever whispered the pronunciation in Clay's ear, and he finished without any further problems.

Then, as a sign of his own personal respect for the Captain's sacrifice in the war, he presented the widow with the CSA insignia which Clay had kept from his own uniform after returning to Cartersville. This gesture clearly touched the woman, as she softly wept as Clay placed it in her hands. She had graciously endured so many hours of missing her husband's companionship during the many years of the war, only to have the newfound abundance of his company violently ripped away from her a few years later.

Ever was treated politely, but with great reservation by all the townsfolk. She was known by these people as the Carpetbagger's charge, the niece of the Irishman sent here to help the Freedmen of the county. She was not quite what they had expected, and her unassuming ways were in direct conflict with the opinions that they had pre-formed of her.

After Clay completed his visit with the widow Nelson, Ever waited respectfully for several minutes before pushing through the crowd of white townsfolk to join the family of Jim Watts, the Negro man drowned attempting to recover the wagon from the creek. They were standing alone beyond the white townspeople, who had kept themselves segregated from the Watts family during the ceremony. However, as this was truly a communal loss, both groups felt an overwhelming need to be a part of the event.

Ever walked solemnly until she came before the black man's family. What she did next sent a stir through both groups. Ever lowered herself before the Watts' survivors, and carefully came to rest on one knee before them. She lowered her head, reaching out to take the hands of any family member who would take her own. The sight of this innocent young white woman, genuflecting before the mourning family members, would normally have caused a great commotion. But under these tragic circumstances, there was a tenderness in her submissive act. Slowly, in a most tentative manner, the hands of Jim Watts' family reached out to take her own.

Ever bowed her head in silent entreaty to the Lord. Her tender milky-white fingers and palms interlocked with the family's calloused black hands, as she prayed with them in silent consolation. Then, she recited The Lord's Prayer aloud, and everyone, black and white, joined in. The physical contrasts were never starker, yet even the most hardened of souls could feel the common currency of loss, of grief, of despair that pulsed through their clenched hands.

"I am so very sorry for your family's loss," Ever said sincerely to them all. "A man's life should never be imperiled for nothing other than retrieving the property of another."

The faces stared at the beautiful young woman, still on a knee before them, when a black mourner said aloud, "But Child, we all was nothing but property to them for so long, they can't help but to still treat us as such."

Ever looked up at them, her eyes glistening. She then picked out the crying and despondent woman before her, who she suspected was Jim's woman. Wiping away her own escaping tears, she asked a simple question...

"Your Jim was a good man, was he not?"

"He was the best of all men," came the answer.

"Then, let us all remember him as such. A good man, a freed man, the best of all men who gave his life helping others. Not because he was forced to, but because it was his nature to always help those in need."

Her words struck a chord with them, and all the women of the group stepped forward. They tenderly grabbed her by her arms, raised her to her feet, and embraced the young Irish woman as a group.

Then, the simplest of foods was provided by both groups. Ever and Clay spent time equally, eating cakes and drinking cider with them. Their visit was greatly appreciated by all.

Clay and Ever returned to the makeshift ferry and crossed the creek one last time. The buckboard had been loaded with sacks of ground goods from the Euharlee mill for the return trip. They departed in reverential silence, with the solemnity of the day's events pressed hard upon them.

Ever turned to Clay and said simply "The Lord cleanses us all through the water. The earth's water gives life, and takes it away, according to His will. But the Lord's water gives us everlasting life, and after drinking from it, no one will ever thirst again."

"Amen," said Clay, bowing his head.

Clay had decided to take the same route back to Cartersville, when Ever surprised him a few minutes later with a request.

"Clay, is it true that General Sherman refused to burn a mansion along the river because a girl he loved was living in it and declined to leave? I had heard this story, and I find it so romantic. Could you take me there?"

"Well, Miss Ever, I can take you there, all right, but you done got that story all sideways and such. You be talking about Etowah Heights. I can surely go a little out of our way and drive you past that mansion, but I reckon I need to share the proper story with ya' along the way, Miss Ever."

"Please be so kind as to enlighten me, Clay," she said. "I wish to know every word of this romantic story, so I can tell it to my children and all their children until the day I die."

Clay looked at the young woman sitting aside him. Her face beamed with expectation. She seemed to be always curious about the war, and how it came to be. It seemed odd to him that anyone did not possess the knowledge of the events that led to the conflict, but that was only because she had not lived through it.

"Well, the first thing you need to know is that General Sherman was very familiar with our great state of Georgia. When he was at West Point, he roomed with a young man from Augusta – Mr. Marcellus Stovall, who later became Major General Stovall of the Confederate Army."

"Isn't it strange that a Confederate General would have gone to West Point in New York?" she asked.

"No, not t'all, Miss Ever. Ya' see, them West Point cadets come from all across the country – nobody knew what a God-awful conflict was coming down the road. Even our beloved General, Robert E. Lee, was the commandant of West Point for a few years."

"So, all these Generals, intent on killing each other, they all knew each other before the war?", asked Ever. The concept had never occurred to her.

"Mostly so, ma'am. Many of them fought side-by-side in the war against Mexico in the time before the War Between the States."

"Remarkable, truly remarkable," responded Ever.

"Well, while Sherman was a young man at West Point in 1836, Marcellus Stovall's younger sister, Cecelia, come to New York for a visit. Sherman had no designs on ladyfolk up to that point, but he fell hard for Miss Cecelia, courted her something fierce, and finally asked Miss Stovall to marry him. "

"You did say this was a romantic story," teased Ever.

"She done turned him down flat, Miss Ever. Miss Cecelia told the young cadet that he had such cruel eyes that she would pity his enemies in war, for he certainly wouldn't. She told Sherman that he would surely crush them."

"Clay, a woman surely knows a man from what she sees in his eyes," she replied. "For instance, from the very first time I looked into your eyes, I could tell what a good man you are. Very compassionate, very loyal. And they say the eyes are the window to the soul. You are a good man, Clay."

The words surged through him, raising feelings in him he had thought were long driven out by the guilt of his wartime experience.

Sensing Clay's awkward reaction to her words, Ever asked him to continue. "How did the young cadet Sherman respond?"

"Sherman told her that even if she was ever his enemy, he would cherish her and protect her from harm, even with his life if he had to."

"How gentlemanly," commented Ever.

"Sherman was no gentleman, Miss Ever. I almost hate tellin' ya' this story, cause it hides the cruelty of the man. Now, he went on to come to Georgia in the 1840's, staying in these parts and all the way down to Big Shanty and Marietta. Nobody says he ever saw Miss Cecelia Stovall again. She went on to marry Mr. Charles T. Shelman of this area, a fine Southern gentleman."

"So, instead of becoming Mrs. Cecelia Stovall Sherman, she went on to become Mrs. Cecelia Stovall Shelman?" asked Ever.

"That's right. And favorably so for her. He fought for the Confederacy during the war, as did Miss Cecelia's six brothers. Before the war, Mr. Shelman had built Miss Cecelia one of the finest homes along the river. It come to be known as Etowah Heights."

"And this is where you are taking me, Clay?"

"Sure am, ma'am. But later, during the war, when General Sherman come through this area in May of 1864, he come upon a recently abandoned mansion on the Etowah river. His troops was looting the place, as Sherman had already ordered it to be burned. The man had no sense of what was just. He waged war on the civilians of the South, just cause they had been in the way of his army. The man was a scoundrel, and still is, iffen ya' ask me."

"But he didn't end up burning Etowah Heights, did he, Clay?" asked Ever.

Clay could see the young girl was still romanticizing this story of Sherman.

"No, Miss Ever, he didn't. About that time an old Negro man

come up to the General. Some say he was the head servant at the house. When General Sherman asked him where the residents were, he told the General that Miss Cecelia Stovall Shelman had taken her better possessions and set off for her home town of Augusta to avoid the invading Yankee army."

Image 9 – Etowah Heights
Source: Etowah Valley Historical Society

"Sherman recognized the name, of course, and after quizzing the servant, concluded that this was the home of his Cecelia. Instead of burning the grand home, he posted sentries around it and ordered that none of its remaining goods were to be looted."

"Did she ever find out that the General saved her home?" asked Ever.

"She knew he had," said Clay "for General Sherman left a letter for the lady."

Having explained this, the buckboard pulled along the drive leading up to Etowah Heights. "She still lives here, Miss Ever. Likely she is inside that home just now, goin' 'bout her business."

"It truly is a magnificent home, Clay. What a pity had it been burned to the ground." Ever had never seen a home so grand, not here, nor in her native Ireland. "What did the letter from General Sherman say to Miss Cecelia?"

"Well, not many has actually seen that letter, but it seems almost everybody done got it mem'rized, figure that! According to the townsfolk, that letter said,

'You once said I would crush an enemy, and you pitied my foe. Do you recall my reply? Although many years have passed, my answer is the same now as then. I would ever shield and protect you. That I have done. Forgive me all else, for I am only a soldier.'

And it was signed by the general."

"What a remarkable story, Clay," she said. "Thank you so much for bringing me by here. I will always remember this day."

"Miss Ever, that is truly a wonderful story for children. Just remember this. When Robert E. Lee marched us into Sharpsburg and Gettysburg, we never destroyed not one civilian's home. Sherman done decided otherwise."

"What are you saying, Clay?" she asked.

"I'm only saying that Sherman didn't have to burn any homes as he come through here. Not churches nor businesses that didn't serve the war, neither. We should not make such a great fuss over a single home he spared just because he was once smitten with the lady of the house. General Sherman was a vicious, vengeful man, and needs to be remembered as such."

Having said this, Clay started the horses once more. Leaving Etowah Heights, they drove the buckboard full of goods loaded in Euharlee back to Cartersville. With the weight of the goods, the wagon creaked at every rut in the road. Only the cadence of these mechanical sounds marked the time they shared after Clay's telling of the Etowah Heights story. For the longest time, neither Clay nor Miss Ever said a word. Clay feared she had romanticized not only that story, but the entire war. That was his thought, until she abruptly spoke.

"What a horrific conflict that war was, Clay," Ever stated, after the long period of silence. "How could so many lives be ruined? How could so many lives, so many mother's sons be wastefully lost? How did it ever come to pass?"

Clay looked at her carefully, and he could see her eyes were full of tears. It seemed the silence that had set in upon them after leaving Etowah Heights had cast her into heavy and troublesome thought. Her emotions were at that point overwhelming her. He felt as if he had been too stiff with her regarding General Sherman. He did not intend to chastise her, but feared he had.

"It was what like you said this morning. I think you put it well, Ms. Ever. The Lord give us all free will. The war was a clashing of those wills. The Yankee folk didn't care for how we lived our lives down here. The abolitionists stirred up the Yankee's emotions. They flowed over in new states like Kansas and Missoura, and when the tyrant Lincoln was forced on us in the election of 1860, it was too much for the South to take. They should have just let us go and live our lives in our new Confederate States of America, but Mr. Lincoln would not allow that to pass. So, there was this war."

It was the first time Clay could discuss the war without his stomach tensing up, without his nerves tightening to the point it strangled his thoughts and whipsawed his reactions.

"So, brothers took arms against brothers, friend against friend?" she asked.

"It was so. In several cases. Even friends who went off to war together would never be the same."

"Like you and that Willet Blackwell?" asked Ever. "He was your friend before the war, was he then?"

Amazingly, Clay found he could talk to the young Irish woman in a calm manner. And surprising to him, it felt soothing to talk to her. She was not judgmental in the least. She was only interested in the facts of the war, he thought.

"Yeah, me and Willet grew up in each other's pockets," quipped

Clay. "Twern't one of us seen without the other. We both went off to war expecting to come back heroes, covered in glory."

"Clay, in town all the talk is that the two of you were in three of the largest battles of the war. Is that true?" she asked.

"That is true, Miss Ever. We was both in the battles of Sharpsburg in Maryland, at Gettysburg in Pennsylvania, and at Chickamauga.

"Where is that, Clay?"

"Just North of here a bit, in Georgia, just before ya' comes to Chattanooga, Tennessee."

"Everybody says you were the Hero of Sharpsburg, Clay. A real sharpshooter. They say you kept the Yankees from following General Lee's army back into Virginia."

Clay wanted to set the young woman straight, show her how these stories got distorted away from the battlefield.

"Now, Miss Ever, I don't never correct folks on these stories, but they got that all wrong. Do you know what a rifled musket is, Miss Ever?"

She looked perplexed. "I don't know anything about guns, Clay? How possibly could I?"

"Well, a musket shoots a ball out of the barrel. That's what we call a smooth bore. But I became pretty good at using a British musket that had what's called a rifled barrel. It just means that the barrel has a spiral groove in it that steadies the ball as it is fired and lets someone like me shoot more surely from a farther distance."

"I see, Clay. So, you were able to kill Yankees at long range. That is why the Yankee General didn't follow General Lee's Army back into Virginia?"

"That's the tale that everybody latches onto like leeches. But it t'ain't true. They think I killed a dozen or so men from long distance. The truth is much worse than that."

"Tell me the truth, Clay," she pleaded innocently. "I just want to know what you were forced to go through, Clay. You and Willet."

He looked at her with a sideways glance. She was interested, but he sensed not from a desire to spread rumors. He felt safe in sharing with her what he could not share with any other person alive.

"Willet and I were separated at Sharpsburg. He was with a group of Georgia militia who was protecting a critical stone bridge over Antietam Creek. The Yankee General Burnside had been trying to get his troops across that bridge, and the Georgia militia just kept mowing them down. 'Easy pickens,' Willet said."

He paused as he could feel the tension pulling taut within, like a boat about to snap its mooring.

"You can tell me, Clay. You are doing fine, please continue" Ever pleaded gently. The sound of her voice calmed him somewhat. He decided to press on.

"They held that bridge for several hours, before falling back. Truthfully, had it not been for Willet and them other Georgia volunteers, me and the men I was fighting with would have had those Yankees circling all around us. Willet and his fellow troops done good, real good."

"Where were you, Clay?" asked Ever.

He hesitated. How much could he really tell this young girl of his shame?

"I was with the other of General Longstreet's troops at a place called the Bloody Lane."

"The Bloody Lane, Clay?" she repeated.

"I just can't, Miss Ever. I just can't talk of it." For the second time he could feel his guts begin to tie themselves up into knots.

"Clay, don't you see. The longer you hold all this inside of you, the longer it will fester and eat at you. You can tell me, Clay. I promise I will never repeat a word of what you say to anyone. You just need to get this serpent's venom out of you."

He knew she was right. He had to share this horror with someone, and she certainly had never laid an ounce of judgement on him. He felt safe with her, that she would not turn on him, nor tell his secrets to even another soul.

He paused in his response. This young girl, purity herself, was calling on him to free himself of his own impurity. He began, not knowing how far he would get.

"At Sharpsburg, well, that part of Maryland is full of farm country, really pretty country, had we not been killin' each other in the middle of it all. Sharpsburg was the single bloodiest day of the war. And these battles are like hell. I was in the worst part of it. There was a country road that was sunken below the fields around it. We was along that road, along the side of it that rose up to the field. After the battle, they named it the Bloody Lane, there was so much killin' there."

"Oh my God, Clay, how did you survive?"

"I got no notion, really. Soldiers was falling on both sides of me, their bodies being throwed back by the balls into the lane behind us. I just kept fighting. I just kept killing Yankees, it was all I could do. They just kept coming at us, wave after wave. But our position was better, and we kept cutting them down in waves."

Then he found himself for the first time unable to draw the next words.

"It's fine, Clay, you are doing fine. Please tell me what you are remembering. It'll bring you peace from having to relive it, forever. I promise."

Image 10 – Sharpburg's Bloody Lane

"I am ashamed to tell you this, Miss Ever, I must of killed thirty men or more that day."

"Clay, you were only doing what you were trained to do," she was crying softly at that point, "I am so sorry to ask you to remember that. But as I said, I am sure it will bring you peace."

"I have never told nobody that. I am so ashamed of that killing that I did there. But it does feel good to confess that to another soul."

"You have nothing of which to be ashamed, Clay," she repeated.

"It is worse, Miss Ever. I don't know how to tell ya' this next bit, but I feel I has to. I just know you will hate me for this," he said.

"I could never hate you, Clay. You are my good friend," she reassured him. She laid a gloved hand upon his right shoulder. It was the first time that she had touched him in his distress.

"Many if not most of them men I killed that day were, I don't know how to say it, but they was..." he paused, "they was Irish boys," he finally confessed to her.

"Oh, my Lord, Clay," she said in shock. Her right hand came up to her mouth, but she never removed her left hand from his shoulder.

"Remember what I told you about the rifle musket and long-distance shooting?," he asked.

"Yes, of course," she replied, attempting to compose herself.

"Well, that is what everybody gets wrong. We was fighting at thirty yards and less from them Yanks along that road. There was a small rise from the lane, less a hill, more like a knoll. They just kept comin' over that knoll. I remember seeing that huge green regiment flag before I ever saw them boys. It just floated so proudly on the breeze as it come over that rise."

"I am so sorry to have forced you to tell me this," said Ever, before realizing he was at a point where he could not stop himself.

"I just took aim at those boys as they come over that ridge. I would drop one boy and take one of two muskets the soldiers behind me had reloaded. I dropped them boys as they come closer and closer to that lane. I could hear the boys I shot dying all around me. I could hear them boys calling for their mamas. I can still hear them. They talked funny the same way you do, Miss Ever, beg pardon. When I don't want to hear them the most, that's when they call out to me. You gotta forgive me, I am so ashamed to tell you all this."

Ever removed her hand from his shoulder and placed it on his forearm. She had realized how the torment he felt was doubly barbed with the guilt of his having killed her own countrymen.

"Clay, you have been through fighting to which no man should ever have been subjected. You were only doing what you were trained to do. There is no shame in doing your duty, to fight the enemy put before you. However, I will tell you something that is truly shameful."

Her voice now had an edge to it that he had never heard before, and he found himself being to tense again. He feared her judgement of him was coming next.

"What is truly shameful," she continued in her tight voice, "is that many of those Irish lads you shot down along that 'Bloody Lane' in Sharpsburg may have been put there by my uncle."

Clay could not believe what she was saying. He felt for her, as the tears had returned to her eyes. Any tension within himself was gone and replaced by his care for his young friend.

"He was paid for each one of those boys he talked into being volunteers, and later was paid great sums for getting them to become replacements for the sons of the richest of families in Massachusetts. He profited off those boys giving their lives. And that is despicable, Clay. You merely did your duty, my uncle had no duty, only his greed to profit from their spilled blood."

Clay could not believe that she had totally relieved him of his own guilt, all the while harboring the greatest of her hatred for her own uncle.

"I am sorry, Miss Ever, for reminding you of all this. For upsetting you such."

"Don't concern yourself so, Clay," she responded, gently massaging his forearm in a reassuring manner. "It does indeed feel good to get it out to someone I can trust. However, for the rest of the afternoon, perhaps we should discuss another topic. And don't worry, Clay, I will never repeat what you have entrusted to me."

"Neither will I, about yer uncle, I mean," Clay replied.

"I fear that is already an open secret among the people of Cartersville. What is not a secret is that he is not very popular here."

They spoke no more of the war, nor of her uncle for the rest of the trip. As they came north into Cartersville, Ever remarked on the quarrying of the Three Sisters Mountain along its south face. The Ladd Lime and Stone company had begun excavating the face of the mountain just after the war had ended.

The firm's mining into the mountain had been going on for several years. The south hillside had been blasted away, with only large piles of crushed rock remaining. These were separated by the size of the stones, with the last pile being nothing more than a fine powder. The hillside had been transformed into multicolored cliffs of about sixty feet in height, with the open pockets of the caves below having been exposed.

"Those colors are so beautiful all along those cliffs. The ochre, the rust, the tan and the red clay all fused and blended. I have never seen such a sight, Clay!"

"It is a bad thing that they are doing to that mountain. We played in those caves when we was young..."

"You and Willet, Clay," Ever asked.

"Yeah, and Deekie, too. Wonderful caves, full of rooms with these big columns of rock dripping from the ceiling and arching to the floor. Since just after the war, they been blasting and grinding these stones. Take 'em out of here in big rail cars. God knows where they go to on those trains."

"You are right about that mountain, Clay. That is a beautiful rise. I bet you can see all the county from up on top of it."

Clay thought of Willet, his camp atop the mountain. Panic seared through him.

"Promise me, Miss Ever, that you will never go up on that mountain. Never."

"Why, Clay?" she asked in earnest. "Why should I not go there and enjoy the scenery?"

"Just promise me that you won't, Miss Ever."

She looked at him, sensed the dread in him, but agreed if only in order to calm him.

"I promise, Clay, I will not," said Ever, adding, "not unless you are with me."

14

ANTIETAM
SEPTEMBER 17, 1862

E verything Clay had told Ever was absolutely true to the knowledge that he possessed. Yet, as an infantry soldier, he was unaware of many of the events that led up to the Battle of Sharpsburg – the battle the Yankees referred to as Antietam.

For instance, Clay did not possess the knowledge of the applied strategy of Confederate General Robert E. Lee. At the onset of the Civil War, then Colonel Lee had been asked to command the Union Armies. Deciding he could not wage war upon his home state of Virginia, he resigned his commission in the Federal Army of the North.

Lee soon found himself in the role of military advisory to the Confederate President Jefferson Davis. Being a man of action and a strategist of battle, Lee found being restricted to the capital of Richmond as a frustrating appointment. He watched as the Union Army closed in around Richmond under the direction of the North's General McClellan. They had indeed closed within less than ten miles of the capital, prompting President Davis to ask his advisor to where they should retreat when Richmond soon fell. It was then that Lee responded famously, "Sir, Richmond must never fall."

The Confederate General countering McClellan had been Joseph E. Johnston. When Johnston was injured, General Lee took over the Confederate troops which he soon renamed the Army of Northern Virginia. Soon, with the aid of his most trusted General, Stonewall

Jackson, Lee pushed back the Union Army away from Richmond and back to the Yorktown Peninsula from which their campaign had initiated.

Tired of fighting battle after battle on the soil of his sacred Virginia, Lee devised the plan to take his army across the Potomac into the farmlands of Maryland, where he envisioned the local farmers would receive his rebel troops as liberators.

Lee put into effect a two-tiered plan in September of 1862, first capturing the federal arsenal at Harpers Ferry, Virginia, and then pressing the main body of his troops into the South Mountains of Maryland.

Lee was not aware that his special order detailing the attack had fallen into the hands of General McClellan. McClellan had earlier been removed from command by Lincoln in the Peninsula Campaign in Virginia because of his lack of aggressiveness and his failure to take Richmond. Later, he had been reinstated as commander of the Union Army of the Potomac. It was then that one of McClellan's soldiers had come across a stash of captured Confederate cigars. Wrapped around these prized smokes was Lee's special order detailing the invasion of Maryland. Holding General Lee's complete plan of battle, General McClellan uncharacteristically moved his Union Army aggressively to meet Lee's Army. The two masses of men came upon each other at the town of Sharpsburg on September 17th, 1862. Off to the east was the rapidly running Antietam Creek. To the Confederates, what followed was known as the Battle of Sharpsburg, while to the Yankees it was revered as the Battle of Antietam.

The single day battle commenced in three main actions. General Stonewall Jackson's troops engaged the Union Army in cornfields north of the town, while General Longstreet's troops held against ferocious attacks in both the sunken road that provided natural cover for his troops, and at positions overlooking the stone bridge crossing the Antietam Creek.

All three venues were extremely hard fought, and deadly in its losses to both sides. The battles in the cornfields see-sawed back and forth in tides of death to both Blue and Gray alike, before the

Confederate lines collapsed back into the town itself where they would eventually hold.

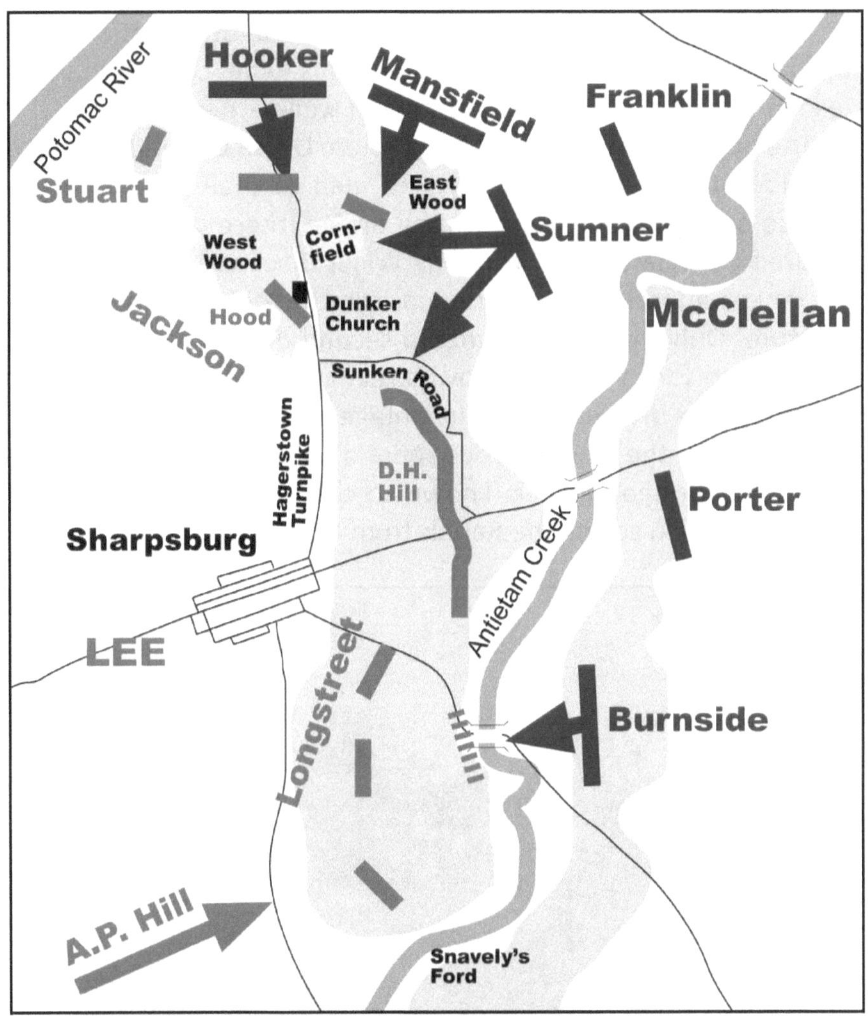

Image 11 – Map of Battle of Sharpsburg (Antietam)
Source: historynet.com

The sunken farm road soon became the Bloody Lane, as the Confederates repulsed wave after wave of attacking Union Troops before being themselves decimated upon it from Yankees having finally gained a superior position, firing directly down the lane. Here Virgil Clay-Harris had indeed cut down dozens of Yankee infantry, with many of them being the Irish Regiments of Massachusetts and New York.

Clay and others were able to escape into another set of fields just behind the bloody lane, as many of his Rebel companions fell dead in the road, giving it its ghastly but well-earned name.

The battle at the Stone Bridge is where Union General Ambrose Burnside hurled wave after wave of men to their death. For on the rise of the hillside opposite the bridge, there were some five hundred Georgia troops, including Willet Blackwell, cutting down the Yankee infantry as they tried in vain to cross over the narrow structure. Only hours later, when a second detachment of troops managed to ford the creek downstream of the bridge, were the Georgian rifles driven from their vantage point.

Even then, the Union troops spent a lengthy time crossing the "Burnside's Bridge" as it is known to this day. The time wasted proved critical in saving the Rebels from utter defeat.

Image 12 – The Burnside Bridge Over Antietam Creek

The delay in crossing the bridge, and General McClellan's failure to commit his reserve troops when the Yankees appeared to be on the very verge of breaking Lee's lines, were two strategic mistakes of tremendous significance. They allowed the Confederates to receive much needed reserve troops of their own under General A.P. Hill from Harpers Ferry. Despite the seventeen-mile march, Hill immediately pressed his troops into battle, stabilizing Lee's lines as the day turned to night.

The next day Lee awaited McClellan's attack. But the Union officer's lack of aggression had returned. The day passed with no significant fighting, and that evening, under the cover of darkness, General Lee removed his Army across the Potomac River into Northern Virginia.

McClellan failed to pursue Lee's army. Not because of long range Confederate sharpshooters as the myth of Cartersville had suggested. To the contrary, the fighting at Sharpsburg was close and near, and devastatingly deadly for both sides.

The Union General's own timidity in pressing the battle was all that was needed to allow what was left of Lee's army to retreat. McClellan's lack of aggression in engaging the enemy was well known. It caused President Lincoln at one point that year to say, *"If McClellan is not using the Army, I should like to borrow it for a while."*

The failure to pursue Lee was also cause enough for President Lincoln to later sack McClellan for a second time from his command. Ultimately, the command of the Army of the Potomac was assigned to General Ambrose Burnside, whose own delay in crossing that stone bridge contributed to the survival of the Rebel Army.

As it was, The Battle of Antietam was the single bloodiest day in the history of the United States. With over three thousand Americans dead, and tens of thousands wounded, to this day its losses exceed those of Pearl Harbor, D-day or the terror attack of 9/11.

While the Confederate Army lost significantly fewer men than that of the Union, these losses constituted nearly a full quarter of Lee's troops.

And in one final ironic twist of this battle, it was a battle where Marylanders were killed and wounded on both sides. For while Maryland is often thought of as a Union State during the war, it harbored great sympathies with the Southern cause. As such, there were Maryland regiments formed in both the Union and Confederate Armies, all of which fought against each other at Antietam.

In fact, Maryland blood had already been spilled the previous year. Many acknowledge, to this day, that the very first deaths of the Civil War were claimed in Baltimore. After the shelling of Fort Sumter in Charleston Harbor, where no one died (save for one poor Union soldier who accidentally shot himself), Lincoln called upon the states to provide 75,000 "volunteer" soldiers. These troops arrived by train, and were marched through east Baltimore, from one train station to the Camden Yard station where they would continue on to Washington DC. These Union troops were attacked by a mob of Southern-sympathizing Marylanders. In these riots, lives were lost on both sides, representing the first bloodshed of the great calamity of this nation.

15

THE SCENT OF THE BLOOM
MAY 1871

Time had passed, and Clay's friendship with Ever blossomed, even though the rose bushes he had planted for Mrs. Gilreath had failed to do so. There was talk that the merchant's wife, while happy that the bushes had taken to the soil and appeared to be thriving, was losing patience with their failure to produce any flowers.

In the middle of the month of May, during an uncharacteristically warm and sunny day, the first of the Gilreath's bushes bloomed a single, lovely yellow rose.

That morning, Clay arrived at the Gilreaths' lawn. He walked along his bushes, as he did on his first arrival each day. Along his walk, he spotted the singular unfurled yellow rose. A thrill of excitement sparked deep within him.

He leaned down to sniff the scent of the first bloom from his efforts, and that is when he had seen the small envelope, tucked neatly below the flowering bush. He lifted it delicately from the soil, as if it were as fragile as the flower itself. Upon it was written his full name, Virgil Clay-Harris, in the most beautiful script handwriting he had ever seen.

He stabbed the envelope against his thigh with his left fore-stump. Then he used his right hand to awkwardly extract the card from it. The card itself was as white as a mountain frost, with a beautiful scene of an Irish countryside embossed upon it. Below this was written in the same delicate script handwriting,

"As delicate a scent as has ever reached a living thing's nose, is the breath of Our Lord on the first bloom of a Summer's rose."

It was unsigned, but Clay placed his thumb just below the seventh word, "ever". He choked back a tear as he realized that she must have been walking these rows of bushes each day before his arrival for weeks, if not months.

It was then that Clay had realized their friendship was marked in the growth of these very bushes. Their friendship had dared to root when she had watched him tend to them from the boarding house porch. It had a thorny first encounter when she had come to his assistance in the spilling of the flagstones. Their friendship budded on those very flagstones, which they would later walk many times together, side-by-side, watching the bushes grow. Their friendship grew heavy with anticipation as the bushes began to bud in the Spring. Bud, but not bloom. That is, until this very day.

He knelt before the bush bearing the lone rose. He placed the card upon the soil, face up so he could read its inscription. He cupped his hand protectively around the gentle bloom.

Clay thought of this remarkable young girl with whom he could talk so easily. He was able to speak to her about so much, for she never judged him. He spoke to her about the war, up to a point, and the result it had in him was exactly the opposite of discussing it with anyone else. Instead of his gut becoming twisted in knots, he felt as if a terrible burden had been lifted from him. It was as if a yoke had been taken from his shoulders.

He was able to speak to her about his maw's deepening sickness. Her own mother had gone through the same illness. She consoled him, and prepared Clay for the day that the Consumption would eventually take his mother. She had a way of calming the angst within him.

Clay then recalled that when he had come back from Chickamauga, he was a broken man. Not just in body, but also in spirit. He had secretly questioned if there even was a God. How could there be after all the death and destruction he had seen and himself been a party to during the war?

It was Ever who convinced him that there surely was a God, through her words that "wars are not His doing, but the clash of the free will he gifted to each of us".

She further convinced Clay that war was the ultimate darkness of man, and it was not the Lords' place to prevent it, just as it was not His place to prevent each of us from sinning in any other form.

Yet it was the budding of this rose that convinced him that God surely existed. For He had sent Ever to this place to become Clay's salvation, to reclaim him from his personal darkness. She calmed the anxiety within him. She returned him to The Lord. It could be no coincidence that Clay was taken on by the Gilreaths just as she came to this small town in Georgia.

No, it could be no coincidence that their lives would intertwine over these rose bushes. Her being in Cartersville was as much the touch of God's hand as was the unfurling of the precious yellow rose before him.

Still on his knees, Clay leaned forward and brought his nose close to the tender petals of the bloom. He inhaled softly and smelled of the rosewater that he had recalled the first time Ever came close to him. Yet, this was even more delicate a scent, as if her spirit had floated by him on the morning breeze. It was the purest of scents, that could not be caught, could not be described in words. He thought himself lucky if he should even be able to recall its essence in his memory.

Clay said her name to himself, and a single tear escaped his left eye, and tracked slowly down his cheek. As he attempted to compose himself, the tear dropped from his jaw, landing upon the upturned card. Although Clay would not notice it, the teardrop landed on the ink of the seventh word. Its salinity mixed with the ink, causing the word to seemingly float bloatedly upon the purity of white embossed card. And the smudged word was "ever".

As Clay prepared to face his day, triumphant in his victory, he thought of Ever. This was her victory as much as his. A wonderful feeling of contentment came over him. He felt that he had at last overcome the demons of the war.

It was a most satisfying feeling that would not last for long.

16

ATTACK ON THE CARPETBAGGER
JUNE 1871

The dusk was thickening into darkness. The night was swollen with a descending mist from the mountains surrounding the town of Cartersville.

Colin Brannigan left his office near the courthouse for the quick walk to the Howell boarding house on Market Street. It was very late in the day. He had been busy, preparing the court papers to invalidate the labor contracts of the man who had defiantly become his nemesis, Colonel Silas P. Austell of the mansion named River's Bend. Brannigan had lost his sense of time and stayed later than usual at his office. He was late for dinner at the boarding house and wished not to provoke worry in his young niece, Ever.

The Irishman walked with purpose as the evening fell with the mist. He turned off the square when he first noticed the sound lingering behind him. In the mist, it initially seemed nothing more than a hushed echo of his own steps. But it raised a quickened awareness within him, and the pace of his already purposeful steps accelerated slightly.

As he progressed along Market Street, he sensed that the echo of his steps had stopped. It was then that Brannigan became very aware that he was alone on the street, shrouded in the thickening night.

He returned to his walk, now only a few hundred feet from the boarding house. He smiled at his own apprehension and thought that he had not been that fearful since his own childhood. It was this business with the Colonel. Why had this stubborn man refused his generous offer to accept an indulgence instead of forcing him to invalidate the Colonel's Freedmen's labor contracts? And then to threaten him in such a crass and unconvincing manner. It was surely an idle threat, as he was an agent of the Federal government. No one would dare lay harm upon him.

Like a bolt of terror, a shadowy figure thrust itself from the darkness upon him. The impact caused the startled Colin Brannigan to yell aloud, "What is this madness!"

The force of the impact resulted in Brannigan being pinned up against the trunk of a large oak tree along the road. As he regained his wits, Brannigan realized that he had been struck by a man, a renegade. His face was covered with a red bandana, but the attacking man's eyes betrayed the disguise. The Irishman could clearly see the gruesome scar descending from the aggressor's right eye, before disappearing under the fold of the bandana.

"Hush, now, Carpetbagger," said Willet Blackwell in a soft voice that implied an intimate relationship. Willet was enjoying the terror running rampant in the pale face beneath his gloved hand covering the Irishman's mouth. "You been stirring up nothin but a hornets' nest since you come here, you Yankee leech."

With this, Willet leaned harder into his pinned prey such that he could remove the dagger from its sheath concealed in his boot. As he did so, Brannigan's eyes became as large as an owl's as he spotted the emblem of the Stars and Bars etched into the blade. He could read the engraved initials, WEB.

Brannigan attempted unsuccessfully to speak through the gloved fingers covering his mouth.

"I told you to hush, Carpetbagger," said the masked renegade. "You and me, we's just going to have a nice talk. Providing ya' behave yerself, but just in case you got other thoughts..."

As he said this, he brought his blade level with Brannigan's face, before resting the tip of the blade upon the man's cheek.

The eyes of the Irishman became enflamed with panic as the attacker slowly scraped the skin of his face, threateningly moving the point of the dagger from his cheek to press on the tender skin just below his eye.

"Maybe I should disfigure ya' like yer Yankee soldiers did to me?"

The pressure on the blade increased until it indented the fat skin of the man without piercing it. Then, abruptly, he pulled back the knife.

"Now, what should I do to convince ya' to drop yer lawyering against Colonel Austell and his labor contracts? I was told to use my imagination," Willet Blackwell said, introducing a new level of terror upon Brannigan. "I know just the thing..."

He then squeezed the hollows of the Irishman's cheeks, forcing him to open his mouth. When he did, Brannigan began to scream. His yells were muffled by the assailant as he worked his gloved fingers into Brannigan's mouth.

"You bite my fingers and I will drive this blade clean through to yer skull, ya' parasite." Then, with his fingers in the Irishman's mouth, he attempted to grasp the man's tongue. "I know what I should do is cut free that ever-wagging tongue out of yer mouth."

Willet played trying to grasp the Irishman's tongue, laughing aloud all the while knowing he was driving a horror upon him. Colin's fear had peaked, his heart pounded within his waistcoat, despite not a drop of blood having yet been extracted from him.

Willet pressed the tip of the blade again, although slightly harder, in the tender skin below the Irishman's eye. "Give it to me, Carpetbagger, lay that wagging tongue of yers in my grip, or loose yer sight forever. What is it gonna be?"

Brannigan could not believe what had happened in only seconds to him. How had this hooligan so rapidly forced him into such a position that he could not resist, call for help, or even plead for mercy. All he could do was submit. He passively laid his tongue in the fingers of his attacker.

Willet grabbed it, letting out a snide laugh. "That's it, boy, just learn who yer betters is!"

Blackwell pulled hard on the thick appendage. As he did so, Brannigan began to whimper like a horribly frightened child.

Willet let go of the man's tongue. "No, no, that's just too much work altogether for a warning. How's about I keep this simple?"

With that, Willet drew his gloved fingers out of the terrorized man's mouth and again covered it with his gloved hand. Then he brought the tip of the dagger to the spot just below his collarbone.

"You will drop yer actions against Colonel Silas, or I will have to shut you up forever. I am leaving you this here as a reminder to let you know that I will do it."

Willet drove the tip of the dagger into Colin Brannigan's shoulder. As the blade broke the skin, a loud muffled scream was heard throughout the street. Willet thought the scream was that of a very soft man, unaccustomed to dealing with either pain or the terrorizing threat of it. His blood immediately swelled in a pool on its blade surface before beginning to run down the chest of the victim.

Willet thought to himself, *This fat-cat Carpetbagger who is so intent on changing our way of life, is now understanding just how painful a change of life can be.*

Willet leaned harder, driving the blade further into the man, increasing the pitifully high pitch of his scream.

"Hey, you there, release that man!" echoed a yell from a passer-by just down Market Street.

Willet was startled by the interruption. He awkwardly withdrew the blade and turned to escape into the night. At this same point, Colin Brannigan raised his newly unpinned arm to cover his profusely bleeding wound. The wounded man's arm clashed forcefully with the blade-wielding arm of Blackwell. The dagger was knocked free of the renegade and lost into the blackness of the night.

Willet, angered that his war blade was then lost to him, thrust Brannigan with all his might against the oak, separating the man's shoulders. The broken man's arched chest was smeared with the black drippings of his blood. As the Irishman slid down the tree in tremendous and unbearable pain, Willet Blackwell slipped into the night before the passer-by could come upon them both.

The renegade escaped, and the passer-by tended to Brannigan as he lay in the grass at the trunk of the mighty oak. In doing so, the good soul came upon the bloodstained knife of the attacker. Assistance then came to carry Brannigan the few remaining yards to the boarding house. At that point, the knife bearing the Stars and Bars and the initials WEB was turned over to the Sheriff upon his arrival.

Alpheus T. Goff, the Sheriff of Cartersville, was certain this was the work of Willet Blackwell. And now he had proof in the recovered war dagger.

17

**RECRIMINATIONS
JUNE 1871**

Clay had come as soon as he had heard of the attack on Ever's uncle. He feared that the attacker might return to finish off the wounded man. The town's doctor, Doc Hardin, had immediately treated Colin Brannigan for shock, as well as his wounds, and set him up to rest in his room at the boarding house.

Ever was inside tending to her uncle. The doctor had pronounced his wounds serious, but not life threatening. Of course, that was only if infection did not set in. The wound was meant as a warning, nothing more. Ever administered to his gash, following the doctor's directions as attentively as she could. As she did so, her uncle's moans softened as the opium that Doc Hardin had given him began to take its effect. He let out a slow plaintiff chant of "Willet... Willet Blackwell...Willet."

Ever had feared that the renegade would reason that the only way to clear himself of being named in the attack was to eliminate the eye witness, that is, the victim, her uncle. The passer-by who had interrupted the assault had told Sheriff Goff that he could not identify the attacker. Either it was the truth, or a message to Blackwell that he would not give him up. In either case, Ever feared that Willet knew this only left her Uncle Colin to identify him.

She felt more comfortable now that Clay had arrived. He sat on the boarding house porch with his Spencer rifle and single Colt

Navy revolver in plain sight. He was sending a simple message to his old mate from the war – *Do not come back, lessen there be a war between you and me!*

Clay sat as the silent sentinel throughout the fog drenched night. Around four in the morning, Ever brought him a cup of hot coffee, and took the seat across the lantern from him. Her uncle was sleeping under the spell of the opium, and she was able to tend to her valiant protector.

"Clay, would it not be better for you to douse this lamp, or even to come inside?" she asked.

He looked at the worry etched upon her tender young face. Despite its strain, the skin still had the angelic glow that he had loved. In this shroud of fog and night, the lantern's flicker kissed and rolled across her skin, giving it a vulnerability that was accentuated by the tension in the muscles beneath.

"Miss Ever," he said slowly, "I need to be out here where all can see me. The lantern's light only helps to that end. They need to know that I am here. They will not come back, not tonight."

Her face began to dance with uncontrolled emotion. Tears filled her eyes but did not drop upon her skin.

"Clay, I am scared that they will hurt you out here. They could shoot you from across the street, and in this night you would never even see them."

The torment within her was stabbing at Clay. He needed to console his young angel.

"Willet, nor any of his men, will never hurt me," he said plainly. "I know this, and you must settle yerself down, Miss Ever. As long as I am here, you are protected."

"Clay, please, please come inside," she pleaded with even more fear rippling through her voice.

He could see the terror settling into her. It was the darkness and the fog. Like the child she still was, she feared what she could not see.

"Willet won't never hurt me, Miss Ever," he said to her. "After Gettysburg, we promised we would always protect each other. We have both lived to that promise ever since. And we will always keep it."

He could hear the echo of Willet's voice - ***No harm to you, no harm to me! Forever, no matter what!***

"What happened at Gettysburg to make you both pledge to protect each other, Clay?" she asked, now only beginning to recover the runaway fear that had quickened her pulse, ratcheted her breath.

"At Gettysburg," he started in an attempt to soothe her further, "we both had to attend to the fear that come to crush us. I think it was the first time we really both reckoned we could die in that war, become just another pair of bodies throwed down across that Yankee grass. I know it sounds unbelievable, but up till that point, we both thought no harm could come to touch us. We had survived so much fightin' that we started reckonin' ourselves unkillable."

"I can't understand how, Clay. No one is invincible," she said.

"Liken I said, Miss Ever, you couldn't fathom it. After surviving yer first battle, with yer fella soldiers fallin' all 'round you, you start thinkin' you are somehow special. That there t'ain't any bullets out there with yer name on 'em. Willet had feeled the same way. We reckoned God was looking after us. I knows it's stupid now, but that's how we felt. But that all changed on the way to Gettysburg."

"How so, Clay?" Ever's voice was tender, it wrapped in comfort around him.

"We was on our way to Pennsylvania, cutting across Maryland. Passed back up along Sharpsburg, where we had fought the September before. Willet and me was assigned to protect a Colonel who wanted to ride back to the battlefield at Sharpsburg. We walked that battlefield with him for a couple of hours. It was near nine months later, but them fields was still strewn with rotting bodies of the boys who had died there, Blue and Gray. I dunno if they was buried shallow nor not at all, but it was as if they was trying to crawl back to the fight. They was nuthin more than bones, scattered bout like wind-strewn scarecrows."

"I can't imagine a more atrocious sight," said Ever, her fear rising as she continued to search the black fog for even more dangerous threats.

"Scarecrows that could not drive away that monster. You see, Miss Ever, that day, Willet and me realized that this war was nothin' but a vicious monster, come to chew up all of us, just saving Willet and me for another sittin'. After that, we were both come to be scared of being laid low. Them brave words we had been telling each other soured in our mouths like over-ripe persimmons - *Glory and honor!* All these Rebel boys laid rotting on the ground where they fell for glory and honor! All them Yanks, too. Willet and me both realized what dang fools we had been all the time. That day on that awful Maryland field we realized there was other farms, other fields where we ourselves could come to fall and forever rot."

She realized he was telling her something that he had never shared with another woman before, perhaps with no one else, save Willet. Here was the bravest of men she could ever meet, admitting to the first time he had dealt with his own fear.

"When, we rejoined the rest of the corps and moved into Pennsylvania, we marched right across that Mason-Dixon line. It supposedly separates the North from the South. From what I saw, them Marylanders t'ain't exactly what I would call Southerners, I mean not like the Virginians are. But when we got to Pennsylvania, there was no denying we was on Yankee soil. I've heared since then that we was marching north to Harrisburg. Then, our scouts and the Bluebellies ran into each other in a little town just cross that Mason-Dixon line. General Longstreet marched us south to that town, to join the rest of the Confederate Army. Word was General Robert E. Lee was ahead of us, figurin' how to attack them Yanks."

"You must have been so nervous, Clay!" Ever was hanging on his every word. She realized how deeply he was diving into his trove of memories – haunting memories at that.

"Truth be told, Miss Ever, I was never more at piece than when we was on a long march. The heat and dust seeps into ya', and by then it was hot and dusty something fierce, but you just keep picking up yer legs and putting them down again. Lulls ya' into a trance, almost. Always settled my mind. I liked to think of home, of maw, of the farm. I would just crawl inside my mind and come to think of everything we was fightin' for."

"I just thought after seeing everything you had seen at Sharpsburg, that those poor boys would have been on your mind," said Ever.

"Well, they sure 'nuff were, just not on that march," said Clay. "By the time we got to that town of Gettysburg on the first day of July, most of the Union army had already come up from the south, from Washington or wherever. They had the high ground, along a ridge. At the end of that ridge was a high rocky hill. The next morning, we was marched to take that high ground away from the Yankees by flanking them around that rocky hill."

"What does that mean, Clay?" asked Ever, "What does 'flanking them' mean?"

"It t'ain't nuthin' but fancy military talk for getting' around the end of their line. They was up on that long ridge, and our unit was sent to support an attack by General Longstreet on a hill that was nuthin' more than a pile of boulders with some trees growing between them, called Little Round Top. The Yanks were up atop of it, but they was also down below it in a peach orchard. We didn't get started to fighting until late in the morning, and that heat was already blazing. General Longstreet hisself lead us to that peach orchard, where we routed them Yankees something good. Then we did the same in a rocky wasteland at the base of that hill called the Devil's Den. It was then, in that place I thought on them boys laying rotting on the fields of Sharpsburg. Not just Southern boys, in general, but many of the very same fellas who died by my side. It was that day I was sure I was gonna die. Right there in the Devil's Den. A lot of my fellow soldiers did just that. And I come to believe I was to join them."

"How terrible, Clay," said the Irish maiden, "And Willet must have been thinking the same thing?"

"Well, Willet was with General Pickett's division, and they was held in reserve that day. Didn't see no fighting that day t'all. But they done got their own taste of horror the very next day. We were sent up that hill to take that high ground from the Yankees. We had been fighting fiercely with them Bluebellies all that day. It was time for the last charge up that rocky hill. Men was dying around me all day. I started to do something I had never done before. I started looking for the bullet that was coming for me. I was plain out scared, Miss Ever, maybe for the first time during that war, I was truly scared that I was about to die."

"You poor thing," she said to him, but Clay continued, looking off into the night fog. "What did you do?"

"I just kept fightin'. Killin' them Yanks hiding among them boulders and dead looking trees and brush. It was fierce, but we done drove them all out, but only after heavy losses of our own."

She thought she was about to lose him. Clay's eyes seemed to stare out into the night. He searched it as if he were searching the recesses of his own fears. Ever still dreaded what the night and the fog hid, even if her protector did not. Yet his foolhardy confidence nonetheless did calm her somewhat. She knew he would not let her stay on that porch if she was at risk.

"At that point we only had to climb that hill and git around those Yankees. We just had to kill 'em, then we could get behind their lines. We could work our way down that ridgeline, taking on them Bluebellies from behind. It would have been the end of the War. All we had to do was take that damn hill."

Ever could see his face draw tense as he spoke. She wondered how long these evil memories had tormented her Clay.

"Unlike that Peach Orchard or the Devil's Den, that hill was covered in tress growing between the rocks and boulders. I remember how glad I was to get out of that Devil's Den, and into the cool shade at the base of this hill. It was after we regrouped, that we come to climb that damn hill. We must of charged them Yanks atop that hill six or seven times that afternoon. It was like we was billie-goats or so, climbing that hill one rock at a time. We'd get so close, regroup, and on our commander's signal, we'd break up the last bit of that hill screaming the Rebel Yell."

"What was that?" she asked Clay.

"It's just a God-awful scream that drove fear into the bellies of them Yanks. They knowed we was coming when they heared it. But this day was different. They fought us like demons. They never did turn and run like most other times we fought them. A few of our men got up into their position atop that hill, only to be shot dead as soon as they got over the little wall of rocks them Yankees was behind. But they was weakening, we knew we was only one more charge away from taking that hill."

"And your thoughts of the dead boys at Sharpsburg had left you by then?" she asked.

"Somewhat, but they still must have been on my mind some. We started that last charge, but it was the damnedest thing. As we climbed that hill, there was no volley of fire from them Yankees. It was eerie quiet. We didn't realize it, but they was out of ammunition. Then, out of nowhere, we heard the screams of these Yankees as they ran down that hill at us with raised bayonets. The shock of it sent fear through our lines, even though we had balls in our muskets, we were too scared to send up a volley. As the first few men were run through, our ranks broke, and our line turned and ran down from that hill."

"Was that where you were injured, Clay?" Ever asked.

"No, that was months later in Chickamauga, Georgia. No, what I had took from me that day was far worse even than losin' an arm. I lost my nerve. And in the hole left by its taking, a crippling fear crawled in. And once that fear creeps into a soldier's being, Miss Ever, it is just a matter of time before fate finds him. Before the jaws of that monster crush him, leaving what is left of him to rot where he lies. I am ashamed to say I dun turned and run just like the rest of 'em. Just plum a coward, like the rest of 'em. I was lucky to live, cause most half our force was either killed, wounded or captured that day. We never did take that Little Round Top hill. I just returned to our camp, just another exhausted coward."

"You stop that right now, Virgil Clay-Harris, for I have come to know you and I know that you are no coward. You are the bravest man I have ever met. You sit here with me tonight, despite the danger to yourself."

Ever then asked, "And Willet? Did you later tell Willet of your day on that hill?"

"Only much later after that entire battle. Like I said Willet was assigned to another of Longstreet's Generals that day – General George Pickett. On the third day of that battle in Gettysburg, General Pickett was ordered by General Lee to lead a charge across open fields right into the enemy positions. 'Pickett's Charge' they call it now, and it turned into a bloody slaughter of our boys in them fields."

The shame swelled within Clay as he told his tale for the first time to anyone. Yet, instead of it converting into a consuming rage intensifying within him, the shame slowly dissipated as he voiced his recollections to Ever. He knew she would not judge him.

"And your friend Willet was not wounded there either?" Ever asked Clay.

He thought it odd that she seemed to treat Willet in the war as a character in a play, separate from the man she had come to despise for having attacked her uncle. She had somehow sifted Clay's childhood friend and fellow soldier from the renegade that now seemed so out of control in this town.

"Willet was not hurt at Gettysburg, neither" Clay answered, "Well, not his body, anyhow. But his soul was crushed during that charge. Sure, he attacked that ridge with the rest of General Picket's men, and he watched the Rebel soldiers in front of him git mowed down by the Yankee artillery and gunfire."

"How was he not injured?" she asked.

"Because, like me the day before, his will was broke. As the men around him went down, Willet had a fear something fierce raise up inside him. Even though he had not taken a ball, he dropped to the ground and laid in the blood of his fallen Rebel brothers and wallowed in fear and shame. He told me this after the battle. He was ashamed. He was ashamed that he laid in that field as Rebel soldiers from behind ran over him to charge up towards that long ridge. Again, them Yankees had the high ground, and they refused to be budged from it. And our boys, they kept on fallin'. Ol' Willet just laid there unhurt until the retreat was called, when he mustered enough courage to raise himself and mix in with the rest of the retreating Rebs."

"He surely was a coward," she said aloud.

Her comment raised Clay's dander a bit. No one who had never been in war could understand the gulf of emotions that flooded through a man's being.

"Miss Ever, Willet t'ain't no coward. I know this by my own eyes. When yer in the middle of battle, feelins like you t'ain't never felt before rise up in ya'. They can be mighty strong, and fear alone can turn a man into stone, just a frozen target for the enemy. I believe that on that day, in the middle of that charge, his feelings for living just come up and grabbed his legs out from under him. Somethin' within him told him to live to fight again. If you want to call that man yella', well I can't stop ya', but Willet was no more yella' than me running from them bayonets the day before."

His words had more force than he had intended. They came to shake her, which is the last thing he wanted. It was just like when he had shaken a fear into Deekie in the pines. In that instance, he realized he missed his Deekie.

"I'm sorry. You are right, Clay, I can't imagine what you men went through on those battlefields," she sighed. "No wonder you two are so closely bound to each other."

"What is it that you mean, Miss Ever?"

She looked at him tenderly. The lantern's light flickered upon his face like the indecision she had about what she would say next.

"Clay," she decided to begin, "I have come to know you deeply over these past months. I respect you Clay, you are a truly good man. You never think of yourself, only about others. As we sit here and talk, I can see the pain on your face. The pain not of what happened in the war, but of what has become of your friend Willet. What the war has done to him. For every bit of goodness that has saved you from that terrible experience, his suffering has raised up within him and consumed the man who was your friend. He has become more than just a renegade, Clay. He has become evil. And it pains you to have to watch."

Clay sat quietly, reflecting upon what she had just said.

"Willet and me, Miss Ever, never told our failings at Gettysburg to no one but each 'nuther. We was all we had to carry that weight. After that battle, we decided we would always be there for each 'nuther, no matter what happened in the future. And to this day we's been livin' to that pact. What I fear is that the day will come when one of us will have to raise up agin' the other. That is the pain you are seeing in me, Miss Ever. That pain I pray will never come to pass."

"But you know that it surely will," Ever said to him tenderly.

At this point, a loud moan came from within the house, and Ever excused herself to check on her rousing uncle. Clay nodded his head as she left and he stayed in the seat on the porch in the bubble of flickering light within the much deeper black of night. The morning light would begin softening the sky in about an hour or so, he thought.

There are two things I know for sure, he thought to himself, *Willet is nobody's coward, and he will bring no further harm upon this house so long as I am here.*

For Clay knew that just as he could never bring harm upon Willet, Willet could never raise up against him. Clay feared the day that this ceased to be.

18

GETTYSBURG
JULY 1-3, 1863

Not much more can be written about the Battle of Gettysburg than has already been put to paper. However, in the context of rendering this tale, the reader must consider a few critical events of the war that occurred before those first three days in July 1863.

First, after the Army of Northern Virginia was driven from Maryland at Sharpsburg, Robert E. Lee continued to pursue the strategy of shifting the warfare from the grounds of his beloved Virginia northward to the very cherished lands of the Union itself.

However, before this was possible, there were many more battles to be fought on Confederate soil. After the Union General McClellan was relieved of command for not pursuing and destroying Lee's army, General Ambrose Burnside was given command of the Union's Army of the Potomac. Burnside indeed did pursue Lee's army into Virginia, and in December of 1862, only a few months after Sharpsburg, amassed a significantly superior force to Lee's army on the hills of the Rappahannock River. These hills overlooked the Confederate town of Fredericksburg, and here Burnside planned a massive frontal assault across the river and into the town itself, which was held by Lee's army.

Burnside then proved he was as easily deferred from attacking Lee as his predecessor. He failed to press the pursuit, instead, he opted to wait for pontoons to arrive from Washington DC. These his army could use to make bridges to cross the Rappahannock River into the town and engage Lee's Army. Burnside opted to wait for the pontoons, despite the fact that the river could have readily been forded, or crossed on foot, upstream without the pontoons.

What was supposed to have only been a few days' wait was administratively fumbled into ten, as the Union forces waited for the pontoons to arrive. During this extended time, Lee withdrew the bulk of his forces from the town itself and dug their defensive positions into the heights overlooking it.

When the Union army eventually did receive the pontoons and pressed the attack, it was preceded by extensive artillery shelling of the town by the Yankees. Fredericksburg, the lovely town halfway between the two war capitals of Washington DC and Richmond was decimated. After overcoming resistance from the Rebels, the Union troops crossed the river and arrived in the shelled-out ruins. Only then did they realize that General Lee and the mass of his troops were themselves in a superior position on the heights overlooking the Yankees, who by then occupied the remains of Fredericksburg. The Rebels were out of range of the Union artillery across the river, and Lee dared Burnside to press the attack up the slopes.

And this is exactly what General Burnside and his commanding officers did on December 13th of 1862. They attacked in a Blue wave upwards towards Lee's Confederate positions. Lee and his leader-ship, including Generals Stonewall Jackson and James Longstreet, waited patiently until the Union Army was within their sights, and then cut them down mercilessly. The Rebel position that was per-haps most punishing to the forces in Blue was General Longstreet's army. They were positioned behind a stone wall atop a rise known as Marye's Heights. Behind this wall, several rows of Confederate musketeers patiently awaited. The Union troops kept advancing uphill to that stone wall, and the Rebels forces kept mowing them down.

After the tremendous success of Fredericksburg for Robert E. Lee, Lincoln once again changed his commanding General. Burnside was replaced by "Fighting Joe" Hooker, who was, like Burnside, also a commander in the last significant Union victory at Antietam.

Hooker opened 1863 by changing the strategy from an overpowering frontal assault, as was used at Fredericksburg, to flanking and encircling Lee's army. That strategy was put to test in early May at a small clearing in the wilderness known as Chancellorsville.

This location was not far from the battle fought the previous December at Fredericksburg. General Lee fooled Hooker into assuming the mass of his army was still at Fredericksburg. In fact, they had moved upriver.

General Lee was ready for the Union onslaught. He dispatched General Stonewall Jackson to outflank the Union's massive lines. The Union Army, seeing Jackson's movements from their observation posts, assumed the Confederates were retreating. When Jackson's troops curled around the far end of the Union lines, he had outflanked those who were themselves attempting to outflank Robert E. Lee's entire army.

At Chancellorsville, the Union Army had been routed by Lee's superior strategy, and they suffered tremendous losses. Yet, perhaps the greatest loss of all was Lee's. Stonewall Jackson had been wounded in the fighting, shot by his own men as he scouted beyond his lines for a night attack. His wounds required that he lose his left arm but were not deemed to be fatal. Lee was quoted as having said, "Jackson has lost his left arm, and I have lost my right."

What was fatal was that General Jackson was found to be suffering from advanced pneumonia. On May 10th, eight days after the battle, he passed from this world, with his last words being "Let us cross the river and rest under the shade of the trees." Robert E. Lee had lost his most effective general. Stonewall Jackson had been loved by his men, feared by his enemies, and respected by all.

As Lee had watched, his outmaneuvering of the Union troops at Fredericksburg and Chancellorsville ravaged the beauty and souls of his native state of Virginia. He convinced Confederate President Jefferson Davis that it was time to strike again on Union soil. This time it would be Pennsylvania, and the strategy was to drive hard to the east, possibly to Philadelphia, cutting off Washington DC from New York.

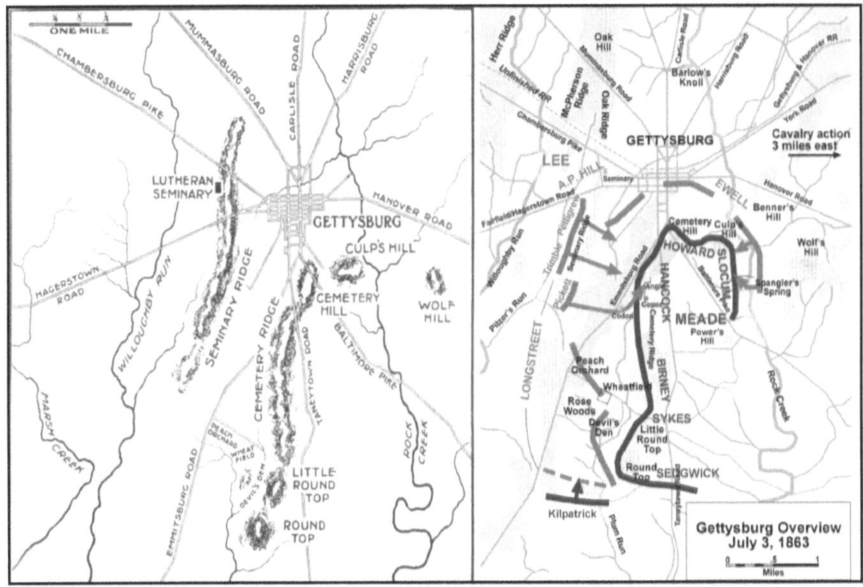

Image 13 - Battle Maps of Gettysburg
Source: commons.Wikipedia.org

Of course, as has long been known, Lee's troops were intercepted almost by chance in the small rural Pennsylvania town of Gettysburg. Once again, Lincoln had changed the Union commander after General Hooker's failure at Chancellorsville. General George Gordon Meade assumed leadership of the Army of the Potomac. At Gettysburg, Lee and Meade squared off in the opening three days of July 1863.

The battle had been precipitated by a rumor. Some Confederate infantry wandered into Gettysburg, seeking a supply of shoes believed to be held there. Shoes and boots were among the highest demanded articles of the Rebel army. Often, after a battle, the dead would be stripped of their footwear because the need was so great.

The mass of Rebel infantry was spotted by the Federal cavalry.

The small Yankee force took refuge in a seminary just outside the town. Commanded by Union General Bufford, they sent to General Reynolds nearby for infantry reinforcements, which would arrive the next day, on July the first.

So, the greatest battle of the Civil War was an unplanned melee that quickly grew into its greatest conflagration.

On the first of July, the Confederate Army attacked the Federal forces at the Seminary. The first of the Union Army had just entered Gettysburg that morning under General Reynolds, who in the opening of the battle was dropped by Rebel gunfire. The Confederates drove the Union forces back through the town itself, and then slightly south to an area known as Cemetery Hill. The Union troops fought gallantly and held until nightfall, after which Lee's troops did not attack them significantly. The failure to displace the Yankees on Cemetery Hill would prove to be a fatal mistake for the Confederacy.

The second day opened with the Union Army heavily fortifying their positions with troops from Washington DC. Soon the Union lines resembled an inverted fishhook, open to the east. The hook itself wrapped around Cemetery Hill in the North, while the "shank" of the Union lines ended near an elevated boulder formation known as Little Round Top.

Fighting all along the battle lines was tremendous throughout the second day. Lee, for the first time in a major battle without Stonewall Jackson, attempted to outflank the Federals at Little Round Top. It was within these forces that Virgil Clay-Harris had been mustered. Several Rebel assaults were made on the hill, and the Yankee forces held. Late in the day, as the Union forces ran out of ammunition atop the boulders, the Rebels attacked once more.

The Union troops, led by Colonel Joshua Chamberlain, defended Little Round Top in an unexpected wheeling, downhill bayonet charge that sent the Rebel forces in a frenzied retreat. Lee's attempt to outflank the Yankees, as he had done so brilliantly at Chancellorsville a few months before, had failed terribly.

The next day brought even more of a reversal of Lee's fortunes. Lee directed General James Longstreet to amass a frontal assault under the direction of General George Pickett. Longstreet is understood to have questioned Lee's strategy, and Lee reportedly responded by saying, "No, General, this is where I have them, and this is where I will crush them."

General Longstreet knew the charge across the open Pennsylvania farmland was suicide. When General Pickett asked if he should proceed with the charge, General Longstreet was so emotional that he could not even voice a reply. He could only nod affirmatively that Picket was directed to carry out General Lee's command.

What proceeded next, known forever as Pickett's Charge, was nearly an identical undertaking to the charge at Fredericksburg that prior December.

Except, this time, it was Lee who sent his troops in a headlong attack across open fields into the guns and rifles of the Federals. This time it was the Rebel forces who were slaughtered mercilessly as they attempted to overtake another low stone wall atop an expansive and open rise of countryside.

Robert E. Lee's strategy had failed in outflanking the Federals the day before at the Little Round Top. The strategy that served his troops so well at Chancellorsville, had failed him at Gettysburg.

On this third day of fighting he had fallen into the same trap as he had lured the Yankees into at Fredericksburg. As the few surviving troops returned that day from Pickett's Charge, with our Willet Blackwell having been among them, General Lee emerged from the protection of the Seminary Ridge tree-line confessing to them all "It is all my fault! It is all my fault!"

Image 14 – Chamberlain Statue on Little Round Top

General Longstreet had foreseen the disaster and had attempted to dissuade Robert E. Lee to cancel the attack. Longstreet recommended they fall back to a defensive position of their own, and not attempt to attack the superior position that the Union Army held along Cemetery Ridge. Of course, General Lee could not be persuaded to do so.

General Pickett was openly eager to charge his men into battle. He did not have the foresight of the slaughter into which he was leading them. While General Pickett survived the attack, the men he led suffered severe casualties, exceeding sixty percent. He would later, after the war, say of Robert E. Lee, "That man destroyed my division."

The three-day battle that took a massive toll on both armies had become the single deadliest battle of the war. And Lee's strategy of taking the war onto the North's soil had, for the second time in just over nine months, failed not only himself, but the Confederacy.

Image 15 - Fields of Gettysburg – Location of Pickett's Charge
(as viewed from Cemetery Ridge and
The Monument to the High-Water Mark of the Confederacy)

19

OBLIGATION AND IGNORANCE
LATE JUNE 1871

It soon came to pass that the wounds inflicted upon Colin Brannigan were not enough to keep him from pursuing his attacker, who he knew to be Willet Blackwell.

The knife that was recovered from the scene of the attack was the confirming physical evidence of what Brannigan already knew. In the Irishman's memory, he could clearly see the descending scar from the corner of his attacker's right eye, before it was obstructed from view by the masking bandana. In his fearful heart, the Irishman could still feel the icy sting of terror that had raced down his spine. It was the memory of the debilitating fear, more so than the stunning realization that the dagger's blade was piercing his body, that Brannigan could not shake. Colin had long ago learned not to allow fear to make him another man's servant. So, he mastered his fear and decided to pursue charges against the renegade.

Willet Blackwell had been apprehended the following day as he attempted to flee the area. It had been an open secret that Willet had long been camped atop the Three Sisters Mountain. From the days of the war, when his marauders were attacking Union soldiers, no one had any interest in finding him there, despite his being a deserter from the Rebel Army. As time went by, his reputation became so blackened by his deeds that no one, including the law, dared to disturb him or his men in their camp.

Yet, the action against the Carpetbagger had escalated the situation. Sheriff Alpheus Goff had an attack on a Federal officer, that is, the Federal Freedmen's Administrator, on his hands. The retribution from President Grant's Government would mean a convergence of Federal troops upon the town of Cartersville. The Sheriff knew these soldiers would bring with them their ire of the South in general. It could only be a prescription for pain for all the residents of this county.

Sheriff Goff had no option but to stake out the trails from the mountain, and in doing so, had apprehended the fleeing Blackwell.

The Sheriff had taken Blackwell despite his own personal inclinations. He had served with Willet during the war. Goff had been captured at Sharpsburg and was held by the Union forces in a prisoner of war camp for several months. After signing a pledge that he would never fight again for the Confederates, he was released. It was a pledge Goff had no intention of honoring. He fought again for General Longstreet at Gettysburg.

Despite his personal sympathies, Goff held the criminal Blackwell in the county jail until his day in court was arraigned. He was under heavy guard, less his gang of renegades should attempt to break him out.

The Carpetbagger was also under heavy guard at Howell's boarding house. Clay had stood watch for the first two nights, but with Willet in the jail, he yielded to round-the-clock guards who were paid for out of Federal funds.

Clay returned home to find that his younger brother Truitt had begun to feel conflicted by Willet's incarceration. "We gotta do something to help Willet, Clay!" protested Truitt during one of the nights before the approaching day of Blackwell's scheduled trial.

"Boy, we t'ain't gotta do nothing such, and we won't neither. Willet got himself in this mess, and it's his mess to get himself outta."

"But Clay, he's the same man who went and saved us from being burned out by the Yankees. How can you turn your back on him now?," bristled Truitt. "He likely saved all our lives that night, 'specially yours."

Clay was worried about his young brother, and what he might do. He had only been a twelve-year-old child that night of the raiding party. It had left a great impression upon him when Willet's gang arrived to rescue them all.

What Truitt did not understand was that Willet and his marauders had never made the transition from wartime. They treated the citizens of the county, even to this day, as if they were at war with them still. Stealing their cattle, terrorizing their citizens and hiring themselves out as agents of the most notorious land owners of the county were all crimes that Sheriff Goff had every right to pursue.

"Listen to me, Truitt," said Clay. "Me and Willet, we been bound at the hip for a long time. We owe so much to each nuther, that is true 'nuff. But, no matter how much we may owe each nuther, there comes a time when a man's actions show what kind of man he will always be. Willet is a criminal, plain and simple. And you being an officer of the court, you gotta let this play out without getting yerself all wrapped up in it."

Truitt could not believe his brother would allow the man who had come to their aid when they needed it most to be offered as a sacrifice to the Union government. He thought of another way to pull Clay into action.

"And What about Deekie, Clay?" he said. "She's all by herself up on that mountain with five of Willet's men. You just gonna throw her aside now, too?"

"Deekie done made her decision to go back up on Three Sisters," said Clay. He had wished she had never left the homestead, but he knew he could not talk her into coming back to him. Not after she saw him with Ever in that wagon.

"No, Clay," said Truitt, "you made up her mind for her, didn't you? Throwing her aside when you got your job at the Gilreaths' spread. Spending all your time on that fine Irish girl. She didn't figure on her own to go back to Willet. You pushed her there with the full force of your ignoring her. And now, your failure to help Willet is gonna put a noose around his neck. That is gonna leave Deekie with nowhere to go, except to become the whore of whichever one of them marauders steps up and takes Willet's place…"

The sharp crack of Clay's calloused right hand upon Truitt's cheek shocked the young man. The force of it was more than Truitt could have expected. It was not a simple punishment borne of Clay's frustration. It was an unexpected unleashing of the violence that resided below the surface of his brother's skin.

"You ever call Deekie a whore agin' and, brother or not, I will thrash ya' to within inches of yer life, boy! You understand me?"

"Yes, Sir," said Truitt, as the eyes of his brother pierced him like Willet's dagger had done to the Carpetbagger.

"Now, Truitt, I won't have no more of this talk of he'pin' Willet. For God's love, boy, sometimes I think all that learnin' you went and crammed in yer head done went and drove out yer common sense."

And there was no more talk from Truitt on this point. Clay's striking his brother had convinced Truitt that whatever actions that were needed to assist Willet were his alone to undertake.

That night, just after this discussion, Clay went up on Three Sisters Mountain. He spoke to Willet's gang of five.

He walked out of the night, surprising them all.

"Hold them guns, fellas. It's just me, Clay," he said to them.

"Damn, Clay, you gonna get yerself laid waste walkin' up on us like that," said Flinch, Willet's number two man. "Why didn't you come up the trail where we got our man posted?"

"Flinch, next time I have to come up here, y'all gonna be just as 'sprised." Clay wanted them to feel at risk, despite all their precautions.

"What are you wantin', Clay? You know Willet ain't up here," said Flinch.

"I just come up here to let ya' all know I ain't got no business in Willet's plight. I am neither fer him nor agin' him. This is his fix to git himself out of."

"Why you tellin' us this, Clay?" Flinch looked the man up and down. Flinch remembered but could not understand why Willet had long ago told his gang that no harm was ever to come to Clay or his family.

"Iffen Willet beats this thing," Clay started aloud, "that's good fer him. Iffen the Federals up and hang him, then that's bad fer him. Either way, it's his scrap. I am here to tell yer all, that until this thing settles itself out, any man in this camp who lifts even a finger against Deekie, I am gonna personally hunt down and gut with but my one good arm!"

Flinch took the message in stride. So, this is why Clay risked coming up here.

"You wanna talk to her? She's in Willet's tent. Go ask her if any of us been unfit with her. We ain't dumb enough to mess with Willet's girl, Clay. Ya' see, we don't get that same pass that Willet allows you."

Flinch laughed at the reference that Clay was known to have been with Willet's girl.

Clay let the men laugh until his silence overpowered them all. He waited, staring each man, in turn, in the eyes, then spoke.

"Know this, each and every one of y'all. Any harm comes to Deekie, and I am coming down on y'all. Any further harm comes to the Carpetbagger, and I am coming down on y'all. Any harm comes to the Carpetbagger's niece, and I am coming down on y'all. And I know each of y'all know I mean what I say here tonight. I will kill each and every one of y'all."

Flinch looked coldly at Clay. "We might like yer tryin', Clay. I should of killed you that night on the boarding house porch. I had you clean in my sights. But Willet said no harm was to come to *Virgil Clay-Harris*. And now you just want us to let the Yankees to find him guilty and string him up?" Flinch was sneering every word through a clenched jaw. "We got yer message, now git on back to yer shack, you ingrate. You don't care that it was Willet and us all that saved your spread from those Yankee torches."

Clay let Flinch's words die in silence of the night, before responding.

"I remember that night, but it don't change a word of what I just told y'all. Just know, with or without Willet up here, any hurt comes to Deekie, Ever or Colin Brannigan, and I will be back. And I will show no mercy."

Without fear, Clay then turned his back on Flinch and disappeared into the black of night.

20

WILLET'S DAY IN COURT
JULY 1871

There were no attacks upon the Carpetbagger nor his niece, Ever. Whether this had to do with Clay's warnings up on the mountain, or the Federals' heavy presence at the boarding house, will never be known.

What was known was that there was not a hand raised against Deekie while she lived atop Three Sisters in the period leading up to the trial. The night that Clay surprised the members of his gang, Deekie was indeed in Willet's tent. Willet himself had not raised a hand against her from the time that she had come back up Three Sisters mountain to him. But despite that, Deekie had not wanted Clay to see her that night, and so he did not.

Deekie had been transformed since returning to the mountain. Willet had Deekie rid herself of the torn and thread-born field dresses that she had come to live in during her time with Clay. Willet had been gracious to her. He had taken her to Savannah to dress her out in some proper clothes. In that port city, Willet bought her riding britches, trousers, and blouses from England for her to wear. He even had her set with a fine hat for riding in the sun. He said he needed to keep the sun off her pretty face. Willet said he wouldn't wear her down the way Clay had working her in the fields. As he said this, she remembered those days, working the fields with Clay, as some of the happiest of her young, but difficult, life.

Deekie was ashamed. She hadn't wanted Clay to see her in these fine boots, these form-fitting clothes, that she had at first loved. It was only after they had returned to the mountain that she realized these were just trappings of a new boredom. Watching Willet and his men steal and plunder the counties surrounding them did not please her. She still had no purpose, other than to be dressed up in fine things to please Willet. And it soon looked like the man she reluctantly ran back to was about to hang.

Deekie worried about what would happen to her once this came to pass.

The day came for Willet's trial in mid-July. The courthouse was thronged with spectators, as it seemed the entire town had come out to see the battle between the Carpetbagger and the Renegade.

Judge Ferris resided as usual over the courtroom. As the morning proceeded, with all the spectator's seats filled, and townsfolk standing in every possible space that would allow it, the courtroom became stuffy and its air thick with discomfort. At one point, during the prosecution's entering the dagger allegedly belonging to Willet Blackwell into evidence, Judge Ferris interrupted the proceedings to direct Truitt Clay-Harris to open the courthouse windows to allow the morning's fresh air to come in. And Truitt did just this.

The prosecution had a very open and shut case. The passer-by who had witnessed the attack had left the county immediately after the crime, and as such, did not testify. However, Sheriff Goff did, detailing the carnage he had observed at the crime scene. The dagger bearing the initials WEB and the etching of the Stars and Bars did indeed appear as evidence. And, of course, the Carpetbagger himself described the attack in his lilting Irish brogue. The morning had most definitely gone against Willet, and all thought that only a miracle would save him from hanging as the trial recessed for lunch.

The lunch period for young Truitt Clay-Harris was anything but a break. After securing the courtroom and placing the evidence that was the dagger in the Clerk-of-the-Court's safe, he had to walk up to the depot to fetch the afternoon's train schedule.

When he did so, Truitt was handed the printed schedule by the depot master, J.C. Wofford. Wofford was a man of about thirty years or so, and he had earned Truitt's respect. He had been nicknamed "Chuck" by the Confederate troops for a card game known as "Chuck-a-luck", which he was known to be fond to play. Truitt could never call him by this nickname, as he respected "Mr. Wofford" far too much. As Truitt began to walk back to the courthouse, the depot master Wofford called out to him.

Image 16 – Cartersville's Train Depot

"Truitt, young man, I nearly forgot, I need to let you know that we also just added a train carrying a freight of stones from Ladd's that will be passing through in the Northern direction at five minutes past three o'clock."

"Yessir, thank you," Truitt said, "I'll add it when I get back to the courtroom."

Truitt Clay-Harris did not add that train to the schedule, which he laid upon the judge's bench, just before the afternoon session began.

It was an interesting afternoon as the defense cross-examined Sheriff Goff before moving onto the Carpetbagger himself.

"Sheriff Goff, you say you found this dagger at the scene of the attack. And its blade was covered in blood?" asked the defense attorney.

"Yep, that's right," said the Sheriff definitively.

"How can you be sure it was the weapon used in the attack?" asked the attorney.

"Cause it was drippin' with the Carpetbagger's, um, er, I mean victim's blood. That's a stupid question!" he barked at the attorney, with the courtroom breaking into an uproar of laughter.

"Order in the court! Order in the court!" screamed Judge Ferris, his gavel slamming furiously at the bench. "I will clear every one of you gawkers from this here courtroom if y'all can't control yourselves."

He then turned to the Sheriff, still in the witness box, and admonished him. "Sheriff, please refrain from commenting on the validity of the questions the attorneys ask. That's why we have the newspaper men here in the court."

The court erupted again, but the judge allowed it to go on, as he was pleased with his own joke.

A short bit later the Carpetbagger himself was called to the stand for cross-examination by Willet Blackwell's defense attorney.

"Your name is Colin Brannigan?" the attorney asked.

"Aye, t'is!" said the Irishman.

"You are the Administrator of the Freedmen's Bureau for this area?"

"Aye, I am so," said Brannigan.

"Why would anyone wish to attack you, Sir?" asked the attorney.

"I have not the briefest of notions, my good man. However, the man that attacked me is a known renegade and a war deserter."

"Do you take bribes, Mr. Brannigan?" asked the defense attorney flatly.

The shocked prosecution objected vehemently. "It is not Mr. Brannigan who is on trial, Your Honor!"

Truitt looked at the courtroom clock. It was three o'clock on the nose. His gut tightened into a knot.

Judge Ferris overruled the prosecution's objection.

Colin was incredulous. "Indeed, Sir, how dare you impugn my integrity. What kind of tactic is this…"?

"It is a very straightforward question, Sir," exclaimed the attorney.

"It is not a question at all, but a mere attempt to undermine the business of my office. How dare this court allow this line of questioning…" protested Brannigan.

"The witness will answer the question," said the judge in an unoffended voice.

It was then that the noise of the train's whistle pierced the courtroom like the shrill call of a hawk above a field of prey. The judged grabbed at the train schedule, which had nothing coming past the courtroom for another hour and a half.

"Clear the court," yelled Judge Ferris frantically. It might as well have been '*Every man for himself*'.

The bailiff remanded Willet to custody, drawing his pistol in the process as if this had been an elaborate distraction arranged by his men. The judge bailed out the rear door, and the gallery of the court was in great commotion as they all knew what was to come.

Truitt's first responsibility was to attend to the evidence, in this case, the dagger. He grabbed it as he headed to pull the sashes on the windows.

The train was already at a full head of steam as it passed the depot and then the courtroom. The mix of steam and coal smoke poured through the large open windows, engulfing the room in a dark, choking fog.

Truitt hung out of the window engulfed in the belching excess of smoke from the train speeding past. It was a rather far distance from the window to the cars of stone moving past him. He wondered if he actually could do it…

———————

Truitt then looked over his shoulder back into the courtroom, but he could see only a trapped cloud of heavy gray fog. The sound of people choking pierced it, but not an eye in the room could do so.

Truitt judged the distance to the moving train. He held in his hand the dagger below the brick windowsill of the court house. The young apprentice realized this to be the very opportunity for which he had hoped. An opportunity for an action he could take to free Willet - to free the man who had once saved his entire family.

Truitt looked up and down the tracks. Given the thick plumes of smoke, no one could possibly see or ever know of his action of tossing the damning knife at the speeding train. Unless of course, he missed the train entirely. How, then, would he ever be able to explain the accusing evidence of the blade, being found alongside the tracks?

Truitt decided he could not live with himself unless he acted. He swung the dagger up with all the energy he could muster, sending the knife flying through an impressive arc in the direction of the train.

He lost sight of it in the plume of smoke and steam being blown back from the engine's smokestack. A second passed before he caught its blade's glint in the sunlight. The dagger was rotating handle over blade as it swung upon its high arc. Truitt could feel the sweat rolling off his brow.

The dagger struck the top of the side of the moving train. It kicked up into the air like the ball upon the maypole being struck by a child. It seemed to hang in the air forever, before descending into the train's last car, directly behind the one it had initially struck.

Truitt exhaled in relief. The train escaped northwards along the rails to wherever these stones were to be delivered. The knife, lodged among the rocks from Ladd's Quarry, was now racing away from the courthouse.

Truitt hung out of the window and coughed just as everyone else had been doing inside. He pulled himself back inside, feigning a choking spell before attending to the windows. As he closed them, he realized that with the train having passed, it would be more natural to reopen them, and so he did.

As the smoke cleared, Truitt "discovered" that the dagger was missing and reported it to the Clerk-of-the-Court, Conyers Trippe, who then reported this to Judge Ferris. Ferris ordered everyone still in the courthouse to be searched.

The man from Willet's gang, known as Flinch, who had been in the gallery throughout the proceedings, was taken briefly into custody and forced to remove his clothing. Having found nothing, and with other reputable citizens having attesting that he had not left the courtroom, he was released. Judge Ferris ordered the courtroom cleared and searched, but, of course, no trace of the dagger was found.

That afternoon in chambers, Willet's defense counsel argued vehemently for a mistrial. He told the judge that they were planning a defense upon the fact that the dagger had been intentionally duplicated and the forgery left at the scene of the crime only to incriminate Willet Blackwell. They argued that Judge Ferris had dismissed other cases in the past when evidence was found to be missing during the trial.

However, Judge Ferris saw this tale for the quickly concocted charade it was. The judge argued that as he could not be sure that some member of Willet's defense team themselves had not absconded with the evidence, there would be no mistrial. The judge glared threateningly at the defense team as he assured he would punish severely anyone attempting to make a mockery of his court. Truitt had been in chambers with the judge at this time, and soon realized that in all the commotion, no one had seen him securing the evidence.

The trial reconvened the next morning, with Judge Ferris rendering the decision that the trial would continue. There would be no mistrial.

Truitt's heart sank upon hearing this. The risk he had taken with his position was done with no other purpose than to secure a mistrial for Willet. The judge had decided that since the dagger had already been introduced as evidence, the trial would go on. Truitt had failed at his attempt to free the man who had once saved his family and their farm.

And so, the trial continued. However, a very interesting effect of the disruption was observed. Willet's defense attorney, who had seemed to be resigned to defeat as the trial began, was now re-invigorated. He strenuously objected to the continuation of the trial, but once it was re-commenced, the attorney focused on the missing evidence.

Why had it been stolen? Only the officers of the court had access to it, why would they wish it unavailable? Could it have been because they knew I was planning to prove the knife a fake planted to incriminate my client? Doesn't this seem odd to you gentlemen of the jury? Is this not simply a situation where the Union Government is trying to hang the man they suspected, but could not prove, killed their troops during the end of the war? Was this not just another case of the Federal Government attempting to manipulate the state's court system to imprison and hang a Southern man they could not indict for cause in Federal Court?

The court case closed and went to the jury. The jury came back after only thirty minutes. As they shuffled into the Jury Box, Truitt was sure this spelled a conviction for Willet Blackwell. His efforts had failed.

"I do want to state that due to yesterday's very unusual course of events, I have requested that Sheriff Goff conduct a special investigation into the matter of the vanished evidence," said Judge Ferris before adding, "however, I had made the decision to proceed with this trial and we will do so. Will the foreman of the jury please rise?"

He did so.

"Has the jury reached a verdict?" asked the judge.

"We have, Your Honor."

The verdict was passed by the bailiff to Judge Ferris, who looked at it without reacting. The judge then passed it back to the bailiff, who returned it to the foreman.

"The foremen will please read the verdict," directed the judge.

The foreman cleared his throat. "We the jury, made up of citizens of Bartow County, Georgia, find Willet Blackwell to be innocent of the charges!"

A great commotion overcame the court, which had assumed that the speed with which the jury had rendered its verdict surely meant a conviction.

"Order in the court! Order in the court!" gaveled Judge Ferris. It was a lost cause. Amid the great throng of residents leaving the courtroom, Willet was released and proudly walked out of the courthouse a freed man.

Truitt watched the shocked expression on the face of Colin Brannigan.

The Irishman could not believe that these local citizens would so blatantly ignore the facts of the case in rendering this injustice.

It was then that Truitt Clay-Harris realized that while he failed in his attempt to win a mistrial for Willet Blackwell, he had opened the possibility for Willet's attorney to stoke the fears of the jury. Their very fears of the Federal Government railroading an innocent Southerner.

Indeed, the next day's paper would feature an interview with the foreman of the jury which stated that this argument led the jury to realize they could not convict, beyond a reasonable doubt, so long as the dagger remained missing.

So, instead of the desired mistrial, which would still harbor the threat of Willet Blackwell being re-tried, young Truitt Clay-Harris had secured Willet his unexpected freedom.

21

THE WITCHING HOUR
JULY 1871

Willet Blackwell returned that night to Three Sisters Mountain. In celebration of his release, his men had stoked a great bonfire, around which Willet and his men drank whiskey in commemoration of the return of their leader.

Deekie sheltered herself within his tent. She had hugged and kissed him when he first came back to camp. She told him that she would wait for him in his tent but would not join him at the bonfire with his men.

Hours passed, and Deekie felt the weight of her own imprisonment grow with each second of freedom that Willet enjoyed. She felt as lost as at any time during her life.

In the small hours of the morning Willet returned to the tent. His breath was sour with the smell of whiskey. Deekie thought she knew what was to come next, but in reality had no idea.

"Flinch tells me Clay was up here warning the boys about interfering with getting' me out of jail." Willet's words were clear, no slurring of his speech.

"So, I heared," said Deekie.

"Warned 'em against harassing the Carpetbagger," he said.

"So?"

"Warned 'em against harassing his niece," Willet said.

"Yeah, I hear he's taken sweet on her," she said.

Willet laughed. "Put on yer riding clothes. I won't have yer Virgil coming up here telling my boys how to behave themselves. You and me are going to do exactly what yer Virgil told us not to do."

"I am not going down into town," said Deekie. "With you or without you."

"Well then, Deekie, we got ourselves a problem. Cause yer Virgil told them not to do something else. Told 'em all you was his girl, and not to touch ya'."

"It's a lie, Willet, he said no such thing…"

She tried to rush past him and out of the tent. He grabbed her wrists and pulled her close to him. "I thought you was through with him, Deek."

"I am, I am," she cried, fighting to free herself from his grip.

"Liar!" he screamed as he pushed her back on her heels, nearly snapping her wrists as he did so. "He wants you back. He wanted me strung up, so he could get his hands on you again. Come up here to tell Flinch and the boys to keep their hands off. You was always sweet on him, and now he's sweet on you, again."

"It ain't like that, Willet. Virgil wants that red-headed fancy girl," she said.

"He ain't gonna want her after I get through with her tonight, Deek. I got a score to settle with her uncle. And you are gonna bring her to me."

"No, no, I just won't do it…" she began.

He hit her with the back of his hand, hard, knocking her to the ground.

"I said you are gonna bring her to me. Don't make me tell you that again."

Deekie could feel her jaw already swelling. It ached like a bad tooth, throbbing and penetrating her. Willet was at the beginning of one of his rages, she recognized with great fear. *Tonight is the night I die, she thought, I should have left while I had the chance.*

"I will not he'p you to get your hands on that innocent young girl, Willet," Deekie screamed.

He brought back his boot, and aimed its pointed toe into her ribs, kicking as hard as he could without shifting his weight. Its force crashed in upon her whole life, reminding her there was no safe place for her in this world.

"But you are gonna he'p me, Deekie," Willet sneered. "Clay still wants you, that much is clear to me, now. But yer Virgil was countin' on my rottin' in jail on those Federal charges, so as he could just come by and claim my woman again. But they was not able to convict me, cause I was just doing what any real Southerner would do - fight back against them Yankee bastards. Them jurors all knew that. They respected that. The Yankees can't touch me, now. And that Carpetbagger will still feel my wrath. And soon."

"Don't you see, Willet, that if you do this, they will only bring fresh charges agin' ya?" she cried between painful sobs.

"I'm not worried for that. For I'll be long gone by the time Alpheus Goff and his deputies come up the trail to Three Sisters. I'll stay here just long enough to see which one of y'all Clay comes to try and take for his own, you or the Irish girl. That is iffen he wants her once I git done with her."

Deekie laid on the ground, seeing a wildness in Willet's eyes that she had never before seen. At first she thought it was due to her actions, her refusing to lure the Irish girl into a trap. But as she watched him seethe, she realized it was neither she nor Ever McLaughlin nor even Colin Brannigan that fueled his irate temper.

It was her Virgil. His boyhood friend, Clay. His fellow Confederate soldier-in-arms. It was Virgil Clay-Harris, who Willet had assured himself as having abandoned him in his greatest moment of need.

And Deekie knew her Virgil. She knew that the bowels of Hell itself were about to be released upon the town of Cartersville.

22

TAKING THE BAIT
JULY 1871

It was two in the morning when Deekie rode up in front of the boarding house. She stayed on her mount and called aloud for Ever.

The federal guard on the front porch had told her to move along, but she continued to call Ever's name aloud. Then, she added, "Clay needs you, Ever."

The guard peered suspiciously about the darkened streets. This was clearly a trap.

"Virgil Clay-Harris is dying," Deekie yelled aloud, "and he wants to say goodbye to ya'."

"I told you to git along, woman…" the guard said.

"I don't believe you," said the young girl's voice from the second-floor window, "Clay is not dying."

"He ain't gonna last much longer!" Deekie yelled from atop the black horse, "Suit yerself! Personally, I'd rather you stay away from him. But I promised him…"

She started to move the horse forward in the direction of Clay's farm.

"Wait!" cried Ever frantically. "What's happened?"

"Willet caught us both together. He drew on Virgil, shot him, then beat me near to death," said the woman. "Just look at my face."

Even in the slight cast of light from the Federal guard's lantern, Ever could see the purplish swelling of Deekie's jaw.

"Go on," said the young girl.

"Virgil killed Willet with a shot from that Colt Navy of his. Dropped him dead. The doc is with Virgil now, but he won't last long. I am going back to him at his farm."

"Wait for me!" cried Ever, in near hysteria.

"I can't wait no more, girl. I'm going back before he is gone," she responded as she paced her horse into the darkness towards the Mission Trail.

It was less than ten minutes later when Ever defied her Uncle and his guard and ran through the darkness along the Mission Trail toward Clay's homestead. Her Uncle told the guard to go with her, but the guard said his orders were to protect Colin Brannigan, and he would not be drawn away from his duty by this elaborate trap. So, they both watched as Ever ran on foot in the direction of Pettit's Creek.

The breath the young Irish girl couldn't catch was thick with emotion, drenched with the saltiness of her tears. Her Clay lay dying after defending his woman, killing that evil Willet Blackwell who had abused her. It all sounded exactly like what Clay would do.

It was then that she came upon the woman, Deekie, atop her mount, walking the horse slowly towards her. Deekie's head was hung low.

"Am I too late? Is Clay gone?" she sobbed.

"No, Darlin', you're right on time."

The voice was that of Willet Blackwell, who had walked his horse up behind Ever, cutting off her path back to the boarding house.

23

FATE'S CALL IN THE NIGHT
JULY 1871

It was the coughing that awoke Clay. His maw was in her final days, spitting up large amounts of blood and clear phlegm-like secretions. The anger of her coughing left her resting breath shallow and weak. Clay knew his mother would not last long, but as he came out of his sleep, he was unaware as to what had initiated her distress.

As he attended her, he could hear movement outside the shack. He wiped his hand clean of the fluids that she had spat up all over him. He reached for the Colt Navy he kept aside the tick mattress in the corner of the shack where he slept.

The knock came loud upon the door. The lateness of the hour amplified it. The intensity of it told of a great urgency.

"Clay! Virgil-Clay Harris! Open up at once."

He recognized the voice as that of Sheriff Alpheus T. Goff. Clay opened up the door and stepped into the moonlit night outside the shack.

"What is it, Sheriff?" he asked, the Colt Navy still in his hand.

"You always answer the door with a Colt, boy?" asked the Sheriff.

Clay looked at him as if he was an idiot asking a fool's question.

"At this hour, Sheriff, if I hear anything bigger than a fox stirring, then, yes, Sir, I do."

"Who you got in there with you, Clay?" demanded the Sheriff.

"Just Truitt and my maw, Sheriff, and she's dyin' of the Consumption," he answered. "You are more than welcome to come inside and see fer yerself, iffen ya' need to."

The Sheriff had the same fear of the Consumption that the rest of the town had. They all knew it was highly contagious, and seemingly preyed on those already weakened by famine, pestilence or just plain old age.

It was then that his maw began another frenzy of cough and wheezing inside the shack. The Sheriff could clearly hear this and assessed that in no way could anyone fake the seemingly multi-tiered hacking and distressed gasping coming from Clay's maw. To him, she sounded only a few hours away from a death rattle. And it would be a mercy upon her.

"Clay, you been with Willet tonight?" asked the Sheriff, ignoring the invite to search the cabin.

"No Sir, I reckon he is up on Three Sisters glorifying his freedom," answered Clay.

"You didn't send Deekie up to the Carpetbagger's boarding house this night?"

"What's goin' on, Sheriff?" asked Clay.

"That little redhead Ever McLaughlin ain't inside with ya', son?"

The pulse of Clay raced. His stomach tightened. His jaw clenched as he was beginning to piece together what Willet was up to.

"No, she ain't in there. Go in and take a long, hard look. Mama ain't goin' hurt you, and you sure won't be bringing no harm on her that she t'ain't already bearin'."

"Clay, we think Willet sent Deekie down to draw out the girl, which she done. Likely Willet has her up on Three Sisters and is likely to bring some harm on her in retribution against the Carpetbagger."

"What are ya' fixin' to do, Sheriff?" His question was tight, as if he had trouble releasing the words through his gritted jaw.

"I am heading back to town to pull together some townsfolk I can deputize, and we are gonna go up there and bring her back."

"He'll be gone with her, and Deekie, and the rest of 'em before you ever git there."

"Not if I can move fast, son. Now you stay outta this mess, Clay. You're still a suspect in all this, but I believe Willet just used your name to draw out the Ever girl."

"What did he tell her?" asked Clay.

The Sheriff looked at the man, wishing he had not asked that question.

"Son, he had Deekie tell her you and Willet was in a tussle. Willet shot you, and that you were dyin'. That you sent Deekie to get her, so that you could see her before you done passed."

"And Willet? What did Deekie tell her about him?"

"She told Ever that you had killed him, Clay."

It was then, that Clay could hear Willet's voice in his ear as they returned in Lee's army, defeated, from Gettysburg - ***No harm upon you, no harm upon me, forever, no matter what.***

24

REVELATIONS OF CHICKAMAUGA
SEPTEMBER 18 -20, 1863

The bonfire atop Three Sisters Mountain blazed defiantly through the night. Clay could see it clearly as he walked at double pace with his Spencer rifle clenched tightly in his hand.

He had been in the cabin only minutes earlier, loading the seven rounds into the rifle when Truitt had climbed down from his loft.

"What's goin' on Clay?" asked his brother.

"You keep watch over Mama, she's right agitated tonight. I hope she makes it through."

"What did Sheriff Goff want outside?"

"He was tryin' to fix whether I was mixed up in Willet's trash, that's all."

Truitt looked confused. "Willet done got acquitted. By the law, he ain't got nothin' to fear."

Clay looked at his brother. "Liken I told ya', Truitt. Willet ain't got no sense to draw on anymore. He's just all bitter and ready to bite anyone close to him. He's like a rabid possum. T'ain't no reasonin' with him. All he knows is force."

It was then that Clay realized just how dangerous tonight was to be. Despite all their joint declarations of no harm to the other, Willet had indeed harmed Clay by his actions.

Truitt watched as Clay loaded the rounds into the Spencer. His eyes began to well with tears. Truitt now realized this very night that it was likely his brother would be killed by the defiant courtroom act of which he had been so proud only hours before. The tears pooled before running down his face. He began to draw heavy breaths and commenced to sob.

"What you cryin' for, Truitt?"

"I done it, Clay! It is 'cause of me that Willet is free." He cried as he went on to tell his brother the tale of pitching the dagger onto the train. All the while Clay kept readying himself for what he must do.

"Don't go up there, Clay. Him and his men will kill you. Let the Sheriff get the men and roust them out." Truitt moved to block the door.

Their maw was now coughing, wheezing and hacking uncontrollably.

"By morning's light, I might be alone in this world," he said to Clay as they looked upon the pitiful sight of their mama.

"Well, boy, yer always gonna have yer guilt to keep ya' company. Now, git outta my way. I told ya' to stay outta this. I told ya' this was Willet's fix to get outta. Well, now you done got him freed just to cause a bigger ruckus. And this one is mine to fix, once and for all."

"Clay, you got but one arm, you can't go up against six renegades with weapons. They will kill ya', for sure."

His last memory of Truitt that night, and perhaps forever, was shoving his brother out of the way as he headed out the door of the shack. He realized that even if he survived the night, he likely would never see his maw again.

As Clay approached the rise of the mountain in the moonlight, Willet Blackwell was in his large tent with Deekie and his prey, Ever McLaughlin.

The flickering light of the bonfire, which still roared defiantly outside, sliced through in a devilish arc. The animated beam seemed to bounce throughout the darkened tent, reminding Ever of the tales of the Witches' Sabbath that she had been told as a child in Ireland.

With the light casting upon the scarred and disfigured face of Willet, as well as the purplish and swollen bruised face of Deekie, Ever realized she was living her childhood terror.

Then, the voice of Flinch echoed into the tent. "Willet, the men are fixin' to move out like you said, you sure you don't want us to break camp and take the tents with us."

"No," yelled Blackwell, "We ain't got no time for all that. Take the ammunition and the store of black powder. We'll raid ourselves more shelter once we lay down stakes somewhere. We just gotta get out of here tonight, before we got all of Cartersville comin' up that trail."

A few seconds later, Willet could hear Flinch relaying his orders to the rest of the men.

Blackwell moved over to Ever McLaughlin, wrapping his arm around her waist. Her hands were bound, but otherwise she was unharmed.

"You sure is a pretty little thing, for being kin to that Carpet-bagger. I still can see the look on his face when they 'quitted me in that courtroom. Same look as when I slammed into him that night on Market Street. Same look as I reckon he has on his sour puss tonight, realizin' his beautiful niece is up here with Ol' Willet."

The girl pulled back from him, her eyes riveted to the horrible scar upon the right side of his face.

"You never seen this up close, have you, my darlin'. Get a good look at it. Yer beau Clay done did this to me."

He took his finger and placed its nail in the corner of her right eye. He traced the path of his own scar onto her cheek, slowly working down to the corner of her mouth. His nail indented, but did not perforate, her alabaster skin.

"Iffen I had my war knife, I might just carve you up and send you back to Uncle Colin. Let him have to look on this mutilation every day. Let him see other men wince as ya' walked by, yer pretty little doll-face all scarred up forever."

She looked away in great fear, only to lay her eyes upon Deekie's swollen features. Ever realized that this warped man breathing heavily upon her was capable of everything he said.

"We was heroes ya' know," Willet said aloud, as if answering a question that had not been asked. "Clay and me and the rest of Longstreet's army. We was riding on a train takin' us from Northern Virginia down to the Battle at Chickamauga. General Robert E. Lee had kept Longstreet from coming to this fight, but Longstreet had gone to President Jefferson Davis directly and got his way. I wish we had stayed with Ol' Bobby Lee."

Deekie at this point realized it was her own question that Willet was preparing to answer – *What happened to you two at Chickamauga?*

"Yeah, we rode that train all day and night. Every Southern town that we passed through had throngs and throngs of people along the sides of the tracks, cheering us on. The women would give the young boys food to throw on up to us. Hell, half of it fell wasted on the ground, but it was a real treat to them of us who caught us a corn muffin or an apple. It was a treat to our spirit to see them folks who we was fightin' for comin 'out to cheer us on like that."

Deekie still sat on the cot within the tent, seethin' as Willet wrapped his other arm around the young girl.

"We got to the end of the line and got off that train and marched right to the battlefield. We had missed the first day of fightin', but all of us was glad to be together again on Georgia soil. Even if it was just over the line from Chattanooga, we was defendin' our own state's dirt, and it felt really good. Not like at Sharpsburg or Gettysburg, Clay and me, we was fightin' side-by-side. And we knew no harm could come to us so long as we was together."

Ever continued to arch her back to afford her whatever distance she could between herself and the whiskey fouled breath of her captor. His hands roamed along her form as he spoke.

"There was a hell of a lot of confusion that next morning as we lined up against the Yankees on a farm down there just west of the Chickamauga crick. Some said the Injuns called that place the River of Death, and from what I was about to see, it was a name hard earned"

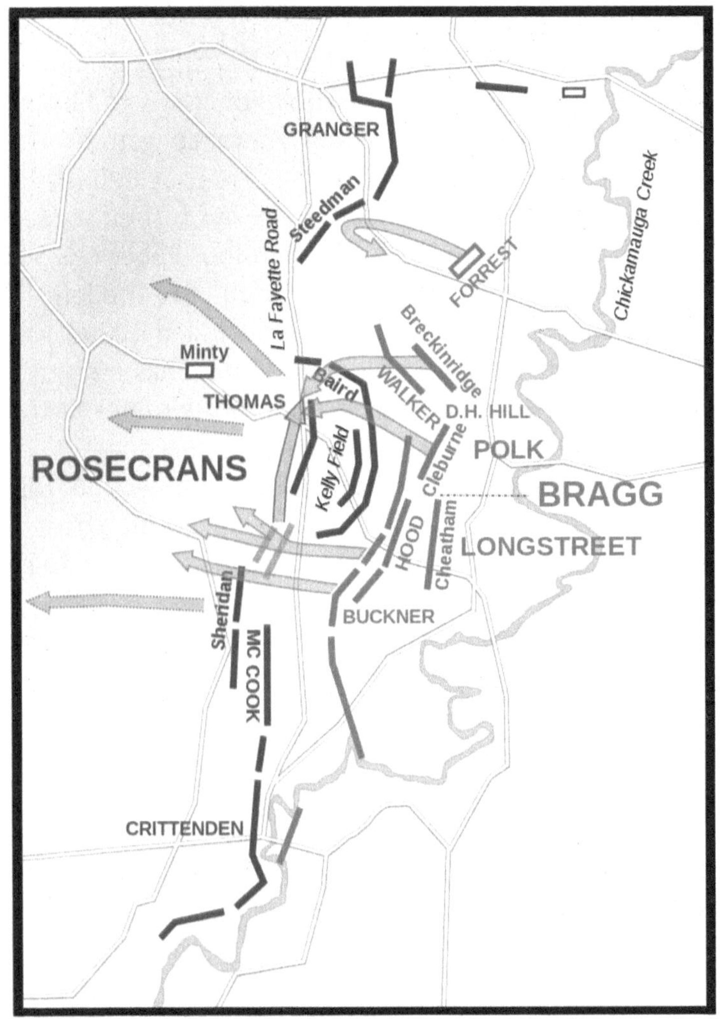

Image 17 – Battle Map of Chickamauga
Source: en.wikipedia.org

"All right, stop. Willet, enough is enough," said Deekie, "leave her be, she never done you no harm."

"Don't ya' want to hear the rest of mah story, Deek. You always was curious 'bout it. Yer Virgil would never tell you of what happened in that great Rebel rout of the Yankees, now would he?"

Willet removed his hands from Ever, pushing her onto the cot alongside Deekie.

"We was routin' them Yankees, too. The Yankee General moved his troops from along the center of their line, to try to fill a gap that didn't really exist. At the same time General Longstreet moved us to attack the center of their line, but 'cause they had just moved, there was nothing there but a big hole. We rushed forward and through that gap in the line with a tremendous Rebel Yell. Soon, we was behind them Yankees on both the right and the left. It was a tremendous slaughter. One of the generals called it '*Bushwhacking on a Grand Scale*!' We mowed down them Yanks before they all panicked and started to flee to the back of their lines. It truly was grand. Best moment of the war, just before the worst."

His eyes had sunken into his impending recollection. His mood became icy and dropped like the settling of a morning frost. Deekie reached her hand onto the back of the young girl, Ever, to comfort her in advance of what might come.

"The Yankees had pulled back into a defensive position atop some high ground called Horseshoe Ridge. We had run all the Yankees off the open battlefield. Clay and I were sent to a deserted farmhouse to make sure it hid no stragglin' Blue Devils. Here we had just fought in great glory in the open field, only to soon be cut down in an empty, ruined farmhouse."

His mood was becoming more angry and bitter by each word of the tale he told. Deekie realized he was preparing himself through its telling for the heinous act he was about to commit.

"Me and Clay went into the kitchen of that farmhouse. There was no Yanks we could see. Just a quarter full bottle of whiskey on the table. Just sittin' there, pretty as a picture. Ya' got any idea how rare that was to have whiskey on a battle field?"

The two women looked at him in terror.

Willet continued. "Clay knowed better, he said to leave it alone. But ol' Willet just had to have a taste. I moved right to that kitchen before we even cleared the whole farmhouse."

He looked at Deekie, who now had both her arms wrapped protectively around the shaking, terrified Ever.

"Yer Virgil," he said, staring at Deekie, "screamed out 'Willet, no!'. Hell, I just wanted that whiskey. I went to that kitchen and put my weapon in my left arm, grabbed that bottle with my right and raised it to my mouth."

He walked over to them. He put the fingers of his right hand under Ever's chin.

"Do you know how sweet that whiskey tasted?" he asked her. She could smell it on his breath, but it was sour, not sweet. It sickened her with a fear that penetrated deep into her. Deekie pulled her away from him in an act of defiance, as they both sat on the cot and he stood over them.

"Well, I will tell ya'," he said, standing upright. "It t'weren't too sweet. As soon as it hit my lips, I knowed it was a trap. It was just sassafras tea in that whiskey bottle. My right arm was in the air holdin' up that bottle, and the musket in my left was useless to me. That's when I seen him, from the corner of my eye. He was hiding in the pantry, a scared little Bluebelly. But he wasn't so scared as he couldn't set this trap, now was he? He must of not had any ammunition, because he dropped down his bayonet and charged at me."

At this point, Deekie feared for them all. Willet dun had a crazed look in his eye as he recalled the ordeal.

"Clay had been moving to stop me, but it was too late. He lunged forward with his musket in his hands. He was just able to get the barrel of his gun between me and that charging Yankee. I swear as true as I am a Southern Son, that bayonet would have gone clean into my heart had it not been for yer Virgil. He had used his musket to block that bayonet upwards. But, liken I said, it was too late. I screamed for my life when the tip of that blade caught the corner of my mouth, then it ripped clean through my cheek right up to the corner of my eye."

He was now back in the face of Ever, bending over the cot so she could see every horrible detail of his scar.

"Mind you, Missy, this was all stitched up after the fact. My cheek was gored clean in two pieces, with just the bottom of my skull peeking out. Can you picture that, my young Irish friend, just a skeleton covered by two pieces of hanging skin of my cheek. I done seen myself a little in the glass of a cabinet."

Willet then turned to Deekie.

"You know what I seen, Deek. I seen the dead bodies that me and Clay seen at Sharpsburg. Did yer Virgil ever tell you 'bout that?"

"No, he never told me nuthin', Willet," she said.

"He told me," offered Ever, "you both were at Sharpsburg on your way to Gettysburg. Those skeletons laid on the ground, as if to crawl back to the fight."

Deekie stared in amazement at her. She wrapped her arms even tighter around the young Irish girl, and said "You poor soul, you should of never had to hear of any of this."

"So, Deek, yer Virgil been tellin our young guest here tales. Tales he even refused to share with you. Ha! Ain't that just too thick!"

Deekie realized that she needed to save this girl from Willet, who just kept going with his ranting story.

"That Yank knocked Clay's musket from him and drew back to finish me off. Clay's motion had took him past me, and I seen my life in a flash. I seen me layin' yellow upon the grounds of Gettysburg, my fellow Rebs fallin' all around me."

He paused as if that moment deserved the respect of silence.

Ever thought to herself, *In your moment of cowardice!*

"That Yankee was somethin' fierce. He must of figured one way or 'nuther he was gonna die, so he might as well kill us both. He drew back that bayonet on his rifle and began his second thrust, this time aimed for my gut. That's when Clay jumped back between us. He stretched out his left arm as he did, and the tip of the bayonet caught the palm of his hand. And I swear what I seen next I could not believe."

Willet took his finger and demonstrated upon the palm of his own left hand.

"Clay closed up his grip around that blade until it come clear through the back of his hand. But he never let go, he just pushed that second thrust clean to the side of me. When he did, though, that massive blade went through his wrist and tore right up the middle of his left arm. He laid on the floor screaming, but I couldn't move. I was holding my blood-soaked face, shaking out of control. I was fixed in my own fear."

Willet walked over to the tent flap. "Flinch, bring me a knife." He yelled out. "I got a matter to settle with that Carpetbagger before we leave."

Deekie rose and stood in front of Ever, "Willet, I'm not gonna let you to bring harm to this girl."

"Deek," he said, "The best thing about pain is it's only for a while. Sure, it stays in yer mind when folk won't look at ya', but yer skin scars over and don't hurt no more. Now, what happened next to that Yankee was permanent. He looked at me as Clay rolled upon that floor in his great, but temporary, pain. That Yankee just snarled at me, and then he grinned a sickly smile with his knowing me and Clay was both helpless. He didn't say a thing, he just panted heavy and brought his bayonet up. He was enjoying knowing he was going to kill me."

"And he should've," said Deekie, seething in anger at what she knew Willet was to do to this child.

"Ya know, Deek, that's what I said to myself. I closed my eyes, I could feel a peace coming over me as the blood drained out of my severed face into my palms. I closed my eyes and was ready to have him send me to the Lord's judgement. But it never come, just the sound of an explosion at my feet. Yer Virgil had taken one of them Colt Navies and shot a bullet up into the bottom of that Yankee's chin. How he ever done that with the butchery to his left arm, I won't never know. Then he shot up two more rounds into this Blue Devil. And when he fell to the ground, Clay dragged hisself over to that soldier and put two more rounds in his heart. He was dead already, but Clay was determined to save me. He saved me only to become the freak I am today, to live forever with the mark of my shame."

Flinch came to the tent's flap and handed Willet a knife.

"Now we're fixin' to get at it!," he said with a sickening grin. Deekie reached for the Colt Navy at her side. Willet continued.

"Clay passed out atop that Yankee. It was as if he had spent his last breaths rescuing me. I passed out just after, remembering my last thought bein' *Well, I always figured we would die together, just didn't figure it to be here today.*"

Deekie could see the inferno that had been raging in Willet's eyes subside into an even more terrifying icy blank stare. Its being void of emotion scared her, as she had seen it before, usually just before he had exploded in anger upon her.

"Of course, neither of us died, just both come damn close, is all. As it was, the Yankee General Thomas held off the Rebel Army for the rest of that fight. They called him the Rock of Chickamauga after that, and hell I guess he deserved it for what he did for 'em. When I finally woke up, I couldn't make out where I was. Turns out, me and Clay was both in a Yankee field hospital called Cloud Springs just north of the battlefield. How we got there, I will never knowed. I woke up to find my face had been stitched up in as rough a way as them Yankee doctors could figure. I soon learned that they had cut off Clay's left arm, too - had to iffen they was to save his life. I just never figured that they would waste their time and supplies treatin' us Rebs, but that was their code. Try to kill 'em, if ya' can't, try to save 'em. Strange, ain't it?"

Willet was talkin' as he played heartlessly with the knife, balancing it upon the back of his right hand.

"Then the damnest thing happened. The field hospital we was in got shelled by our Rebel artillery. They though it was a Yankee command post. Good for us, though, because it allowed for me to escape. The hospital was plum out of Chloroform. One of the shells ignited the Ether they then turned to use in the operating room and the whole place went up in flames. Clay was still under, but I grabbed him and went outside and found a wagon. Laid him in the back and drove like hell down the LaFayette road, which at that point was under the command of our boys. I got Clay back, but our doctors said he was burning up in fever and was no way going to live. I asked if I could bring him home. The commander knew Clay good, respected him, and allowed it. But he told me I had two weeks myself to git back to the fight, that my scar would heal, and I could keep on killin' Yankees. So, I got Clay back to Cartersville as fast as I could."

Willet paused, as the flood of recollections seem to overcome him.

"I thought he would surely die on me, but that man is as stubborn as a crossed mule. Two days on the roads of Georgia, and he just hung on. Burnin' like a matchstick."

"And for all this, you fixin' to take yer anger out on Virgil against this poor girl," cried Deekie.

The girl, Ever, was terrorized. She had visualized every second inside that battlefield farmhouse, only to understand why Clay could never speak of it. But the vision of the bayonet ripping through his arm looped unendingly through her mind.

"Deekie, now you know me better than that," said Willet. "What I am about to do to this 'lass' ain't 'gainst yer Virgil. Nope, what she is about to go through is simply 'gainst her uncle, that theivin' Yankee bastard. No, Deek, Clay's a hero. I know, because I made him one. When I brought him home, and all the townsfolk saw how butchered up he was, I was the one telling the story of how he had saved Bobby Lee's Army shootin' some dozen Yankees from long range as we pulled back from Sharpsburg. It was all made up, of course, but that story stuck like a tick on a dog, didn't it? I knowed he was goin' to die, but I didn't figure my Deekie would abandon me to go fix him up now, did I?"

"You just always been jealous of Virgil, ever since we was kids, and cuttin' up this defenseless girl is just yer way of getting back at him. Just admit it, Willet."

"I will admit that I'm gonna enjoy this plenty," he said as he moved toward Ever, her hands still bound as she sat on the cot.

Deekie leaned back away from the girl. Willet thought that she had come to her senses, getting out of his way. Then he realized that she had pulled her Colt Navy and had pointed it directly at him.

"I won't let you to do this, Willet. You can hurt me, that's one thing, but I won't let you to spill the acid of your black heart upon this innocent soul."

Deekie cocked back the hammer.

"Don't you never pull a gun on me unless you mean to kill me, Deekie," he screamed in an uncontrolled rage.

25

THE RAGE OF VIRGIL CLAY-HARRIS
JULY 1871

Minutes before the scene in the tent, Virgil Clay-Harris approached Three Sisters Mountain. He had bypassed the guard posted at the bottom of the path that led up through the pines to the camp. He crept instead slowly through the thickness of the forest, deliberate in his motions to ensure he was unnoticed. He shifted his weight slowly from foot-to-foot, making sure no dried-out growth snapped under his advance. He crept slowly but steadily, climbing upwards through the trees toward the clearing where the great bonfire roared.

Soon he was gazing out onto the camp itself. The radiant dance of the bonfire turned the dead of night into a flickering ghost of daylight. Clay could see two of Willet's men chucking logs onto the raging fire. He could hear them clearly.

"I plum don't understand why we be feeding this here thang when we are fixin' to leave just before first light," said the man nearest Clay. "With this much timber this beast is gonna burn clean into 'morrow evening."

The other man looked at his cohort with an expression of disbelief.

"You ever think that Flinch and Willet might want just that? Any townsfolk thinking of coming up here will think again on seeing this raging beast. They'll be sure we are still up here, when, in fact, we will already be hours ahead of them."

Clay could see their Henry rifles atop the wagon that was just uphill from the fire. On the back of the wagon sat two boxes of ammunition, and a larger case marked "Explosive".

Then Clay noticed there were not two rifles but three. This is when he glimpsed the third man coming out of the woods, with a large metal scoop that likely had been stolen from a dry grocer.

It was long thought that Willet and his men had been dealing in stolen black powder, a commodity which was in great demand. It was needed by all those who fired cap and ball weapons, and also was needed for the repacking of the metal cartridges that were quickly replacing them. It was a devil's gold, and no one worshipped at its altar more than Willet's gang.

But this third man was filling his scoop and spreading it into lines arcing back from the fire into the woods. He was careful not to get too close to the fire, but Clay knew that should one ember already spreading through the night air like angry fire-flies land upon the powder, the resulting blaze would light these dry woods aflame. It was then that he realized that Willet had ordered these woods to be burned upon his gangs' clearing out. Clay knew Willet well and thought he would get them all moving just before daybreak, only a couple hours away.

Clay knew he had to act fast.

He counted the men in his mind. The one guarding the lower path, the two feeding the fire, and another spreading the black powder. This was four, and only left two others – Flinch and Willet.

As if demanding to be counted, Flinch appeared by the fire.

"Willet wants a blade. Who's got one handy?" Flinch called aloud. "C'mon, now, quick-like, the boss's got a score to settle with that Carpetbagger. Gonna slice up his pretty red headed niece before sending her back."

"Well, I want my blade back, dammit," said the man closest to Clay's position. "I took that blade off a dead Yankee at Allatoona Pass. It's good luck."

The man took the knife from the sheath hanging from his

waist, then taking its blade in his hand, he presented the butt handle to Flinch.

"Well, you are gonna need a riverboat of luck getting this fine blade back from Willet. You know how he likes his knives," said Flinch, laughing aloud.

Clay followed Flinch with his eyes to a large field tent just uphill on the other side of the fire. He saw the renegade pass the knife into someone, and then could make out moving shadows inside the canvas. *So that's where Willet and the two girls were,* he thought. He watched as Flinch moved back towards the three men around the fire.

"That's enough wood on that fire, boys," yelled Flinch. "And that's enough of that powder on the ground. I think it's damn foolish to waste any of it, but Willet wanted to leave something special for anyone comin' up here after we move on. The rest of that powder is goin' with us. Y'all get that wagon ready to roll and I'll lay out the rope fuses. 'Cause as soon as the boss is done dicin' up that Irish gal, we's movin' out."

Clay's blood boiled within him, hearing these thugs so callously speaking of what Willet would do to Ever.

He then watched as Flinch reached into a trough that had been used for watering their horses. He pulled out two lengths of saturated hemp rope and dragged them towards the fire. They were long enough to lay in the fire and connect up to the arcs of black powder spread on the ground. Willet had planned for the ropes to dry, and then burn, until igniting the powder and setting the woods ablaze sometime after they had left.

That was when Clay knew he had to act, before the three men retrieved their Henry rifles from atop the wagon, and while Flinch was pre-occupied laying the wet bands of rope. Once he started firing upon them, the guard he had bypassed at the bottom of the trail would come to join the fight. He would then kill this straggler.

"You seen enough, boy?" came the voice from behind Clay.

His blood, which had been boiling with rage, instantly ran like ice in his veins. Clay heard the lever action of the Henry rifle behind him.

"Turn 'round real slow like. Why do you think these boys have ol' Buck down there watching the night, son? 'Cause I got eyes like a stag in the moonlight. I saw you so far off, even before ya' started trackin' through these woods. Well, I was right behind ya' the whole time. Iffen you raised the barrel of that Spencer, I would have dropped you in yer tracks."

Clay turned to see the face of the man who had bested him. It was clean shaven and alert. The barrel of the man's Henry was already levelled at his chest, from only inches away. Clay damned himself for being so foolish, for being so proud of his own woodsman skills, only to have been shamed in the end.

Clay thought one last time of Ever, her innocence, her purity, and of the tip of Willet's blade threatening both. In his mind, he then saw Deekie's beautiful face one last time.

"Willet had once given us orders to never bring any harm upon you or yer family, boy. But you's outta luck, 'cause when he come back from jail tonight, he told us to kill ya' iffen even yer shadow dared to fall on the mountain tonight. And I am going to enjoy laying you out." The man saw no revolver holstered on either of Clay's hips. He saw no weapon other than the Spencer rifle available to his right hand.

"You fire that weapon from this close range and that black powder is sure to ignite these woods up in flames," said Clay, stalling for time.

Buck fell for it. "Hell, boy, iffen that bonfire ain't set off them powder trails yet, then I don't see where this gun's muzzle fire will."

Given the seconds that Buck used to describe his reasoning, Clay had hoped to, in some way, distract the man who had drawn down on him. But all was in vain, there was no distracting this rifleman.

"Goodbye, Clay," he said softly through a sickening smirk.

It was at that very second the voice of Willet, coming from the tent, bellowed throughout the camp.

"Don't you never pull a gun on me unless you mean to kill me,

Deekie," boomed from the large tent. Every man's head turned instinctively to the raging voice of their leader, including Buck's.

Clay thrust forward and used his left shoulder to push aside Buck's rifle, as the renegade fired past him into the night.

The other men, already moving to retrieve their rifles from upon the wagon, froze for a second upon hearing that unexpected shot. They feared, at first, that it had come from Deekie's pistol, but, then, realized the sound was of a rifle from the other direction.

The three men then knew an intruder was in camp, and they rushed to the wagon and their guns. Flinch scurried up the hill to the tent and to Willet's aid.

Clay had made Buck's first round miss through his quick action during the distraction of Willet's yell. Buck had not dropped his weapon and then cocked the Henry's lever to pump a second round into the chamber.

As Buck raised his barrel to shoot, Clay released his Spencer rifle from his hand, allowing it to slowly fall to the left and to the ground. As he did so, the glint of the firelight in the rifle caught Buck's eye. Clay dove for the ground to his right.

Buck then turned his attention away from the falling Spencer rifle. He knew it meant that Clay was now unarmed. Clay had dived only a few feet in front of him in a futile effort to escape. Defenseless or not, Buck thought excitedly of being the one renegade that finally was to drop Clay in his tracks. Buck swept his rifle in a jerking motion as he excitedly triggered it too early. The second round exploded harmlessly into the night.

It was answered in a dual echo of thunder. Two rounds slammed into Buck. He dropped the Henry rifle as he fell to the ground. He laid on the ground, feeling himself slip into darkness. His last thoughts were '*Where did they come from?*'

Buck was sure he hadn't seen the Colt Navy Revolver on either of Clay's hips. When Clay's Spencer fell, Buck was sure that he was unarmed. But unknown to the renegade, Clay had worn his belt holster across his torso under his shirt. It hung under his left shoulder, and, as it was reversed, it presented the gun nicely cross body to his right hand. As he dove away from Buck, he had reached inside the loose garment and drew the gun. As he hit the forest floor, he took aim at the distracted Buck and fired twice.

Clay knew the man to be badly wounded. He could see the life draining out of him. But Clay couldn't take the chance of having him draw any other weapon on him. Clay raised himself and slowly walked over to the man laying flat upon the forest floor.

"Goodbye, Buck. Ya' should've killed me when ya' had the chance," said Clay over the near-lifeless body. Clay fired a third round into the man's heart.

The rounds from the other renegades' rifles then began whizzing past him. Clay spread himself out flat on the forest floor. Should he take Buck's Henry rifle with its larger number of rounds, or grab the Spencer?

Never trade a weapon you know for an unfamiliar one, he could hear in his mind. He was a soldier again. His training raised up in him. *Stay calm, make your rounds count*. The shots coming against him were wild and undisciplined.

Clay dragged himself back to the Spencer. There were seven rounds to be chambered from its tube magazine. And by his count, only five men left to kill. Including his boyhood friend, Willet.

No harm to you, no harm to me, rang out ashamedly in his ears…

Clay trained his Spencer's sights on the three men crouching in firing positions from behind the wagon, slightly uphill from the bonfire. They were pumping their rounds wildly into the night.

Stay calm, make your rounds count. The only thing in shorter supply on a battlefield than ammunition was patience. Clay held fire and scanned the men and the wagon behind which they fired.

The wagon was chocked by a large limb lying wedged under the front wheel farthest from him, so as to keep it from slowly rolling down into the blazing bonfire. Clay sighted on the middle man, waiting for him to raise his head. He knew if he took out the man in the center, it likely would flush out the men fore and aft.

Then his target raised his head just above the wagon ever so slightly, peering into the darkened woods. Clay drew and held a deep breath, before gently squeezing the rifle's trigger. The round ripped just above the man's right eye, sending him sprawling backwards upon the ground.

The renegade in the rear hunched down instinctively behind the wagon. But the man in front began to flee from behind it.

"Get back here, can't you see he wants to drive us out into the open," yelled the man at the wagon's rear.

Clay levered and cocked the Spencer, which was more awkward than the repeating action required for the Henry rifles. The Henry only required a man to lever and trigger, the cocking being part of the levering action. But Clay knew his Spencer, and stayed with it, despite having the dead man's Henry laying nearby.

Clay trained his rifle on the fleeing man, hitting him on the shoulder. The round dropped him, pitching him in a spiral toward the ground. The injured man then rolled down the hill in great pain, coming to a stop only a few feet from the bonfire. After a brief second of collecting himself, the man began to crawl back uphill in a great panic, back to the cover of the wagon.

Shots from the man remaining behind the wagon were flying again wildly in Clay's direction. The shooter was now lying flat behind the rear wheel of the wagon, not offering much of a target to Clay's uphill aim.

Clay again levered and cocked the Spencer. He took aim upon the crawling man, who had just about reached the wagon's front wheel. His next shot missed short of the man, puffing up dirt just inches in front of him.

Clay cursed himself for rushing his shot. "Make each shot count," he said aloud softly.

The near miss only brought a greater urgency upon the wounded man to take cover. He had pulled himself up the incline to just below the wagon, when Clay chambered and fired a shot clean into his chest. The man writhed in pain, but not before, in a final desperate act, he reached towards the wagon's front wheel to pull himself up.

Instead of grabbing the wheel, he grasped the log wedged under it acting as a chock. In his death throes, he pulled it clean of the wheel, and the wagon began to slowly roll downhill towards the bonfire.

"Damn!" said Clay aloud, realizing the predicament this placed them all in.

The man behind the wagon's rear wheel must have had the same reaction, for he sprang to a crouch, and dropped his rifle in order to grasp the back of the wagon with both hands, arresting its downhill momentum.

Clay could then only take aim upon the man's boots, as every other part of his body was obstructed by the wagon. The man was desperate to keep the wagon from rolling down an into the bonfire.

Then, Clay remembered the massive quantity of black powder in the box atop it. Despite this, he drew aim upon the only part of the remaining renegade he could – his boots.

Clay squeezed the Spencer's trigger, his shot catching the man's foot as an awful squeal filled the air. The man fell, clutching his wounded foot. The wagon then rolled slowly downhill, picking up speed as it trundled dead center into the bonfire.

The wagon came to rest upon the mount of blazing embers within the fire. Clay could see the man he had just shot in the foot, hobbling as best he could away from the fire. His pace was frantic, despite the pain in his leg which must have been tremendous. Clay lowered the rifle from his firing position and quickly ran after him.

After climbing several yards uphill, Clay took aim upon the man. He measured the herky-jerky movements of his prey and readied to shoot.

At that second, before he could trigger the Spencer, the flames of the fire, shielded only by the mass of the wagon, waited no longer and ignited the black powder. The explosion was tremendous, throwing Clay forcefully to the ground.

He rolled over onto his back to see an inferno raging above him. The tops of the pines were ablaze. Two arced curtains of flames instantly raged along the forest floor. The smoke was overwhelming.

Clay looked for and located the tent. He was relieved to see it was nearby, but his escape down the mountain appeared to be cut off by the walls of the raging blaze, and the suffocating smoke from the powder.

Clay could hear the hobbling man screaming in pain. It was not the sound of a man merely in a panic. The pitch was far too high, far too hysterical. Clay recognized it from his days upon the battlefield. It was the horrifying sound of a man lit aflame. He had heard the same pathetic scream upon the fields of Gettysburg, when one of the Confederate field artillery units took a direct hit from the Yankees. The sound of another man burning alive was one that no man could ever force himself to forget.

The burning soul in front of him was the third renegade who had tried to hold back the wagon. He had also been the man spreading the black powder through the woods. His clothes had likely become covered with it. The explosion had lit the powder on his clothes, whose flames then engulfed him. The renegade wrenched and pitched in agony on the ground.

Clay fought the smoke, fumes and nauseating smell of burning flesh to mercifully put a Colt Navy round into the frenzied, fiery figure, ending his misery, and leaving him lifeless upon the ground.

Clay moved quickly to the tent. Flaming branches were already falling upon it. The canvas itself was aflame. He shoved the barrel of the Spencer within the flap, only to find the two girls huddled together in terror in the tent's corner. They were choking on the smoke from the massive burn of black powder.

"Help us, Virgil," cried Deekie frantically.

"Where's Willet and Flinch?" asked Clay as he raised them to their feet.

"They done run like cowards soon as the shootin' started," answered Deekie, still clutching Ever protectively. "They wanted to save themselves. They left us here alone."

"Let's git off this mountain," said Clay. Coming out of the tent again, he realized they were completely cut off from escaping downhill by the blazing woods below them. The inferno had spread at an alarming rate, even in the few seconds since the explosion. Clay feared they all would perish in its smoke and flames.

"Virgil, this way, they got a way out through the caves. Must have been where Willet and Flinch run off to. It's our only hope." Deekie grabbed his wrist, as his hand was still wrapped around his Spencer, and led him up the slope to the escape route.

The three of them climbed higher up the mountain until the slope levelled and began to drop down beneath them. The fire followed them, advancing with a fearful speed.

They came upon a small clearing a few hundred feet from the cliffs that had been created by Ladd's Mining company. Deekie found the safe route that Willet had showed her the first night when she had returned to the mountain.

It was merely a rope tied off against the large trunk of a tree that then disappeared into a wide hole in the ground.

"It drops down in to the caves that we used to play in, Virgil. It will get us off this burning mountain. They don't normally keep it hangin' in the cave, it's usually rolled up at the base of this here tree." Deekie pointed to the large pine to which it was tied. "So, I reckon Flinch and Willet must have just used it."

Through the smoke and fumes Clay could see morning was about to break. "It's too dangerous, Deekie. Willet and Flinch could be waiting for ya' in that cavern."

"Virgil, this here whole mountain is going to burn up. Now help me pull that rope up quickly. Them boys might have shimmied down it, but neither Ever nor me got that much strumpf. And you certainly ain't doin' no shimmyin', no way, no how."

They could hear the crackle of the woods burning towards them as they pulled the rope free from the hole. Ever shuddered in fear, as the events of the night had immobilized her. Her face was a relentless wrench of terror, her eyes were but a constant flood of tears.

Clay realized they needed to tie off a loop by which he could lower these women into the safety of the cavern. He could not tie the knot needed with his sole hand.

"Give me that, Virgil. This is no different than tying off a cinch for ya' to pull a plow through yer daddy's fields," said Deekie confidently.

"You still got mah Diddy's Navy revolver?"

"Only thing that saved us from Willet, Virgil…" she said.

She fashioned a harness loop and told Virgil to go first.

"No, Deekie. Willet's still out there. You got that Navy six in case he comes on ya' close. I can cover y'all from up here with this Spencer once y'all git outta these caves. Mornin's breakin', and with this fire, the whole of Cartersville will be out soon."

"All right, Virgil. Me first, then Ever. How are you getting' off this mountain?"

"Never mind me, just you git on into that hole…", said Clay, grabing her gently.

Clay then placed the loop around her and lowered Deekie into the darkened hole. After several feet of negotiating the tight ground that seemed to close in on her, the bottom dropped out from under her into complete darkness. Clay lowered her into the eerie silence, as all time seemed to stand still in the blackness of the cavern.

Then her feet hit the slippery floor of the chamber. She gained her balance and then tugged twice on the rope as they had agreed. She could then feel the rope pull up in singular strokes, as provided by the one-armed man above.

Deekie scanned the silent blackness of the cave. She pulled out the Colt Navy Clay had long ago given her. She felt its protection wrap around her like a blanket. She cocked its hammer as a warning to anyone that might be hiding in the darkness. They might not be able to see her draw the weapon, but they would unmistakably recognize the sound of its hammer cock.

Clay had retrieved the harness. Ever was nearly hysterical as the fire continued to close tightly around them. He wrapped it around her, telling her not to let go of the rope, no matter how much the harness dug into her rump.

He nearly had to push her into the large hole that lead to the drop. She screamed, fearing the tightness of the ground around her. It made her think of being lowered into a grave. She sobbed until the soil dropped away from under her and she was suspended in the darkness of the unknown depths below her. Then she could hear the tremendous echo of Deekie's voice beneath her.

"You are just above me, Ever. Stay calm, I almost got ya', and Virgil ain't gonna drop ya'. Not Virgil, no way." Deekie kept talking to soothe the young girl's terror.

She grabbed Ever's feet, which only caused the lass to let loose a horrific squeal. "It's me, Ever, I got ya', girl, you're safe now."

Deekie tugged on the rope after clearing Ever from it, but it did not raise. Deekie could feel it just hang limply in the darkness.

"Ever," said Deekie, "grab the back of my shirt, and don't let go. I got the Navy in my right hand, and I need to know you're behind me. I don't want to come this far only to shoot you in this cave's murky darkness."

They stumbled through the blackness which was intermittently only interrupted by shadows and ghosts of their imaginations. Their progress was painfully slow, until they came upon a pair of stone columns arching from the cavern's ceiling to the floor. Between them, they could feel a large stone ledge.

"This is Devil's Altar. We named this so when we was kids. So that means the way out is this way."

Deekie had reached back to remove Ever's hand from her shirt, taking it in her left hand. She then slowly led the frantic young girl into an adjoining chamber. Unlike the last, this was showing a softening glint of the morning's light, guiding their way out.

Clay had taken himself as far as he could from the burning forest, its flames closing in around him. His skin was already singed from its close quarters. He brought himself to the top of the cliffs that had been created by Ladd's quarrying. He waited until he saw the two women emerge from the enlarged mouth of the cave. *Deekie and Ever had made it*, he thought.

A great joy filled him upon seeing them escape into the quarry yard of Ladd's Lime and Stone. He knew then that all his actions that night had been justified, for now they were both safe. The sun was on the rise, and already off in the distance he could see towns-folk moving towards the mountain.

Then the great satisfaction he had harbored within him sud-denly plunged the very depths of the cliffs upon which he stood. For this is when Clay saw the figures of Willet and Flinch come from behind a stone-pile and move in on the girls.

Clay quickly laid himself flat atop the cliffs. He took up a firing position with his Spencer. He could clearly see the revolver that Flinch had pulled on the girls. From this distance he could hear nothing, but as the dawn had now broke in earnest, he could clear-ly see every bit of action. He aimed his sights on Flinch as Willet moved close in on Ever.

Clay could see Deekie drop the Colt Navy to the ground, as Flinch pointed his own pistol menacingly at her. Willet had pulled Ever close to him and held his knife high in his right hand, just in front of her face. He was enjoying terrorizing her, just before he re-leased her and slapped her violently with the back of his left hand. She collapsed to the ground.

Clay could see, but not hear, Willet's laughing, scarred face. He was now standing over Ever, menacingly brandishing his blade. He then knelt just above Ever, and Clay feared Willet had worked him-self up to the point where he would actually stop frightening the young girl and begin taking the blade to her. Perhaps he had merely gotten enough of his disgusting enjoyment of her horror. Clay could see Ever's face clearly, and she was screaming in uncontrolled ter-ror, possibly from Willet telling her exactly what he was about to do with his knife.

Clay had to act. He convinced himself he could not shoot at Willet out of fear if he missed, he could hit Ever. He decided to shoot at Flinch, still standing in front of Deekie, his gun pointed at her. The two renegades did not realize he was atop the cliffs, and Clay hoped the surprise of his dropping Flinch would give Willet shock enough to flee.

Clay sighted in on Flinch's chest and squeezed the Spencer's trigger. The shot rang loudly in his ears. After an eternal moment, the round found Flinch's head, dropping him to the ground, his revolver falling free from his hand.

Clay was elated, satisfied with the shot, but noted the sights were low at this distance. He hurried to lever and re-cock the Spencer, expecting Willet to flee, but preparing himself in case he should lunge at Ever with the knife in a wild rage.

When he took aim again, he was surprised to see Willet standing over Ever, looking up at his firing position. Willet's arms were extended wide from his shoulders, his right hand still holding the knife with which he had been threatening Ever. Willet made no effort to flee. He was making as large a target of himself as he possibly could. Clay could see Willet was shouting something aloud.

Clay was too far away to read his lips, and certainly could not hear him, but nonetheless he knew exactly what his one-time friend was saying.

"No harm to you, no harm to me, forever, no matter what!"

Clay knew that Willet thought his former friend could not, would not, fire upon him. Not after all they had been through together. But even for Clay, this time Willet had gone too far. His rage had spoiled everything that had once been pure and innocent. Clay knew exactly what Willet would do to Ever if he failed to fire upon him.

He took Willet in the Spencer's sights. He knew he had to pull that trigger. Willet just waited in his stance of self-sacrifice. Clay's nerves tightened within him. As he drew his deepest breath, tears came to his eyes. He steadied himself.

He remembered Willet rescuing him from the Yankee Raiders. As he looked down the sights of the Spencer rifle, he realized that it was this very rifle that Willet had seized from those soldiers, and then had given to him for his own protection.

The very gun Willet had given to him would be used to take the renegade's life. Clay choked down that memory and gently squeezed the Spencer's trigger.

Again, the shot rang out loudly, echoing in his ear like the tolling of a funeral bell. The second that it took the bullet to travel the distance was eternally long. As Clay waited for the round to find its target, a heaviness overcame him. A nausea found root in his gut. Even in the brightness of the morning sun, a darkness enveloped him.

As Clay watched, Willet remained in his outstretched, sacrificial pose. Then, Clay saw a small puff exploding in the dirt behind Willet's head.

Clay had missed. He had tried to kill the monster that once had been his friend but could not. Although he had not intended it so, at least on a conscious level, the round had missed.

Clay moved to rechamber another round into the Spencer. Only after it failed to do so, did he realize his last shot had been his seventh and final round. He cursed himself for not having grabbed that dead man's Henry, for if he had he would have as many as another seven shots. The Spencer was silent, and Clay's ability to act was denied him. He had no more rounds with which to reload the rifle. He still had two shots left in his Colt Navy, but these were useless at this distance.

He ignored the fire that had, by then, cut off any escape path from the cliffs. He couldn't leave, and he could no longer protect Deekie and Ever. All he could do was force himself to watch that which he could not bear to see. Clay would not turn away. This was his fate, this was the punishment that had been reserved for his many sins upon the battlefields.

He watched as Willet realized there was not another shot coming. A sinister and decrepit smile slithered across his face. Willet lowered his arms and moved to kneel once again over Ever.

As he turned, Willet's body suddenly stiffened, then twitched erratically. The knife slipped from his hand, falling point down into the dirt. The threat of its tip buried in the Georgia clay.

Then, atop the cliffs, Clay heard it. At least the faint echo of it.

Bang! Pause, Bang! Bang! Bang! Pause, Bang!

Willet's body wretched and pitched, the five shots sent him flailing to the ground, writhing in agony. He landed next to Ever, who at this point was screaming hysterically. She crawled backwards in a panic from Willet. In a few short seconds his body would be still in a deepening pool of his own blood. Those seconds of watching Willet die would haunt Ever for the rest of her life.

Deekie came over to console the young Irish girl. It was Deekie who had just retrieved the Colt Navy revolver Clay had given her and emptied it into Willet Blackwell. Now she tended to the hysterical Ever, uncut but deeply scarred.

Deekie would later say that she could take no more abuse. Or perhaps that "she herself might could, but in no way would she ever allow Willet's rage to pour out upon another woman. Or even a girl. Not now. Not Ever."

26

AFTERMATH

Clay awoke to find an angel hovering over him. The rays of heaven beamed through her fine down-hanging strands of red locks and reflected upward from them to highlight her unblemished porcelain skin.

"Ever, my sweet Ever," he said through the tightest of shallow breaths. Each time he drew in, his side ached in the most debilitating manner.

He winced.

"Oh, Clay, it is so wonderful to hear you say those words!" A smile of the purest joy spread unconstrained across her face. "Doctor Hardin said that Laudanum would be leavin' your system about now. He thought the pain might bring you around."

Clay's memory teased him, the images in his mind were blurred, and seemed to melt into a fog the harder he tried to recall them. He looked up at Ever's face, as beautiful as always, and bearing no scars. He knew this was good, that he had protected her, but he could not yet remember the specific events of his time atop Three Sisters Mountain.

"Where am I?" he asked, wincing again in pain.

"Why, Clay, you are healing up in Miss Howell's boarding house," said Ever in her lilting Irish brogue.

"Healing up from what?" he said, his memory still a slurry of dark recollections. Clay reached up with his arm to touch her face, feel its smoothness, to assure himself the medicine had not played tricks with his mind.

"Clay, you had a terrible fall. We feared that you would not survive it," she said sweetly. "We feared we would never hear you speak again..."

Her eyes swelled with tears once more. She had been crying, that he could see. Her face was as beautiful as it had always been, but something was different. The solace that was her purity had been replaced by a great stress. Clay could see in her eyes a tension that had never been there before. The strain in her cheeks belied a heart that had been greatly scarred.

Then, a trail of memories came like vapor into his mind. They were not clear and distinct, but more like cloudy feelings than actual recollections.

"Miss Ever," Clay said softly, becoming aware that he had dropped the title of respect, "Please tell me that Deekie is unhurt..."

"Virgil, I am fine, don't fret, just take to healing yerself," called out Deekie's voice from a chair along the wall. She rose and walked over to stand by his bed, on the opposite side from Ever.

"Deekie," he said with a widening smile, removing his hand from Ever's face to hungrily grasp Deekie's hand. "I was afeard I lost you forever..."

The words creased his face as he spoke them, bringing tears to his eyes and a tremble to his lips. He squeezed her hand tightly, and she squeezed his in return.

"You both will excuse me, but I must tell Uncle Colin of your awakening, Clay," said Ever, as she moved to depart from the room. "Besides, I will give the two of you some time together."

Despite her every desire to remain by Clay's side, Ever left the room, closing the door softly. She then went down the hall to her room and broke down in tears. The joy of Clay's awakening had triggered a fresh avalanche of her own horrific recollections.

Clay had followed Ever out of the room with his eyes. He then turned his shoulders to look upon Deekie's bruised, but still lovely, face.

"Deekie, why do I hurt somethin' fierce?" asked Clay. The movement of turning brought him fresh volleys of pain.

A honied smile unfurled on her face, as the question reminded her of long ago, when he came back from the war. Then, she had nursed him back from the fever that all were sure was to consume him.

"Virgil, you always did have one of the densest pig-heads I 'bout ever seen on a fella," said Deekie. "Stop movin' round so."

It was then that he could hear it, more than see it, in his mind – **Bang! Pause, Bang! Bang! Bang! Pause, Bang!**

"My Diddy's Colt Navies..." he started to recollect.

"Is that all you think of, Clay? Don't fret, I got 'em both," answered Deekie. "They are safe with me."

"Good," he smiled. A wave of relief passed over him. "Did they he'p you and Ever?"

"Virgil, you really don't remember, do you?" she asked. "Yes, they helped us. They saved our lives. And they saved you. You were so brave."

Deekie caressed his face with her free hand, still holding Clay's hand with her other.

"They's all my Diddy ever left me, but they saved my skin twice now. They saved me in the war, and Willet too, in fact."

The mention of Willet's name cast a pall upon Deekie's face.

"Oh, no," cried Clay, "Willet didn't make it, did he?" The memories awash in Virgil Clay-Harris' mind were garbled and slurred.

"Virgil, you listen to me good, now. The Willet we knowed growing up has been gone for a long time. His heart was filled with a sickness. You saved Ever and me from him."

"I can't believe I killed him," Clay screamed out, before murmuring **"No harm to you, no harm to me, forever, no matter what!"**

"You couldn't kill him, Virgil. You had a clean shot from them cliffs, but you missed. You couldn't do it. So, I did..."

In Clay's mind the words precipitated the memory of the round embedding itself in the dirt behind Willet. Then he heard it for a second time – **Bang! Pause, Bang! Bang! Bang! Pause, Bang!**

"I had to kill him, Virgil," said Deekie, "he was all set on cuttin' up Ever, and I couldn't let that happen. When he backhanded that poor girl to the ground, and you shot Flinch down, I scurried after your Colt Navy. After you missed him, I cut Willet down. I had to. I just had to."

"Yes, I reckon I remember now," said Clay sadly, seeing his friend laying in the morning light, bleeding out.

"After that, you tried to climb down from that cliff," Deekie said. "I guess the heat from the raging fire forced you to. I never seen a one-armed man give it more of a go than you did. You wedged your backside and your feet in a crevice along that cliff. You butt shimmied about a third of the way down before that gap opened up beneath ya'. Gravity done did the rest. You fell the remaining forty feet or so."

"I can't believe that fall didn't kill me…" he said softly.

"It would have except after ten feet or so, ya' slammed into a rock ledge with yer ribs. Busticated three of them, right there, before you spun off, falling into the pile of crushed rock below. Doc says if it had not been so finely pulverized and piled so high you likely would have died. I told him better. I said that you was too damn stubborn to die after Chickamauga, and your head ain't got any softer over the years."

"And you two carried me here?" Clay asked, wincing once more.

"Heck no, that plunge and that fire that forced it had done drawn out most of the county. Along with all that shootin' and the explosion atop Three Sisters. The Ladd mining people brought you out here on a cart. You been out of it for the last three days."

"Where's Truitt? Where's Maw?" Clay asked.

Once again, he could see the shadow of death crawl across her face.

"Virgil, the same disease that robbed Ever of her mother has taken yours. Yer maw succumbed to the Consumption two nights ago. That's why you are here. Doc Hardin said that shack was too contagious for you to be healin' up in."

"Then where is Truitt?" asked Clay, accepting his mother's death and the peace it afforded her.

———

"He is burying her this afternoon on a plot of land on your homestead," Deekie said tenderly.

"Then, I has to be there…" said Clay trying to raise himself, only to have vipers of pain strike at him.

"You can't be, Virgil, you are too busted up. Doc says no way you leave this room. But ol' man Horace from across the street says he's holdin' your job until you are healthy again. He also said that his boss is picking up your tab while yer here at the boarding house, including all the doc's fees."

"I gotta pay my respects to Maw," Clay said, trying to raise himself from the bed, until the weight of his pain crushed him back into it.

"Here, now, Virgil, swaller this," said Deekie. "Doc said a dose of this Laudanum would ease your pain, he'p you rest."

"I don't want it," protested Clay through a tight grimace.

"Well, Virgil, you are takin' it, like it or not," she yelled, pushing his hand down to the bed and forcing the large spoon into his mouth.

"Now, I ain't pullin' this spoon out till yer swaller."

Which he did. "Ew, Gawd. This stuff is more bitter than rotten peaches."

Clay's face was a contorted snarl. The medicine sank warmly through him, and in a few minutes his thinking began to fog over once again.

"Deekie, you sure done got pushy all of a sudden like," he said aloud, not meaning to.

"That's because I'm through letting anyone hurt me no more", she said. Her face was still bruised something fierce, but it would be the last time in her life it would be so.

AUTHORS' HISTORICAL AND STORYLINE NOTES

Eventually, Clay healed and moved back onto the spread on Pettit's Creek with Truitt. Deekie moved in with them both, and the three of them were happy there for some time.

It is important to note here that we have taken a significant, but important, historical license in the writing of this story. The roses of Rose Lawn date well after 1871 and were the undertaking of Mrs. Sam Jones. For the sake of this fiction, we have dated their planting earlier in the hands of Virgil Clay-Harris at the urging of Mrs. Nelson Gilreath.

Colin Brannigan fully recovered from Willet's assault upon him. His young niece Ever was not so fortunate. The luck of the Irish eluded her. Even though she had not been physically harmed in any way, the terror of that night on the mountain would revisit her again and again. Colin Brannigan had promised his dying sister to take care of Ever, and so he would. In a few months, Brannigan resigned his Freedman's Bureau commission and moved with Ever back to his home in Boston.

While many of the first settlers of Bartow (then Cass) County were born themselves in the lands of England, Scotland and Ireland before emigrating to America, our Colin Brannigan, and his niece, Ever, are of course fictional characters.

The Federal Freedman's Bureau and its ability to negate labor contracts of former slaves was a very real element of the Reconstruction of the South.

By which it is important to also note that the presidency of Ulysses S. Grant was known for its inherent corruption. His administration, 1869-1877, occurred at the same period of the height of influence of the political machine of New York. Grant's administration was embroiled in a scandal at New York's Custom House, with alleged pilfering of the collected tariffs.

At the same time in New York City was the rise of the Tammany Hall political machine. Named after the Society of St. Tammany, it grew from its simple beginnings of assisting newly arrived immigrants to become the Democratic Party organization controlling nearly all functions of life in the city. The levels of corruption were astounding even for this period of the beginning of America's Gilded Age. The head of which was William Magear Tweed, an American born of Scottish descent, who came to be known simply as "Boss Tweed".

Tweed's constituency was of a largely Irish immigrant population. He was already under fire by the New York City newspapers, but it was the political cartoons of Thomas Nast in Harper's Weekly that he truly despised. He was known to have said, "Stop them damn pictures. I don't so much care what the newspapers say about me. My constituents don't know how to read, but they can't help seeing them damn pictures."

Boss Tweed came to the precipice of his demise when he approved the march that degraded into the "Orange Riots" in New York City in 1871. Catholic and Protestant (Orangemen) Irish factions clashed leading to the deaths of some 60 civilians, mostly all Irishmen. Boss Tweed, who's Tammany Hall had at first disapproved the march, had later given in to pressure and then approved the Orangemen protest. Tweed and his cohorts were held responsible, and soon were accused of corruption and of stealing millions of dollars of the taxpayers' funds. Despite all his power, he died of pneumonia in a New York jailhouse in 1878.

The role depicted in our story of Irish soldiers fighting on behalf of the North is very accurate. In fact, the Irish fought in regiments for both the Blue and the Gray. Indeed, the Union Irish Brigade under the command of the Irish-born Brigadier General Thomas Francis Meagher lost over four hundred of its soldiers to the Rebels at Antietam, with over 60% of its total regiment being killed or wounded. Meagher re-staffed his regiment, only to have the majority of his Irish troops killed months later during the Battle of Fredericksburg.

Which brings us back to our fictional hero Virgil Clay-Harris. At

Sharpsburg (or Antietam), he manned the infamous sunken farm road that is until this day remembered as the Bloody Lane. Clay fired upon Meagher's 69th New York Infantry, who were marched under their lovely emerald green regimental battle flag over the knoll and directly into the middle of the Confederate lines. While our hero Clay is fictional, these events are historically very accurate.

Likewise, the depiction of Willet Blackwell firing upon Union troops attempting to cross Antietam's "Burnside Bridge" is factually precise. Just over 500 rebel Georgia Volunteers kept over 11,000 Federal troops under General Ambrose Burnside from crossing Antietam creek for several long hours, saving Lee's army only a mile or so north on the raging battlefields of Sharpsburg.

Also based in truth is the fictional depiction of Clay and Willet revisiting the battlefield as they marched on to Gettysburg. Photography was then just emerging as the latest technological advancement. There is explicit photographic evidence of the skeletal remains of those who wore the Blue and the Gray strewn across that Maryland battlefield even nine months after the battle itself.

Coming back to Cartersville, the room in which Clay healed at the close of our tale had a window that looked out across Market Street, and upon the Gilreaths' lovely lawn. All the rows of rose bushes were fully in bloom, and they made for the talk of the town. Well, once all talk of the scoundrel Willet Blackwell was exhausted, that is.

Market Street was eventually renamed Cherokee Street, perhaps in recognition of the dishonor done to those Native Americans who once rightfully lived here. It is factual that the home of Nelson Gilreath was originally built on land cleared on Market Street. The Howell boarding house is, however, a very fictional element of our story.

Nelson Gilreath was indeed a major business leader of *the town of Cartersville* and did certainly renovate his cottage with the Second Empire architectural style in 1870, before adding an attic and additional rooms onto his house in 1872.

Ten years later, the house was purchased and inhabited by the Reverend Sam Jones. As noted earlier, the roses of 1871 are but an artistic license. They were needed to tell the story. In reality, the roses of Rose Lawn were the work of Mrs. Sam Jones, and this actually dates their planting after 1882. The Gilreaths relocated to Main Street, where Nelson would live until his death in December of 1889.

Reverend Sam Jones, a charismatic circuit preacher soon became known throughout the nation. His preaching soon was in great demand throughout the Northeastern cities and across the Western states. Even the original home of Nashville's Grand Ole Opry, the Ryman Auditorium, was originally constructed as a permanent venue for Sam Jones' sermons. Even with his incredible successes and travels, Reverend Jones always came home to Cartersville and his beloved home on Market Street. In 1895, in an amazing engineering feat for its time, what had been the Gilreath cottage was hydraulically jacked, and an entire ground floor and basement were constructed beneath the original structure. This completed the structure that is known today as the Rose Lawn House.

Image 18 – Rose Lawn House of Reverend Sam Jones

In the year following the close of this tale, that is, 1872, the town of Cartersville was incorporated as a city by act of the Georgia legislature. The first mayor of the *City of Cartersville* was Abda Johnson. However, Paul Gilreath, son of Nelson, would go on to become mayor of the city on three separate occasions, from 1904-1907, from 1910 – 1911, and from 1916-1917.

While Judge J. R. Ferris is a fictional character for the purposes of this tale, the judge that actually presided over the first proceedings in the Cartersville courthouse was Judge J. R. Parrott. He presided over the first courthouse session in 1869, but unfortunately died in 1872, before the completion of its full construction in 1873. The problem of train smoke billowing in the courthouse was very real and is well documented in the county archives.

The Bartow County Courthouse stayed in operation alongside the railroad tracks until 1902, although complaints about interruptions by train traffic persisted.

A second courthouse was built with the gilded dome over Cartersville, further away from the tracks. Opening in 1903, it remained in service for ninety years as the county courthouse, it then yielded to the modern day county courthouse and administrative services building in 1992.

The depictions of the Cartersville train depot within our story are historically accurate. The depot to this day bears the scars of its May 20th, 1864, Confederate defense against advancing Union troops. The scars of bullet holes are still visible upon its edifice even today.

Depot Master "Chuck" J.C. Wofford actually ran the Cartersville train depot from 1865 until 1912. He died the following year. It also appears during this period that he may have served as the Cartersville City Mayor on three occasions, from 1881 to 1883, during 1885, and from 1888 to 1889.

The train lines running through Cartersville have become an inextricable part of its history. The lines had many names, including the Western & Atlantic RR, the Cartersville & Van Wert RR, the Nashville Chattanooga & St. Louis (NC&StL) RR, which later became part of the Louisville & Nashville (L&N) RR. Remaining portions of all were eventually absorbed into CSX.

Just before the Civil War, Mark Cooper created the short-lived Etowah Railroad which connected his Cooper Iron furnace with the Western & Atlantic railroad at Stegall's Station, near what is today Emerson.

Most of the other active characters in this Cartersville drama are, of course, fictitious. These include Clerk-of-the-Court Conyers W. Trippe, Sheriff Alpheus T. Goff, and Colonel Silas P. Austell. The Colonel's River's Bend Plantation also never existed.

And while discussing Cartersville, and its local surroundings, the story told by Clay to Ever of General Sherman and Miss Cecelia Stovall Shelman's Etowah Heights home is so very true. It is likely well known by most of the residents of the county. Miss Cecelia did live out the rest of her life at Etowah Heights until her death in 1904. Despite having been saved from the Yankees torches during the war by General Sherman himself, this grand edifice sadly and ironically burned to the ground in an accidental house fire in 1911.

General Sherman's actions throughout Georgia are documented within our story faithfully. He was a man committed to "Total War", and in the broadest sense viewed civilian possessions and property as being of potential military support. He intended "to make Georgia howl", and certainly did so.

One last reference to General William Tecumseh Sherman needs to be noted. Protestant himself, the General married a devout Catholic, Ellen Ewing. His son, Thomas, against his father's wishes, became a Jesuit priest.

Father Thomas Ewing Sherman visited Cartersville in 1906. He had been invited by President Theodore Roosevelt to join a cavalry unit visiting Civil War battlefields. Father Sherman's trip created a great stir within the South at that time, whose newspapers presented the son as attempting to retrace the steps through all the territory devastated by his then deceased father. Given the national attention he was garnering, Father Sherman cut short his Georgia trip after his overnight stay in Cartersville, and the newspapers deemed him to be in "full retreat".

The trip of Clay and Ever to Eurharlee on their mission of compassion is fictional, although the authors fully expect such relief was likely provided by one Southern community to another in times of great distress. The Euharlee bridge collapse of 1871, and its taking the life of Captain Elihu Nelson, was indeed a real-life tragedy that called for greater oversight of the construction of bridges in the area. The county was in need of a master bridge builder who could protect its citizens from the deadly torrents of this waterway.

Then, Washington King, the son of the famous Architect, Engineer and Bridgebuilder Horace King, along with Jonathan H. Burke, constructed the covered bridge in 1886 that still stands today. It was designed using wooden lattice planking connected with wooden pegs, or trunnels. It carried traffic over Euharlee Creek for the next ninety-four years, until it was replaced with a modern concrete bridge in 1980.

It is only fitting to note that Horace King, who died one year after the covered bridge was built, was a former slave. It was their mastery - he and his son, Washington and Jonathan H. Burke - of the art and science of bridge building that finally conquered Euharlee Creek. The creek, incidentally, was named by the Cherokee and means *"She laughs as she runs"*, which seems entirely appropriate.

Image 19 – Euharlee Covered Bridge

Three Sisters Mountain, after the events described herein, became known as Quarry Mountain, then simply as Ladd's Mountain. The caves within it were certainly real, as was the remains of an ancient Native American stone structure atop it. The renegade camp, the shoot-out and the fire are all fictional elements of our story.

The mining that took place there after the time of this tale, in reality, greatly consumed the caves within, and expanded the face of the cliffs to their current height of over three hundred feet. Mining operations continued well into the next century.

The name Three Sisters Mountain, as well as its being mined by Ladd's after the war, are both documented in the book "The Light of Other Days", authored by a resident of the area during these times, Miss Caroline Couper Lovell.

Finally, the role of our fictional Carpetbagger, Colin Brannigan, is not unprecedented. In his autobiographical "Two Wars", General Samuel G. French (CSA) recalls an Irish Carpetbagger from the Freedmen's Bureau in his county in Mississippi after the war. General French was a major Confederate Leader at the Battle of Allatoona Pass during the war. He survived both the Civil War and the earlier War with Mexico.

Our tale ends in 1871. Only a few years later, in 1873, Clay and Deekie would set off to Texas to find out what had become of his gun-smithin' *"Diddy"*. Alas, it is a story to be told in another time. However, the timing of this tale is most interesting in that in 1873 Colt released the successor to its well-loved Navy Revolver.

Known by many names, the Colt Single Action Army Revolver,

> *aka* the SAA,
> *aka* the M1873,
> *aka* the Model P,
> *aka* the Peacemaker,
> *aka* the Colt .45

surely went on to become one of the legendary guns that won the West!

The same Wild West that called out like a siren's song to Virgil Clay-Harris.

Image 20 – Confederate Soldier Statue Outside The 1903 Courthouse in Cartersville

ACKNOWLEDGEMENTS

This book would not have been possible without the tremendous resources of Cartersville, Euharlee and Bartow County, including:

1. **The Bartow History Museum** and its Archives, especially the access to the bound newspapers from the period up to 1871.
2. **The Euharlee Welcome Center and History Museum**, especially pertaining to information relating to the 1871 bridge collapse.
3. **The Etowah Valley Historical Society**, their wealth of historical information, their image library, and their allowance of our use of the Park Hotel and Etowah Height images.
4. **The Rose Lawn Museum of Cartersville** for their wealth of information pertaining to the time period, and their allowance of our use of the Gilreath Cottage image.
5. The following reference and resource materials:
    a. <u>**The History of Bartow County, Georgia (Formerly Cass)**</u> by Lucy Josephine Cunyus, Southern Historical Press Inc., 1933.
    b. <u>**The Light of Other Days,**</u> by Caroline Couper Lovell, Copyright 1995, Mercer University Press.
    c. <u>**Two Wars, The Autobiography and Diary of General Samuel G. French, CSA,**</u> Blue Acorn Press, 1901.
    d. <u>**Sketches of Bartow County,**</u> Compiled by J.B. Tate, year of publication unknown.
    e. <u>**The Cartersville Centennial 1872-1972,**</u> published by the City of Cartersville, 1972.

f. <u>**The War of the Rebellion: Official Records of the Union and Confederate Armies**</u> provided by the Bartow County Library Reference Collection in Cartersville.

The authors would also like to acknowledge the extreme helpfulness of the staffs of the following national battlefields, assisting us on our visits during our preparation of this novel:

Chickamauga, Georgia
Sharpsburg (Antietam), Maryland
Gettysburg, Pennsylvania
Fredericksburg, Virginia
Chancellorsville, Virginia

And, Finally, the Authors Wish to Acknowledge Our Gratitude to the People of Cartersville, Past and Present, Who Through Their Tremendous Efforts and Arduous Undertakings Have Created Such a Rich History and a Wonderfully Pleasant Community.